An Absence of Faith

ISBN 978-1-312-82908-4

An Absence of Faith

David W. Gordon

Claymore 1745 Press

2015

ISBN 978-1-312-82908-4

First Printing: 2015

ISBN 978-1-312-82908-4

Claymore 1745 Press
New York

Claymore1745@yahoo.com

Ordering Information:

Special discounts are available on quantity purchases by corporations, associations, educators, and others. For details, contact the publisher at the above listed address.

U.S. trade bookstores and wholesalers: Please contact Claymore 1745 Press via email at claymore1745@yahoo.com.

For My Mother –
For all that I am, I have you to thank.

Acknowledgements

The origin of this novel stems back to my childhood. The beginnings can be traced to the first real tragedy of my life, the death of my Nana. She was the first person, truly close to me, that I lost. The death of so powerful a force in my life shook the foundations of my relationship with God. So, each of the characters in this novel, though separate and distinct, remain aspects of my connection to God. That simple truth is, all at once, uplifting and terrifying.

Originally conceived as a graphic novel, *An Absence of Faith* was a visual and literary expression of my confused relationship with religion, God, life and death. *An Absence of Faith* is a dark novel. But, it is also a novel of hope and faith. In that, the characters are an expression of myself. They reflect the darkness and the light within. Because of that, *An Absence of Faith* was written long ago and remained unpublished. Moreover, it remained unseen by friends and loved ones because of how deeply personal the story was to me.

As I grew older and the shock of loss was deadened by experience, I allowed my wife to read the novel. There is no denying that it disturbed her. She wouldn't allow me near her for quite some time. Yet, she understood something about the book that I could not. The characters were not just reflections of me; they were reflections of all of us. Where I, in my hubris, thought that these feelings were mine alone, she recognized that they were nearly universal.

Over time, I allowed a few others to read *An Absence of Faith*. My thanks go out to Margaret Fox, Christine McNeil, Jason Schuchat, Kerry Price, JoAnn Bronschidle, George Mohl, Anna and Brian O'Connor, and Nicholas Oliverio. With their help, I grew more comfortable with the idea that others might share my doubts, my anger, and my hope. So, if you find yourself in *An Absence of Faith*, you have them to thank. After all, the title of the book is somewhat of a deliberate misnomer.

Prologue

"Evil is obvious only in retrospect."

Gloria Steinem

Jessica Connors knew her father would not be proud of her at this moment. Not that she cared about his approval. In fact, she couldn't care less about him or anything he said or did. Jessica was a girl with serious daddy issues. Rebelliousness was something she had taken to new heights before she left home. She made giving her father an attitude into an art form. The morning she turned eighteen, her bags were packed and rolling out the door. She left before her father had a chance to kick her out and told herself that she'd never look back. A proverbial walking cliché, she found herself alone in New York City. No job, no money and no family.

A girl on the streets made ends meet how she could. The first time she slept with a man for money she cried through the whole experience. The stench of stale cigarettes and cheap cologne, mixed with sweat and curry, still haunted her. It was enough for a hot meal and a bed though. She realized something would have to change.

She met Jennifer Mathers at a working corner and the two became fast friends. They pooled their talents and the money they earned from that team-up and got a little apartment of their own. Jennifer had the brain, Jessica had the daring. They referred to themselves as Jumping Jiggles, "She jiggles, I jump." Soon enough, they were escorting wealthier men.

The system worked well. Jessica would be the bait while Jennifer acted as the dessert. Hunting men in the higher-end bars of Manhattan or Queens, Jessica would approach the target, flirt hard and dirty as if she were drunk and desperate. Lots of cleavage, a hint of perfume and a lipstick that wasn't trashy but one her father would have balked at anyway. When the man's desires had risen to near uncontrollable heights, in came Jennifer. The two girls would greet each other as old friends with hugs that lasted a bit too long and kisses that came questionably close to the lips. A suggestive story about an exploratory experience in college and the target was ready to burst. Jessica would then hint that the man could join them if he chipped in for the experience.

Tonight, however, she was flying solo. Jennifer was away with friends and Jessica was looking for companionship. Not the kind that paid, necessarily, though she would take that kind readily enough. Tonight, she was looking for a man who was strong and disciplined. She wanted a quiet, stern type that she could do exceptionally dirty things to, and then send packing. If she considered her Electra-like motives for a moment they would have disturbed her deeply. But, Jessica Connors was not one to linger on self-analysis or reflection for long. She was a girl of action and tonight she was going to get some. Jessica was on the hunt. What she did not know was that she was being hunted.

"Excuse me. Do you react well to bad pick-up lines or would you prefer I just introduce myself?"

"Wow," she thought, "This guy is hot." Jessica found herself staring straight into a set of bluish grey eyes. They reminded her of dolphins swimming in the ocean. Eyes so piercing, the kind that looked through you, straight into your soul. Surrounding them were a set of strong, chiseled cheekbones and an eerily clear complexion. To top it off, a thick head of dusky black hair, perfectly tossed between too much care and too little. This guy didn't need a pick up line, he just needed someone to look at him.

The hunk was diffident in his response, "Sorry. I'll leave you alone. My apologies." He began to walk away.

Jessica was on the hook and was being reeled in. "No. No. My name is Jessica. Nice to meet you," she blushed.

He smiled and she took the whole of him in for the first time. Big, broad shouldered but not overly muscular. He was fit and strong, but not obsessed with his body. Clothes, gray slacks topped with a casual collared shirt, were designer but not pretentious. His sleeves were rolled slightly showing thick, powerful forearms while leading the eye up to a set of solid biceps. Too late, Jessica realized that she was gawking at him. He smiled, satisfied that she wasn't going anywhere.

"Can I buy you a drink?"

Her answer sealed her fate.

~

She fumbled for her keys with one hand while holding the back of his head with the other. He held her with one arm and lifted her off her feet. Making out with this guy reminded her of her first orgasm. It was frightening, and it was exciting, and it was something she didn't want to end.

Her keys discovered, Jessica hastily stabbed at the lock, her hands quivering with excitement. It took her several tries before she inserted the teeth correctly. As the key slid in, she could feel her body moisten with urgency. Jessica pushed the door open and stepped inside. Holding him by the gap in his shirt buttons, she gave a soft tug at him and shut the door. She tossed aside her faux designer leather bag and pressed her lips to his. Victor was far more careful in setting his bag down just inside the door.

The two barely made it to the couch before the first layers of clothing fell. Jessica tried to shove her man onto the couch but her hands seemed to hit granite. Instead, she found herself tossed onto it, barely missing the end table's edge.

"Hey. Careful. I'm fragile," she admonished while tugging at his black leather belt. He grabbed her hand away and fell on top of her, holding her arm above her. "This guy knows what he wants," she thought. Jessica allowed her neck to crane upwards as he licked and kissed from her shoulders to her ear. Unwillingly, she let out a little moan of pleasure. "Not so fast, girly," she thought trying to refrain from getting too caught up in the moment. "Slow. Slow down," she chastised herself. "He may have a plan; but, so do I," Jessica thought. She used her free hand to rub between his legs, grabbing and tugging, applying all the lessons learned in her craft. He rose and released his grip on her, presenting himself before her. Jessica, smiled to herself. She had the upper hand now. Dropping to her knees, she made quick work of his pants and his self-control.

Jessica teased him as she shimmied out of her dress, allowing her hips to do the work hands would normally have done. Her hunk of a man grabbed her by the hair and forced her back onto the couch. Jessica took this as a sign that he was ready and reached down, dropping her panties to the floor.

"Do you need protection?" she asked not as a question of if, but rather of who would provide it. He shook his head and dropped onto her. He went to work on her neck again and Jessica allowed herself to be taken away with the sensation. Her clients were never very interested in her satisfaction and so she was determined to enjoy the moment. He nibbled and tugged. She moaned and giggled. He grabbed her breast and squeezed.

"Easy, lover," she said. She loved the take charge kind of man, but knew you had to establish boundaries or things could get out of control.

His tongue worked its way up to the nape of her neck and Jessica released a long, slow moan. "Please," she begged knowing she wanted him. Her arms scrambled around his waist. Seeking. Searching. He grabbed her arms and tucked them behind her. Using one hand he secured her wrists together so that she could not use either arm. "Please," she begged, wanting him more every moment. His hand glided up her body, teasing her. Cupping his hand over her mouth, he silenced her passionate demands. His lips found their way to the top of her neck, just underneath her jaw. She gave out a muffled moan again but this time something was distinctly different. "That hurt!" was the simple thought she had. Jessica did not yet realize that she was going to die.

Her body tightened against his grip and she tried to free her hands but couldn't. She tried to scream but couldn't break through his hand. Again the searing pain struck her neck where he was once kissing her. This time she tried to bring her knee up into his groin, but couldn't get any force behind it. She felt a warm stream of liquid running down her neck, seeping down between her chest. Out of the corner of her eye she could see blood dripping over her breast and panic began to set in. Jessica writhed and screamed but could not escape his grasp. She tasted salt as her tears were seeping down into her mouth under his hand. "I don't want to die!" was all she could think. Then, a third, a fourth, a fifth, each one even more painful than the last. "Oh, God! He's biting me!"

She could feel blood underneath her now. The couch was being soaked in it. She was covered in it. He pulled his head back from her and she could see her blood dripping down his face. Worse yet, she could see a stream of crimson spraying from her neck onto his chest. Amidst her shock, a ridiculous thought came to her, "This idiot thinks he's a vampire!" The thought of it reminded her of a fear of clowns. How can something so silly be so terrifying? But it was. Gut wrenchingly so. He wasn't a vampire. That would have been one bite. She could feel him savagely gnawing at her, tearing and rending the flesh on her neck.

Jessica continued to struggle against her attacker but her strength was giving out. She felt weak and cold. He held her down and watched her struggle against his grasp. She looked into those penetrating grey-blue eyes and saw something horrific. She hadn't seen dolphins, but sharks. In those eyes wasn't joy or hate or any emotion at all. He looked at her strangely, her blood dripping down his face and chest. It was as if he was studying her. He was watching her die and curiosity was the only emotion that seemed to emanate from him. He was cold. She was growing colder. She began to shiver. Then, after a few moments her body stopped shaking and he released his grip on her.

For a moment, he stood over her and watched her intently. Then, as Jessica Connors bled out onto her couch, the man she had brought home with her walked calmly into the kitchen and removed a knife from the butcher's block. He stood, fingering the edge. Satisfied, he walked back towards her. Jessica whimpered and begged but there was little air and less energy for her to do so. She wished her father were here. He wasn't coming. She knew that. He hadn't ever really been there for her.

Chapter I

"The only thing necessary for the triumph of evil is for good men to do nothing."

Edmund Burke

"Call 911!" Kate Manning spoke in low, urgent tones but her sister, Julie, had already dropped her bags and was reaching for her phone. "Tell them shots fired, plain-clothes female officer on the scene, requesting immediate back up and ambulance." All of Kate's five-foot-seven, trim, athletic frame dashed across the small manicured lawn. Wrong evening to wear tight pants, she thought, as she came to rest against the brick and concrete just underneath the window. Quickly, she waved her younger sister away from the building. She would have yelled at her to get to safety but she could not. Julie moved off as ordered, not breaking stride in her conversation with the 911 operator. Kate, realizing her shoulder-length brown hair was down and a potential obstruction to her view, tied it into a quick knot behind her and drew her side arm. With three lightning-fast steps she was at the front door of the home. Not exactly the shopping excursion her sister had promised. "It will be a chance for us to relax. No kids, no work, just us. Dinner, some wine and some great bargains. How can you argue with that?" Then again, Woodside, Queens, wasn't exactly the murder capital of the world so who could've predicted this.

Kate knelt at the door listening for any indication that danger lurked just inside. Everything was quiet. Still, that didn't mean safe. The sun had nearly set, giving off the faint glow of a dying campfire. She craned her head upwards, her flat black 9mm Glock held firmly in her hands. Quickly, she snatched a glance through the storm door screen. Kate pulled the door open, every creak sounding like a car alarm and the hiss of the pressure hinge might as well have been the roar of a jet engine. It was an open floorplan, the door opening on a large parlor room with sofas no one ever sat on. Kate cleared each side of the room, sighting down each angled plane with her weapon. Satisfied, she went to check on the victim.

A woman, mid-forties, with a frosted pixie cut and an expensive yoga outfit lay on the foyer floor. The cream speckled tile was painted in blood. The grout ran like irrigation tunnels, funneling the woman's blood into a checkered pattern around the floor. A small entry wound just to the left of her nose belied the enormous damage to her head. Kate gently shifted a golden cross from the victim's neck and checked for a pulse but already knew the answer. Large boot prints had bloodied the carpet and led to a door just to her left. The trail of footprints was alive in red, but died off as the carpet slowly drank in the victim's blood. Kate had enough time on the job, six years now, to know the assailant was looking for something, or someone.

She moved tentatively, trying not to make any noise as she proceeded through the house. Glancing at the walls, Kate saw pictures of the woman with her husband and children. Two children, a boy and a girl. They looked to be about four and six, respectively. No sign of robbery was present. "Please don't let this be a domestic," Kate pleaded to herself. One person had already been killed. Whatever the motive, the person she was pursuing would not hesitate to kill her. Kate reached the door and found it slightly ajar. Stairs led down to what looked to be a finished basement. She peered through the small opening but there was insufficient light to give her any indication of what she might face beyond those carpeted stairs. Kate opened the door swiftly and led with her gun. The room was darker than the foyer and living room area she had just come from. No glint of sunlight here. She hugged the wall, just as she was taught in the academy. It's one less direction she needed to concern herself with. One room at a time Kate cleared the area. Nothing. Silence.

The distinct report of a gun broke the silence. No muzzle flash. It came from upstairs. Kate moved quickly, retracing her steps, secure in the knowledge that she was safe at least in this area of the house. Kate grew more cautious as she reached the stairway door that led back to the living room. Popping out and clearing her lanes she saw someone at the door and quickly took aim.

"Kate!" Julie yelled, her hand over her mouth in shock as her eyes took in the dead woman swimming in a pool of her own blood. Kate lowered her weapon and chastised her sister, a school teacher that cared more for others than herself. "Julie! Get back!"

Julie looked at her and Kate could see her sister trying to process what was happening. "I called it in. I was worried," Julie illogically whispered now.

"You cannot help. Get out of here," Kate barked. Without waiting, Kate began to creep up the stairs.

She found the stairs full of family photographs. Baptisms, picnics, first day of school, weddings; everything that made up the fabric of a meaningful life was hung on those walls. They reminded Kate of everything in life she had yet to accomplish. They reminded her of her sister's walls.

The first room at the top of the stairs was a bedroom. White colonial door emblazoned with various Disney Princess wall stickers. Kate slipped into the room and her worst fears were realized. A little girl lay bleeding on the pink carpet. Her purple Rapunzel pajamas darkened where she was shot in the back. Kate felt for a pulse, hoping, but she was gone. There is too much blood, Kate thought. She bit her lip, fighting the tears and moved on. Faintly, Kate could hear sirens in the background. Help was coming but it was too late.

Against all her training, Kate skipped the next two doors. Her instincts told her she knew the end of this story. She reached the final room in the hallway, what she assumed was the master bedroom. Slowly, she used the muzzle of her gun to tilt the door back. There he was! "Drop the gun!" Kate yelled. "Drop it, or I will fire!" Again the man did not move. Kate fired one round, center mass and almost as quickly as the round left the chamber she was up and moving forward. It was over.

A man, rather what remained of him, rested against the wall of the bedroom. He was dead before Kate put a round into him. The back of his head was spread halfway up the wall. In his lap, a photograph of a married couple was covered by bits of blood and brain. He was younger, thinner and had more hair but the man in the photo was clearly the same. His wife had longer hair, softer features but it was unmistakable. Shit! Why did it have to be domestic? Then Kate realized someone was missing. The boy! She has to find the boy. Kate dashed off into the other rooms searching frantically for him. "Police!" You can come out! It's safe now!" Kate's voice resonated back and forth from fear and hope. Nothing. No sign at all of the boy.

"Kate!" the scream was Julie's, bloodcurdling but impossible. It came from the first bedroom.

"Oh no," Kate gasped and raced to the little girl's bedroom. Her sister was there. Her little sister. The one who teaches third grade was sitting on the pink rug, surrounded by Barbie dolls and dress up dresses and picture books and the corpse of a little girl. In her arms, rested a dying four year old little boy.

"He was in the closet," Julie sobbed. "Why?" she asked again and again. Kate had no answer. No one in Heaven or on Earth could.

NYPD arrived on scene first. Kate didn't know any of the responding officers personally, but after some quick name dropping had established some mutual colleagues. They took control of the area and administered first aid. Paramedics arrived three minutes after the first NYPD officers did. None of it mattered though. The boy died on scene. Paramedics took him away in the ambulance doing everything they could to revive him but hope had been lost some time ago. Kate understood that. She considered the strange look on all of the first responders' faces when a kid was involved. It's like they couldn't see the child, they could only see their own kid. An intense group of people become something tighter, laser-like in their need to stop bad things from happening to little kids.

"Manning," one of the officers called to her. Kate was sitting on the sidewalk with Julie who was visibly shaken and shivering. Neither of them had talked to one another about what just happened. They just sort of sat together and took solace from their closeness.

"Yup," Kate muttered looking up at the officer. He was a big guy, muscular and fit.

"You going to hang for the detective or do you want me to take you home and have him call you?"

Kate hadn't considered having to recount the experience and she definitely didn't want her sister to have to do so. It wasn't going to matter what she wanted though. They were both witnesses and would have to give statements. Kate put her arm around Julie and pulled her sister tightly to her.

"We'll stay," Kate's voice quivered, "Thanks anyway, though." He smiled empathetically at the two ladies and moved back to his patrol car. The officer opened the trunk and took out a blanket, brought it over and wrapped the women in it. Kate thanked him with a wordless smile.

The detective that arrived was one Kate knew well enough. His name was Jack and they had spoken on the phone several times before, but this was the first face to face meeting between the two. Kate was glad Jack was assigned to the case, at least for her sake. His presence helped to speed the process tremendously because he wouldn't question Kate's memory or experiences.

"Hey, Manning. Wish we could have met under better circumstances." His voice was slightly higher than she remembered it on the phone. She wondered if he was shaken up a bit. He didn't hesitate to get right to business though. Kate respected that about him. "The Wilki family. Mother Joanna, age 38, daughter Jenna, age 7, son Kyle, age 5, father William, age 41. Apparently, mom and dad were in quite a custody battle. Dad has a rap sheet strewn with domestic complaints, so he wasn't about to get the kids. My guess is he figured if he can't have them, then no one can. You ladies gonna be okay?" No, Kate thought. Not at all.

As Kate predicted, Jack took her word at face value and moved quickly through the questions. Kate took a deep breath and tried to remove the emotion from her statement, "We were walking to Mister

Softy for shakes after shopping most of the day. I heard shots fired. I told Julie to call it in and get away from the house, but you know how little siblings half listen." Jack nodded but did not interrupt. "The front door was open and the female was down. I checked her, but she was DOA. I headed into the house and started clearing rooms. I figured Julie already called for back-up."

Jack began to interrupt, "Kate you shouldn't have . . ." but Kate ignored him.

"That's when I found the girl." Kate paused a moment to steel herself, "The little girl was gone. I tracked the guy to the master bedroom, ordered him to drop and then put a round, center mass. When I entered, I saw he had done the work for me. I heard Julie call out from the girl's bedroom. That's when I realized that Julie had followed me in. She had discovered the little boy hiding in the closet."

Kate hesitated, knowing what Jack wanted to ask. She had been on the other side of things like this enough to know. She also didn't want her sister going through it at the moment. "Please, just don't give me any crap right now Jack, I really don't need it." It was a preemptive warning.

Jack was, for the most part, gentle with Julie. He understood he couldn't expect the same sort of response from her. The one time Kate told him to cut the crap, he didn't fight her, he just moved on. Kate knew she'd have to apologize for that someday. When Jack was finished he had muscle man drive them home. As they were pulling away from the house, Julie, mom to a beautiful six year old miracle named Anna, let her tears flow.

"God help them," she whimpered, "I used to see Joanna and the kids at Stop and Shop. I didn't know. God, help them," she began to chant.

"He's a little late for that," Kate chided, masking her sorrow with anger. "Damn late for that."

Chapter 2

"Question with boldness even the existence of God; because, if there be one, he must more approve of the homage of reason than that of blindfolded fear. "

Thomas Jefferson (1743 - 1826)

Victor Sloan sat in the back of a yellow cab alone with his thoughts. He pondered the path he was taking now. From everything he had heard, his cab should have been driven by an unkempt Indian man who spoke little to no English. The cab, he had assumed, would be dirty, loud both in exhaust and Hindustani music, as well as reeking in curry. Yet, Victor found none of these things to be true. Yes, his driver was of Middle Eastern descent but the man spoke perfect English, listened to pop music and had a clean and otherwise fresh smelling cab, especially considering the bouquet of red roses Victor had brought with him. Victor smiled to himself. "You cannot believe everything you read."

"Fordham Street pier, right?" the driver yelled over the music. Well, at least cab driver manners are questionable, Victor thought.

"On City Island, yes," Victor replied. Victor had switched cabs on three occasions for this trip. His current driver would be his last before he arrived at the Department of Transportation ferry that would take him to Hart Island Cemetery. The ferry usually only ran on the third Thursday of every month but Victor had obtained special permission to visit the island. After all, his mother was buried there.

Hart Island is a potter's field. It is a public cemetery supported with tax dollars where people who cannot afford burial are deposited into mass grave sites. Visitation is severely restricted and even when one comes to the cemetery to visit, they can only go to a gazebo as a place for reflection.

Managed by the Department of Corrections with graves dug by prisoners, it is no wonder that the site isn't exactly tourist friendly. Victor considered petitioning the Department of Corrections through appropriate channels but figured money would expedite the process. A few well-placed connections and cash laden envelopes later and he was on his way to see his mother's grave site.

Victor paid the driver and then walked to the chain link fence to await his contact. The fence, reinforced with a large X, with a lock and chain seemed to guard things no one would want. Large stacks of industrial supplies, long since abandoned and unwanted and dozens of large industrial gray trash bins lined the fencing where it could not be opened. The bright colored rust, so akin to bureaucratic neglect, punctuated the scene. A Department of Corrections van arrived shortly after Victor did. The long white van with blue letters and orange clad passengers stopped at the gate and awaited entry. In short order, a middle-aged man appeared and opened the gate. He spotted Victor as he waved the van through.

"This is a restricted area," he said, pointing to the sign that said as much.

Victor smiled and stated, "I understand. However, I made arrangements for transport to Hart Island Cemetery. My name is Victor Sloan. I believe there is a ferry?"

The name seemed to bring immediate recognition and the middle-aged man waved Victor through the gate. "You can wait over there," the guard said, pointing to a small square of unoccupied concrete.

Victor looked out over the water towards Hart Island. It wasn't far at all. In fact, it looked easy enough to swim to if he was so inclined. There was no need for that, however. An orange and black ferry designed to transport vehicles over to the island looked as if it were about to make a return trip. Victor looked at the red brick building across the way. It was classic nineteenth century New York industrial. Utilitarian, meant to stand for centuries and absolutely no frills. A large smoke stack of the same variety jutted into the sky. Victor got the sense that it looked more like Auschwitz than it did a boys reform school or insane asylum, both of which the island once was before becoming one of the world's largest mass graves.

The ferry pulled into place and the van drove onto it.

"You'se need to use the bathroom, you betta do it here. There ain't no facilities over on the island." The guard's Brooklyn accent seemed at odds with the use of the word, "facilities." Nevertheless, Victor waved him off.

"I am quite fine, thank you."

The guard waved him onto the ferry like a princess in a parade. In a few short moments, Victor and his orange clad comrades were headed across to Hart Island.

Victor was shuffled off to the side as the ferry unloaded. A guard gave him a "come hither" motion and Victor did as he was told. The guard handed Victor a light jacket and a hat that would allow him to blend in and look like a corrections officer.

"Be back here no later than 4:15, got it?" he said.

Victor gave a nod and put on the items he was handed and picked up his flowers. He had no idea what this man's cut of the money he paid was and could not care less. Just so long as he was granted access to the grave site.

Using his iPhone compass, Victor began to head towards the part of the island his mother was most likely buried on. The island was about a mile long, just over one hundred acres. Hundreds if not thousands of white markers, thick angled poles about three feet high, were placed on the grounds denoting the spots where approximately one-hundred-fifty adults were buried. Immigrants, criminals, unidentified tourists, anyone who was unwanted or unidentifiable found their way here. The island also housed stillborn infants by the thousands.

Was Mother here because she was a criminal? Maybe she was here because her next of kin could not be contacted. Maybe she was here because her family could not afford it or just maybe she was in a potter's field because they had not wanted her elsewhere. For Victor, this was the beginning of a journey of discovery, but more importantly, one of closure. This trip marked the beginning of the end.

When he reached the spot he most likely assumed was the location of his mother's mass grave, Victor paused and looked around. The area was punctuated by trees and was grassy but not anything like a private cemetery. Large areas of dirt lay off in the distance where heavy equipment had dug or covered over holes. A gentle breeze and the scent of the river made Hart Island seem equal parts park and construction site. Nothing felt cemetery-like to him. Victor eased down on one knee and unwrapped the flowers he had brought. Gently he spread them on the ground making a semi-circle around him. He took a deep breath and began speaking into the wind.

"Mother, I've brought you some roses. You always loved the smell of roses. Remember how you used to pass Jerry's flower shop near our apartment? Gregory and I would watch from the window, waiting for you to come home in the morning. We could see you stop and smell the flowers, but you always lingered on the roses. They were your favorite. Do you remember how I would do simple chores for Jerry in exchange for a rose for you? You told me once that the red rose was a symbol of love and that each time I gave you one, you knew I loved you more than the world. You made me feel special when you received the rose from me. I felt loved."

Victor dropped down onto both knees and sat on his haunches.

"You never really needed me to make you feel special though, did you? You had so many other men to make you feel special. They paid you to make them feel special, just like I did. They bought you and you let them use you. Is that what I did too, Mother? Did I buy you with roses? No matter. You were a lie and I know that now. A careful crafter of deceptions, meant to fool men. A snake! You might as well have offered each man an apple from the tree of knowledge."

Victor stood now, his foot crushing one of the roses underneath it.

"The virus destroyed you. It showed the world what you really were. A temptress and a whore! Repugnant and vile!" Victor was screaming now but there was no one to hear him. "I will show him. I will show Gregory that there was nothing to you. That there is nothing inside any of you! He will know how empty and vain you all are. I will prove it to him. No matter how long it takes, I will show him that he is wrong."

Chapter 3

"When you close your doors, and make darkness within,
remember never to say that you are alone, for you are not alone; nay,
God is within, . . ."

Epictetus (55AD – 135 AD), Discourses

A man is only as strong as his faith. For Father Gregory Sloan, that would mean he was a rock. Gregory was devout in his faith, unwavering in his commitment and determined to serve God. After all, he had made a promise and Father Gregory Sloan never broke a promise. Not since he was a little boy had he broken his word. The thought of that fueled a feeling of guilt inside of him that he fought hard to crush.

Gregory took off his simple black rimmed glasses and pinched the bridge of his wide nose. He was a simple man. Everything about his appearance confirmed that. Short, trimmed hair, clean shaven and of medium build, Gregory was a man who would never stand out in a crowd. Right now, his head thumped in time like the bass of a rock band's speaker. Today was a challenge he had not expected.

The man in the confessional was unseen, but Gregory felt he knew him well enough. He had dealt with these sort of men since he was a child and had little patience for them. "Father, please forgive me. I have sinned," the man concluded. When a person came to confession and asked for forgiveness, Gregory had noticed that they could be categorized in four groups. The first, kids who came because their parents required them to. The second, those that came out of habit or dedication to their faith. Third, and most rare of them all, was the person who truly sought counsel for their problems. Finally, those that wanted forgiveness but had little intention of changing who they were. The first two groups, Gregory was used to. He could fly through those sessions, doling out a selection of prayers without much effort. The final two groups were a challenge to him. Those that earnestly sought his advice were rare, but ones he truly felt dedicated to helping. This guy, he fell into that fourth group. The one that had no real interest in being a better man. That group made Gregory angry.

"Tell me again," Gregory hissed. The man let out a sigh and begrudgingly did as he was told.

"I had sex with a call girl," he began. Gregory noted that the first time he had spoken, the man referred to her as a hooker. This time, he attempted to soften his sin a bit with semantics. "I paid for sex. Forgive me, but my wife hasn't come near me for a year and, well, I couldn't resist. I needed it."

Again, a subtle shift in how the story was told. Last time it was because he was having marital problems. This time it was because his wife had not had sex with him in a year. Gregory noted the attempt to blame his wife, not himself for his actions.

"I couldn't help it," the man pleaded.

Couldn't help take advantage of a desperate woman, Gregory thought, unable to tamp down the fury welling inside of him.

"God will not forgive you," Gregory blasted the man.

"Wha? Father, please . . ." the man's shock was total. Gregory inhaled deeply and waited. "Father? Father, please say something," he pleaded. Gregory gave the man the only answer he could.

"You must seek forgiveness from not one, but two of God's children before God might forgive you. Absolution comes when one corrects mistakes, not simply admits to them." Through gritted teeth, Gregory forced out, "Good day, my son."

Gregory stormed out of the confessional before the man could respond. An altar boy was restocking the accoutrements that had been depleted from the morning mass.

"Go away!" Gregory demanded. The boy did not move. In fact, he had not even registered that Father Gregory was even speaking to him. He simply continued on with his work, oblivious to the rage approaching him. Gregory dashed forward and shocked the boy.

"Go! Go now! You have done your work. Go home!" he yelled.

"Ye . . . Yes, Father Gregory," the boy stammered, terrified, dropping a box of candles and running down the aisle towards the front of the church. I was never that young, Gregory thought, chastising himself. He knew his anger was misplaced. He had misplaced anger in spades, he thought. Anger was something he wrestled with his entire life; a cross to bear, the weight sometimes becoming too much to carry. Nevertheless, it was his to bear, and he knew he should not ask others to carry it for him.

His church in Woodside, Queens, was a leftover from early in the twentieth century. Built by Irish immigrants who had moved into the area, displacing the dominant German population that had occupied the area previously, the church was a brown brick façade that showed all the frills of a poorer population putting their heart and soul into something. Today, it was a bedroom community that boasted one of the most diverse populations of any area in the city, much less the world. Gregory had led an effort to get the various religious leaders to work together to better the community and ensure tolerance in a post 9/11 world. His efforts had gained him the respect of Catholics, Protestants, Muslims, Jews and others. He had a knack for bringing people together and helping them see all that they had in common. He was proud of his successes, but haunted by his failures.

The church was empty now. Gregory hated an empty church. It gave him time to think and that was when the darkness came. He sat on the edge of the altar. Gregory looked around him, seeking solace in the imagery of the church. Stained glass windows depicting the most important events of Christianity surrounded him. An image of Mary, the Virgin Mother, holding a newborn Christ caught his gaze. A candle burned bright in front of it. So innocent, he thought. I was never as innocent as that. God could not grant me that. Even as a child it was stolen from me. He stared into the flame of the candle and slowly, the darkness crept in on him.

Strange that Gregory remembered the bright light. He was young then, only eleven when the man came to the door looking for his mother.

"Mom?" Gregory whispered. "Momma, I'm scared. Please wake up," he begged.

He remembered the pounding. Thump. Thump. Thump. The glowing television that told the man someone was home. If he could have only reached the light; turned it off somehow.

"Open the door, you bitch! I know you in there and I wants my money," the man yelled through the door of the apartment.

Gregory could see his shoes under the door. "Sssshhhh," Gregory whispered to his younger brother. "He won't get in. I'll protect you, Victor. I promise."

God knows, mother could not. She was on the couch, in her underwear and a tank top, legs spread wide and head flopped back. Gregory wasn't even sure if she was breathing. Another round of heroin in her veins meant another day where Gregory was left to take care of himself and his little brother. A hypodermic needle, a bottle of Jack Daniels and two terrified children lay near her feet.

"Please, God, don't let him get in," Gregory prayed.

"Damn it! Open this door, you slut!" More pounding, kicking. Then, as suddenly as it had begun, it was over. "It don't matter. You can't hide forever, ho." The light from under the door peered through crisp and clean. There were no feet outside the door anymore.

Gregory waited a moment and then started to rise. Victor clung to him.

"No! I am scared," the little boy pleaded. Victor was eight and Gregory did everything in the world he could to protect him and shelter him from the life they were forced to live. Victor didn't understand the drugs. He didn't understand what his mother did for a living and Gregory didn't want him to. Gregory soothed Victor's worries.

"It's alright. I need to check on Mom. I'll be right here. I'm not leaving." Gregory shook off Victor's grasp and went onto the couch. It creaked and popped even under his light weight. The thing was a

Salvation Army give away and smelled of wet dog and stale cigarettes. The cushions couldn't be turned over because one side was worse than the other. Gregory took his mother's face in his hand and gently shook it. He was too young to understand the significance of a pulse or body heat. For Gregory, if his mother moved, she was alive; if not, he didn't even want to think about it. "Please God, don't let her be dead," Gregory whispered in near silent prayer.

Out of fear and frustration, Gregory began to jostle his mother. He shook her harder and harder as the terror grew within him.

"Don't you leave us alone!" he yelled. Victor sobbed on the floor while Gregory vented his anger. "Mom? Mom, please wake up," Gregory begged, giving up on shaking her.

His anger spent, gaining nothing, Gregory pleaded with God. "Please give her back to us. God, if you let her live I will do whatever you want. I'll become a priest. I'll work for the church if you want. Please, don't take my mom," Gregory's sobs grew heavy. Victor tugged at his older brother's pajama pants.

"Gregory, is Mommy dead?" Fear pervaded his blue-gray eyes and Gregory could feel his hand shake. The rage returned and Gregory began to pound on his mother's chest. He hit her again and again. Angry that she would do this to herself. Angry that she would leave them alone. Angry at God for ignoring him. All of his fury unleashed, Gregory collapsed on her and cried.

Suddenly, their mother woke with a start. Coughing and hacking, she was oblivious to everything that had just happened. A once youthful face, worn by abuse and neglect, looked around the room trying to remember, or worse, trying to forget again. Those same blue-gray eyes that her sons' possessed scanned the room in confusion. She focused on the television and grimaced.

"Same old Mets," she muttered in frustration. Gregory hugged her but her arms remained limp at her side. Victor climbed frantically up her leg and sat on her lap.

"Mommy, Mommy," Victor kept repeating.

"Ssshhh," she said, "I'm okay."

"God gave you back to us, Mommy. I prayed and I prayed and God gave you back. It's true Mommy!" Gregory was awash with joy. But, that joy and God's gift to them would only be temporary.

Gregory returned to the confessional. His memories had brought him to tears again and he did not want anyone to enter the church and see him crying. He hid in the small box and allowed himself to sob. Then, he heard the distinct sound of the door open from the other side. A confessor had arrived. Gregory wiped his tears and waited. A voice spoke.

"It has been many years since my last confession." The voice was eerily familiar.

"Brother Gregory, do you wish to hear my confession?" Victor chose his words carefully, calling him brother, not father. Gregory's body stiffened at the sound, recognizing the voice and the word choice immediately. It was his younger brother.

"Victor?" With recognition came a smile from one brother and a sense of terror from another.

Victor leaned close to the gold embossed fleur de lis panel that separated the two men and whispered triumphantly, "Come now, my brother, you have not forgotten me so soon, have you? After all, I have brought you a gift."

Gregory shuddered at the thought that his brother might be inches away from him. Leaning towards the same panel he muttered, "Victor, is that you?" Victor leaned back against the wall and adjusted himself, smug in the shock his arrival had caused.

"I have come to get something off of my chest. Isn't that what the confessional is for?"

Nervous, Gregory choked out, "Then you have come to the right place."

Victor's smile cut wide across his face. He held the neatly wrapped package on his lap. He fingered the red ribbon, tied in a perfect bow. "It has begun."

First, Gregory questioned what, if anything, had begun. He pondered the meaning of his little brother's statement for a moment and then came to a dark realization. No. No, he couldn't. He wouldn't. Gregory's thoughts ran wild.

"Open your present, Gregory," Victor instructed, rising to leave.

Gregory heard the door creak and blurted, "No. Wait!"

Victor turned and gave one final chilling statement, "Remember your promises," and then he was gone.

Gregory knew that he could confront Victor now. He could run from the confessional and catch him. What good would it do, he considered. Victor had never been one for conciliation so Gregory wondered what ulterior motive rested behind the gift Victor had mentioned. Instead, Gregory waited. He hesitated a few minutes until he knew his brother had time to leave.

Gregory walked casually to the other side of the confessional box and opened the door. On the seat, rested a present; a shiny silver hat box, wrapped in a thick red ribbon. Gregory knelt in front of it and removed a small business-card sized envelope from the top. Opening, he read the card. Four words were inscribed in perfect calligraphy. "You cannot stop me." Gregory dropped the card and shuddered at the thought racing through his mind. Please God, don't let it be, he begged. He won't. He's just playing a joke. That's all, Gregory convinced himself, trying to gain the courage to open the box. Gregory tugged at the end of the silk ribbon and it unraveled, gliding away from the box. He used two hands and lifted the lid up, looking inside. He uttered a shocked set of "no's" as he dropped the lid to the floor. Within the box, nestled in tissue paper, was a human heart.

Chapter 4

"From the deepest desires often come the deadliest hate."

Socrates

The first officer on the scene had thrown up in the entryway. He was on the job for around eighteen months and had not seen an ounce of blood in that time. The worst he had faced was a man who had threatened to stab him if he issued a traffic citation. The man didn't have a knife, but he arrested him anyway. The newbie tried to get out into the hall before he blew chunks, but hadn't made it. He stood outside the door, head hung in shame. He didn't even look old enough to drink.

"Kate Manning, homicide," she said, introducing herself to the young officer. "This is Mike Cooper," Kate added, pointing at her partner.

"Oliver Guggenheim," he said, barely raising his head as he wrote furiously on a pad, then added, "like the museum. No relation though."

Kate's eyes darted around the hallway. She was looking for any sort of prints on the walls. Her eyes went up and down the wood molding. It was showing its age and had been painted too often without being sanded down. She could positively identify at least three different colors. Paint hung loosely as if preparing to rappel from a bridge. She scanned along the edges, her eyes arriving at the doorknob. Double locks, neither of which showed any signs of forced entry. They were clearly much newer than the paint.

"No forced entry and no visible prints that I could see," young Oliver Guggenheim said, watching Kate's eyes. Mike's eyes went wide and he gave the kid a look of certain fear and quickly shook his head. Mike knew better than to interrupt her.

Mike, an imposing man to most, took Oliver by the shoulder and walked him a few steps away.

"Talk to me, Ollie. Walk me through from dispatch until now," Mike asked. The kid shook his head a bit.

"My friends call me Museum," he corrected.

"Okay, Museum, whattya got for me," Mike said, friendly as always. It was one of the things that made them a good team. Kate sniffed for details, Mike worked the people.

Museum handed Mike a pad of paper and gave his report. "Responding to a call from Jennifer Mathers who reported her roommate had been murdered. Arrived on scene at 2:12 pm and found Mathers sitting on the stairs. She was distraught. So much so, I called for an EMT," Mike nodded, listening and taking notes on his own pad. "I left my partner with her and went up the stairs. No sign of blood evidence or anything out of the ordinary. I checked the doorframe, floor, stairs and rails. The door was ajar. I entered the premises and . . ." Museum's voice trailed off.

Mike quickly asked a question to draw attention away from the embarrassment, "Any other points of egress?"

Museum, shook his head, "Never saw anything like that, man. Girl was butchered."

"Mike, I'm ready," Kate called over to him. The two would enter the scene together.

"Good work Kid. You did everything you were supposed to do," Mike reassured him.

"Thanks. I'm sorry about the . . .," Museum stammered, but Mike cut him off.

"I didn't see a thing, Museum. Not one thing."

The kid smiled and shook Mike's hand, knowing that Mike had saved him countless hours of ribbing at the hands of other cops.

"Can you hang here and make sure nobody comes in without our say so?" Mike asked handing back the pad Museum had handed him. The kid really had done everything right. He had even kept a log of anyone who had been on scene, including time in and out as well as what department they were with. Mike and Kate had been added to the list while they were talking. "Every officer should be as thorough as this kid," Mike thought.

Museum stiffened like a soldier, "Will do."

The smell of stale vomit lingered at the door. Kate handed a pair of latex gloves to Mike and pushed through the door. The metal door moved silently on its hinges. It drifted softly until it struck something unseen behind it and then slowly returned towards Kate's outstretched hand. The small tiled area near the front of the apartment was free of footprints. Kate noted that there were some small specks of dirt, a few tiny stones, former stowaways from the bottom of shoes. The area had not been freshly cleaned, but Kate could smell bleach in the air. No attempt had been made to cover any tracks, at least at the entryway. The steady, rhythmic hum of traffic bounced around the apartment walls. That would have concealed some noise, Kate pondered. She entered first, her blue-gloved hand barely touching the door. Mike followed behind her.

The apartment had an open floor plan. The kitchen, off to the right was small but neat. No clutter on the counters, nothing left out. Behind the kitchen, towards the back of the apartment was a closed door. Kate assumed it was the bathroom. Circling around from there were two open doors that led to the bedrooms. The center of the apartment was dominated by an open living room. Kate ignored the head of the victim jutting above the couch and worked her way from the edges of the room inwards. She noted the lamps, two of them, probably Ikea. Neither of which had been knocked over. A tall fake plant stood in the corner, again, still standing. She looked at the settlement of dust on an end table. A picture, two scantily clad women at a bar that Kate didn't recognize, stood undisturbed.

Mike walked behind her, observing as well. They had developed a routine of sorts that didn't need to be discussed. Kate did the initial look over, Mike dealt with available witnesses first. In this case, there were none to be found. Then, they did a walk through together, never talking or distracting one another. Once complete, they would compare their findings, free of influence from the other. This helped in several ways. It allowed two opinions of the scene to form free from any tainting thoughts. They could test their theories on one another quickly. It would also keep one of them fresh for an evaluation of the witnesses. Kate, the more aggressive one, would use their findings to challenge witnesses. Mike, on the other hand, would use what they found to corroborate what witnesses had told him. It was their good cop, bad cop routine one could argue, but it worked well for them.

Both of them, satisfied that they had gained what they could from their initial walk through, turned to the victim. Museum wasn't kidding. The girl had indeed been butchered. She sat nude, propped straight up on the couch, a massive circle of blood spread from the couch to the floor. A putrid cocktail of excrement, urine, blood and bleach all blended in the air. Her head was tilted back, her mouth agape. Her hair hung behind her, seemingly out of the way. Painted on her forehead, was a blood red cross. There was a large wound on the left hand side of her neck. Kate considered it for a few moments. It wasn't a slash or a stab wound. It struck her as a gash. Something reserved for victims of construction accidents or those who had been ejected from vehicles. The origins of that wound would be something to inquire with the medical examiner about. Dried blood trailed down the victim's body from it. Kate figured she had bled out pretty quickly based on the size and location of the wound.

There was an eerie silence about death. It wasn't like a person was sleeping. There was no breathing, no subtle wheezing of a slightly stuffed nose. Elusive movements that would cause cloth to rub against skin were wholly absent. Death brought on an oppressive silence that forced a person to hear only themselves. The contrast of one's own life and the shattering permanence of death was sobering. It forced a person to consider how fragile they were. Kate tried to shake off the thought, but the scene in front of her made that impossible.

The gash in the victim's neck was gruesome, no doubt about it, but it wasn't what had sent Museum fleeing from the room. The victim had been flayed and gutted. Kate had been through a number of crime scenes. She had seen gore and death but never like this. A straight cut had opened the victim from breast bone to navel. That line was then crossed like a T just under the victim's breasts. Her skin had been pealed back like a vest, laying bear her abdominal muscle wall. That, too, had been opened with a measure of precision Kate had never encountered before. Her rib cage was clearly visible amidst the carnage. Her intestines crawled outward like a nest of snakes that had been accidently disturbed. There were other organs, too, that hung limply from the large hole that had been opened in her. Jutting out from all that horror was a single long stemmed rose that looked as if it had grown from within. Kate recalled the case study one of her college professors had them do on Jack the Ripper. The scene reminded her a great deal of one of the victims but she couldn't recall exactly why. Kate wasn't certain which organs remained and what might have been taken. Something else to discuss with the M.E., she thought.

Soon, the apartment would be abuzz with technicians, busily collecting evidence. Kate would act as the queen bee, instructing the drones on what to do, where to go, and the things she wanted bagged and tagged. Most of the techs she had worked with before and would instinctively know what she wanted. While she supervised them, Mike would start the long and frustrating task of canvasing the neighborhood, knocking on doors. He would question, console those who needed it, and catalogue a long chain of people, who, in all likelihood, had nothing of value to contribute to the case. Real cases were not like crime dramas on television. Often, they took months to solve if they ever got solved at all. Reality was, most cases went unsolved. Kate would love nothing more than to wrap this one up in a tight forty-two minute serialized bow; but, she knew that wasn't in the realm of possibility.

It was time for their initial discussion. Kate walked to the door but Mike lingered, noting some last detail. She waited patiently for Mike to come out. When he did, she silently waited for his assessment.

"Hey, Museum, no one allowed on scene until the M.E. arrives. Clear?" Mike ordered, the Marine in him slipping to the surface.

"Yes, Sir," the kid responded as if he had just received orders from a drill instructor.

"Do me a favor and radio your partner. Tell him to stay with the roommate. He needs to go to the hospital with her and stay with her until we get there." Again the officer sounded off and then immediately began to relay the orders to his partner.

"Walk with me," Mike said to Kate. They strolled down the stairs and out into the relatively fresh air of Jackson Heights. The area, just east of the Brooklyn-Queens Expressway wasn't the most affluent area of Jackson Heights, but it wasn't a bad neighborhood by any standard. Lots of private parks, co-ops, and a smattering of wealthy individuals characterized this part of Queens. Kate had worked the area for six years, Mike almost five. This was the type of case every detective dreams of and then immediately regrets wishing for when it comes to them.

Mike waited as a woman passed him with a stroller and another little kid at her side. When she had put enough distance between them, Mike began, "No signs of forced entry. No signs of any real struggle. Victim died as a result of massive blood loss, likely the result of the trauma to the neck. Not sure what caused that wound, but it wasn't a blade. Killer cuts her open with surgical precision, probably removes something from her, replaces it with the rose. He cleans up nice and tidy, leaves through the front door, calm as a cucumber. We'll have to swab the bathroom. Hopefully, he left us something behind."

"He would have had to bring a bag. A change of clothes with him. No way he could have stayed clean," Kate added, not disagreeing with any of her partner's assessment. "This was an experience for him. The cross, the rose, the time he would have taken," Kate visibly shuddered replaying the final moments of this woman's life in her mind.

Mike reached out and softly held her arm. "You okay, Kate," he asked warmly.

Kate shook him off, "Yeah." She was put off by Mike's concern and loved that he worried about her. That didn't make sense to her, but it was how she felt. Sometimes she could focus around him, and sometimes, he was the only thing she could focus on. They had started out as partners, had become friends, but recently, things were evolving into something Kate didn't quite understand.

"I doubt this is over," she said, eyeing the street pretending to look around for clues, but really avoiding Mike's tender eyes.

Chapter 5

"Life is really simple, but we insist on making it complicated."

Confucius

"Manning? Hey, Manning," Mike called across the office. "Kate, you okay?" he asked bringing the volume of his voice lower.

Mike was a tall, fit former Marine in his early thirties. At six foot three and two hundred ten pounds, he was an imposing figure of a man. A high and tight haircut hid the beginnings of a few early grays that were dotting an otherwise dark brown head. Yet, as scary as he could be in height, size or demeanor, if you took a second to get to know him; he was an enormous teddy bear.

"Detective Manning," Mike said in a sing-song voice as if he were talking to a three-year old.

"Huh?" Kate finally realized that someone was talking to her. She looked up at her partner with a blank expression.

"Would you like me to get you some tea?" he asked. Kate stared at him, glazed eyes and no answer gave away her fatigue.

"Huh?" she said again. Mike took her chin in the crook of his hand and gently shook her head back and forth.

"I said, do you want me to get you some tea?" the words were overly exaggerated as if he were speaking to someone partially deaf. Kate's response was an enormous, uncontrollable yawn that took over her whole body. She stretched her arms high into the sky and pointed her feet straight down to her toes. She nodded her head amidst all of it and Mike bowed in deference to her, "As you command, my lady."

Kate liked Mike. She had liked him the moment they were partnered together. He had everything a female officer could want in a partner. He was imposing. Handy when it came time to intimidate a perp. He wasn't sexist. Helpful and altogether rare when paired with a female. He was also calm. That might have been Kate's favorite quality about him. Mike had a way of approaching life that relaxed those around him. He didn't get angry easily. He wasn't reserved so much as he was Zen-like. Kate figured his approach to life came from being around so much hardship and death. When you see the things combat Marines have, everything else in life isn't worth stressing over. Kate had worried that he was going to be one of those, "I can kill you in two and a half seconds," sort of Marines; the ones that are all bravado. Mike wasn't that at all. He had a presence that didn't need words to convey his strength.

Mike returned with a Styrofoam cup of tea and plopped it on Kate's desk. He picked up the file in front of her and thumbed through it. It was the domestic murder suicide she had stumbled on with her sister. The pictures did more than enough to convey a scene that Mike wished his partner had not had to see in person.

"You file your discharge report yet?" Kate shook her head as she sipped her tea. "I've had partners that have shot all manner of perps, but you are the first to shoot a dead guy," he chided her, shaking his head to add to her shame. Kate was obviously hurting, but Mike didn't know exactly what was going on in that racing hamster wheel of a brain of hers. "You okay?" he asked quickly, returning the file to the desk.

"Sucks. Wish they would just kill themselves, you know? Why do they have to go with the whole, 'If I can't have you, no one can mentality,' and murder kids instead of just themselves?" Mike reached into his pocket and pulled out a Reese's Peanut Butter Cup and placed it gently on top of the file. Kate smiled at the thoughtfulness and picked it up. It was cool to the touch. They were an addiction of hers that she tried not to indulge too often, but she never refused a gift, especially one that had come from the refrigerator. Mike knew her too well, she thought.

"Listen Manning, you ladies do screw with our heads and the male brain isn't the most sophisticated organ. No excuse for this idiot; just saying," Mike said as he held up his hands in a *"don't shoot the messenger"* pose.

Kate dropped the last bit of peanut butter cup into her mouth and opened the file. She buried her head in it, wondering if Mike's last comment had some double meaning. To say that their relationship was complicated was an understatement. They were partners. They were friends. They had also slept together recently and neither had brought the subject up again after it happened. Kate had done the walk of shame back to her apartment sometime in the wee hours of the morning and since that night, everything was back to normal. Outwardly normal, but Kate's head was riddled with nervous energy and millions of questions. She was just terrified to ask them. She was also terrified that she wanted to ask them. So, the two of them sort of existed in a state of limbo that looked normal but had an undercurrent of mass confusion.

"I got in touch with the girl's father," Mike informed his partner. Kate's back stiffened. "Well?" she asked. "Pretty much a horrible convo, as you might expect. We had the local PD show up to inform him and expect my call; but, it wasn't real for him yet. Guy's name is Thomas. He didn't give me anything we didn't already know or piece together ourselves. Jessica was a troubled teen. They fought all the time. He blamed himself for failing her, pushing too hard, not trying hard enough. She turned eighteen and bailed. That was the last he had heard from her."

Mike flipped Kate's pen up and down through each of his long, powerful fingers. She watched the sinew in his forearms dance like the strings of a piano being played by a maestro. She tried to shake it off and focus on the case. When she spoke, she deliberately looked away from him so she wouldn't be distracted again. Kate asked all the questions she knew Mike already had.

"Known enemies?" She asked knowing it was futile. Mike started to chew on the edge of the pen. Kate glanced at him, already breaking her rule and becoming distracted by him again. She chuckled audibly and held her hand to her mouth. He just needed the little pincer glasses and he would have looked like FDR with his long cigarette pinched between his lips, bouncing up and down

Mike looked at her somewhat confused and flippantly replied, "Nope." He hesitated a moment and then admitted, "I didn't tell him how she was making her living." Mike looked down at the floor, "I didn't think he needed that right now."

A search of the girl's apartment had made that assumption plain. Two pretty girls, living together in a nice apartment in Jackson Heights. The two girls worked as part time baristas at a high-end coffee shop two blocks away from their apartment. There was no way that could fund the lifestyle they had. The apartment was full of cash, condoms and adult novelty items that might make even a porn star blush. It was a credit to Mike that he didn't crack a single joke the entire time. Kate knew that had to have been incredibly difficult for him to hold in.

Kate thought Mike was a great cop and an even better detective. If he had an Achilles heel, it was that he genuinely cared. In this business, that could ruin you. Burn out, suicide, or doing something stupid; those were the things caring led to. "So he's a dead end then," Kate cut off that part of the investigation. "What about other family? Mom? Siblings?" Kate queried.

"She was an only child. Mom died of cancer when Jessica was three. They never really knew each other." Mike sighed deeply continuing to gnaw on the pen, "Dad blamed himself for spoiling her too."

Kate thought of her own upbringing. Her mom, too, had died when she and Julie were young. Kate remembered her more than Julie but not much. Most of what she could recall was from pictures and home videos. She was pretty and sweet. Kate recalled her favorite video moment. Her mom was asleep. Dad had decided to bring her breakfast in bed. Julie had made toast, Kate had cracked the eggs and scrambled them. The kitchen was a colossal mess, but the three of them were so proud of what they had done. The girls brought the food in on a tray: orange juice with toast and scrambled eggs. Dad video-taped the whole thing. As Kate and Julie tried to put the tray on the bed, everything tumbled. Mom woke, shocked by ice cold orange juice, screaming from the cold. The girls cried. Mom hugged them and sat in a bed full of orange juice and ate her breakfast and pretended to enjoy every morsel.

Kate missed her. The whole family had a hole in it. No matter how hard her dad had tried to fill in for her; he just wasn't a mother. Kate tried to be a mother to Julie but that didn't work out as well as she had hoped. Kate understood the dangers of growing up without a mom. Girls made bad decisions, dads tried too hard or not at all. Worse, sometimes, the dad's couldn't get past their own pain and resentment. Kate Manning and Jessica Connors had lived parallel lives. They had just chosen different ways of pissing off their fathers.

"How did it go with the M.E.?" Mike asked.

"You were right," Kate admitted, not putting up the fight she normally would in saying those words.

"Told you it would be the heart he took. Anything else?" He asked with mock smugness.

"That was the only thing missing," Kate affirmed and tossed the candy wrapper at him in disgust.

"The wound on the neck was a bite," Kate said, letting the shock of it linger before she spoke again. "M.E. said the killer bit her at least a dozen times. Literally ripped out her jugular with his teeth."

"That's possible?" Mike asked with a furrowed brow.

"Apparently. This is not the case I need right now," Kate said as she stared at the growing mountain of paperwork on her desk.

Mike shoved Kate over and sat at the computer. "Come on, I'll help you fill out your discharge report and then we can go visit Ms. Jennifer Mathers in the hospital. Find out if she remembers any interesting clients that needed more than they offered." The twinkle in Mike's eye let Kate know that the first joke about the sex toys was bubbling to the surface and would boil over any minute.

"Well, I sure hope her bed vibrates," Kate smirked as she beat him to the punch.

"Kate, talk like that, and somebody will need to spank you," Mike said with a deadpan smile.

"You wish," she fired back flipping him the middle finger. "Oh, and you can keep my pen!"

~

Jennifer Mathers was in New York Hospital under guard. The NYPD officer at the door checked their credentials and then waved Mike and Kate in without a word. Boring duty, indeed, but it was part of the job. She was alone, asleep in the room. The television was on, but the volume was so low it barely registered. "I hate the smell of hospitals," Mike whispered. Kate thought of the last time she was in a hospital. She was visiting her father, hoping he would recover from his stroke. He didn't. He died on a plastic mattress with crappy white sheets without anyone who loved him around him. He was supposed to get better, they said. Kate and Julie had gone on with their work, expecting to check him out of the hospital. They thought they would have to fight with him to eat better and take care of himself. They never got that chance.

"He knew how much you loved him," Mike said, realizing now what Kate must be thinking. He rested his hand on Kate's back, just above her belt. His hand rubbed her slightly and this time Kate didn't push him away. Sometimes, she loved that he could read her so well. Other times she resented the hell out of him for it. Her father read her like a book too and she had resented him for it. Kate's emotions started to well up, swarming her, closing in on her, like Time's Square on New Year's Eve. She felt crowded. She needed space. Quickly, she stepped to the side and let Mike's hand drop from her.

"Ms. Mathers," Kate said firmly, trying to wake her and avoid what had just happened. Kate didn't look at Mike. She didn't want to know if he was staring at her with hurt eyes. She couldn't deal with that right now. "Jennifer, we are detectives with the NYPD," Kate said as she saw Jennifer's eyes lift and her head tilt. They were puffy and red with sadness and fear. She barely looked like the same girl in the picture at the bar. There was no carefree joy, no buzz of excited energy. Jennifer still looked like she was in shock. "May we ask you some questions?" Kate continued, ignoring the confusion that comes with sudden waking.

"I'm sorry . . . who are you?" the woman asked, dazed.

"Detective Kate Manning and Detective Mike Cooper, NYPD," Kate said, pulling up the plastic guest chair from the corner of the room. "We'd like to ask you some questions about your roommate."

Jennifer bit her lower lip and tried not to cry. It didn't work. Tears fell in moments and then the horrible grieving sobs that shake an entire body took over. Kate waited them out but Mike couldn't bare it. He reached to her and held her hand.

"I'm so sorry you had to find her like that," he said gently. "We are going to do everything we can to find whoever did this." Mike lifted her hand and held it near her face. He looked into her eyes and said, "We'll keep you safe and I promise you, we won't tell anyone." Jennifer seemed to comprehend his meaning. Most people in Jennifer's line of work didn't want to talk to cops. Jennifer nodded her head and Mike smiled back at her.

"Jennifer, can I call you Jennifer?" Kate asked, even though she already did. The woman nodded and Kate continued, "Is there anyone you know who might have been willing to hurt Jessica?" She shook her head and choked on her tears again.

"Jennifer, we need to know if there might have been a client of yours that got too close? Maybe a recent one that seemed aggressive?" Mike asked softly.

Jennifer again shook her head, "No. No one."

"Did the two of you have any doctors as clients? Any surgeons?" Kate took over again.

Jennifer looked puzzled, "I think so, why?"

Kate went to answer but Mike stopped her. "Just following up a lead," Mike said, wanting to save Jennifer from the explanation as to why they suspected someone with medical experience.

"We will need a list of your clients," Kate demanded. It had come out of her mouth more harshly than she had intended, but Kate still felt agitated at how naked Mike made her feel. He could see through her, as if all her secrets were merely words on a page for him to read at his leisure.

Jennifer started to cry again. She was lonely and scared and totally exposed. Her whole life was crashing around her and the one friend in the world she had was brutally murdered in her apartment.

"I promise, we won't go after them or you. We just want to catch this guy, alright? We want to make sure he can't do it again and that's all we're interested in. Deal?" Mike's voice was serene, like a lake at dusk on a still day.

"O . . . Okay," Jennifer said staring up at Mike, "I'll help you."

Mike took out a zip lock bag from his pocket that contained a cell phone. "Do you know Jessica's cell phone passcode? It would save us a great deal of time and might help us track the man who did this to her."

"5309," Jennifer replied. "Like the old eighties song. It was her password for everything."

Kate cut the conversation short and started walking from the room. "We'll be in touch."

Chapter 6

"The greatest deception men suffer is from their own opinions."

Leonardo da Vinci

Victor sat in a corner booth and listened to the traffic drone along. It wasn't just any booth, though. He remembered this one well. The same orange vinyl, the same white and brown laminated table. Victor held the menu up. Even it was the same, though the prices had changed more than he had expected. This had been his mother's day job. Waitressing tables, telling men her sob story; then, getting them to reach into their pockets out of pity for someone that deserved anything but.

"Can I get you something to drink while you look over the menu?" The waitress was a college-age woman, probably very early twenties. Thick red hair, soft curls and a complexion free of even the slightest blemish. Victor considered her. She was attractive but a bit thick for modern day tastes, probably squeezing into a size eight when a ten would be more appropriate. Her tone suggested that she would rather be in a hundred other places than this diner at this time. She hated her job and her attempts to hide that disdain were thinly veiled at best.

Victor lowered the menu and smiled at her. The two looked each other over, quickly taking the other in. The waitress blushed in embarrassment. She had given a very fine looking man the same treatment she gave everyone. That, she regretted, and instantly tried to make nice. For Victor's part, he took notice that her top three buttons were undone. Her breasts were large, size D's squeezed into a C-cup and pushed up with gusto. They were her weapons of choice. Victor was certain that patrons tipped them well as long as they could get a good, steady glance at them.

"May I have an iced tea, unsweetened please?" Victor asked politely, then quickly added, "Sara." as he read her name tag.

The waitress stumbled an apology, "I . . . I'm so sorry. I didn't mean to be rude it's just that . . . well, usually when a man sits alone in this place they tend not to be the . . . um, nicest kinda people, you know."

Victor tucked his bottom lip in and shook his head. "What do they do, smack you on the behind like they do in the movies?" He then smiled at her, knowingly, then faked a chuckle at the thought of it. Sara smiled and laughed as well. With a toss of her head, she flipped her hair back over her shoulder. Victor stiffened as he watched the whore play her game.

"It's happened, I swear!" Sara retorted, waving her hand in the air.

Victor replied with an evasive but ever so suggestive, "I can believe it," as he let his eyes drift down from her face.

"Thank you. That's very sweet of you. One unsweetened ice tea coming up," she said, stressing the "un" in "unsweetened" like a bad pun.

When Sara returned with the drink she asked, "Are you ready to order, honey?"

Victor noticed the change in tone, the subtle addition of "honey" at the end of her question. This is how they operated. They were opportunistic. They wasted no time on a target they felt they could not win over. Victor breathed deeply, trying to quell the rage within.

"What is your favorite dish, Sara?" he asked as he exhaled. Sara thought he was flirting and joined right in.

"Well," she started as she slid into the seat next to him and took hold of the menu, "I like the surf-and-turf combo. You wouldn't think a diner could do it up right; but, the cook keeps it simple, you know? He doesn't muddy it up with crazy flavors."

Victor understood exactly what she was doing. It was the most expensive item on the menu. He gave a deep, "Hhmmmm," and then said, "If it is your favorite, then it must be great. I will go with that."

Sara smiled and snapped the menu shut. As she rose, she used his leg as leverage, placing her hand on his thigh. It lingered longer than it needed and Victor tightened uncontrollably. Sara started towards the kitchen and said, "I'll do it up right for you!"

The meal was subpar but not as awful as Victor had expected. Sara had refilled his drink three times and checked on him twice over. She flirted with him and at least three other patrons in the diner that Victor could see. Admittedly, Victor was the prime target for her, but that didn't stop her from keeping a few other fish on the hook.

When she returned to clear his dish, she dialed up the charm to ten. "Did you love it as much as I love it?" she asked batting her eyelashes at him.

"Regrettably, no," Victor said leaning back in the chair. Sara gave a disappointed look, but before she could say anything, Victor stopped her. "There is a place down in mid-town, Le Bernardin, ever hear of it?" Victor asked as he examined his own hand. She shook her head. "It's a few blocks from the Museum of Modern Art," he added now looking her in the eyes. "I'd love to take you there so you can taste their surf-and-turf. Maybe I can tour you around the museum and then top off the night with dinner?" Victor suggested not taking his eyes from hers. His confidence was intoxicating and Sara desperately wanted to say yes to this gorgeous man in front of her. She had met too many creeps in this place though. Too many times, she had said "yes" and had gotten burned.

"That's kind of you, but no," she said, rejecting the offer. "I just can't. Too many times I have been asked out here and things have gone bad," she explained. "I hope you understand," she implored.

Victor smiled at her and replied, "I am not surprised that you get asked out often. I thought it was worth the risk to ask." Victor reached into his jacket pocket and drew out his wallet. He dropped two hundred dollars on the table and then neatly stacked them atop the bill. "It has been a pleasure, Sara," he said picking up his iced tea and taking a sip.

Sara picked up the bills and said excitedly, "I'll be back with change," hoping that wasn't what he wanted.

Victor simply waved his hand and stated firmly, "No need."

Sara stopped in her tracks and seemed to pause for a moment. She turned around quickly, her fiery red hair flipping around as she did. "You know what?" she said, smiling. Victor smiled back at her. Here was the truth of her. "It's not like every guy on the planet is some sort of creep," she continued, as she jotted down her number on her order pad. Tearing it off, she walked it over to Victor and tucked it under the side of his plate. Victor glanced down at it as she walked away. In big bold letters it read, "Prove me wrong!" with the exclamation point resting over a small heart. Included with it was her phone number.

Victor had made his choice. He would end her. He would send this tease back to her maker in a box.

Chapter 7

"The dead cannot cry out for justice. It is a duty of the living to do so for them."

Lois McMaster Bujold

A casket is a horrible enough thing, but two of them in miniature just sealed the deal, Kate thought. Julie had asked her to attend the funeral, but Kate had fought her hard on it.

"It will be cathartic," Julie pleaded.

"What does that even mean?" Kate lashed out.

Julie slumped her shoulders and gave Kate a, "*I cannot believe how borderline illiterate you are*" sort of look.

"Don't give me that look. Say what you mean, mean what you say," Kate blasted her little sister with exactly how their dad would have reacted to the use of the word cathartic.

"It will help you deal with your emotions."

"How will doing Christian calisthenics be good for my emotions?" Again, Kate brought forth her father's words.

"Ugh! You are such a pain in the ass! Don't come then you frigid bitch," Julie slammed her hand down on the counter and stormed out of the kitchen.

The game was afoot now. This was a battle that they had fought before. The rematch was a familiar dance. They both knew where to hit; where to hurt one another.

"Don't walk away from me," Kate yelled, following her into the living room.

"Keep your voice down," Julie turned and yelled back even louder. "Anna is asleep!" Kate took a deep breath and tried to calm herself. She was the big sister. She was supposed to be the role model. She heard her father chiding her over and over in her head.

An Absence of Faith

"I'm not going," Kate said as softly but as firmly as she could.

~

Kate sat next to Julie at the funeral. She had caved, like always. The two fought, Julie cried. Kate dug her heels in over something ridiculous. Then, a day or two later, Kate would be overcome with guilt and relent. She would never admit to being stubborn or wrong. She would just show up and nothing was said about it. That way there wouldn't be a second fight. It was their unhealthy pattern of behavior. Julie wasn't sure if she had ever heard anyone in her family other than herself utter the words, "I'm sorry." Her husband, Donald, had taught Julie the tremendous value in those words. How they took responsibility for your actions and relieved the victim of responsibility. They went a long way towards healing. Kate just wasn't interested in that.

"The Lord is my Shepherd, I shall not want; . . ." the priest said. He was a younger man than Kate had imagined. He stood at the altar podium, surrounded by flowers and gilded easels with giant photographs of the mother and the children. Kate did not see a single picture of the father. On the wall, nearest to them, was a collage of family pictures; outings to the park, camping at the lake, baseball games, apple picking. The priest continued, "He makes me lie down in green pastures. He leads me beside still waters; He restores my soul. He leads me in paths of righteousness for His name's sake. . . ."

Kate pulled away from the photos. She didn't understand how this made anyone feel better. Let's look at all the great memories we had and think about how we'll never be able to have any more, she thought. How is continuing to stare at what you lost going to help you cope with it? Kate's solution was to put it into a box and don't ever look back. Opening the box wasn't any use to Pandora and it won't do any good to anybody else either.

The coffins, the central focus of the church, could not be ignored. Kate had tried and failed to ignore them. The two small caskets flanked their mothers on either side, like they were holding hands walking down a steep path. "Even though I walk through the valley of the shadow of death, I fear no evil; for You are with me; Your rod and Your staff, they comfort me. . . ." Kate thought of the children hiding, terrified. To be so scared of your own father. To be murdered by the man who was supposed to love you and protect you and sacrifice for you. She could hear Julie sniffle next to her. Kate didn't look at her. She was feeling the grief as it seeped from her pores.

Kate tried to focus elsewhere. She looked around the church. Distraught and saddened family members in tears, they held each other. Kate saw the grandparents slumped over in their seats. "Surely goodness and mercy shall follow me all the days of my life; and I shall dwell in the house of the Lord forever." Did they believe in goodness and mercy now, Kate wondered. Was this God's mercy on two innocent children? "We remember Jenna and Kyle with loving hearts and we mourn their loss so early in life." To take them violently from a world they had barely known! Kate felt like a cornered animal. She couldn't run, couldn't escape!

She grabbed the book from the pew in front of her. A Bible. This was something she had not held in her hands since her father's funeral. She opened it to a passage her mother used to read to her. Kate thought of the few memories she had of her mother. Mom used to say that the Bible would bring her hope, she recalled. Tears fell from Kate's eyes. Small drops appeared on the pages and the ink began to run. Her father used to say it would put her to sleep. Neither was right. Instead, it made Kate angry.

"It seems so unfair that innocent children can be taken from this world. They had yet to experience all the joys and sorrows that come along with our earthly world."

Kate's hands closed the Bible. The book slapped together and made a loud popping sound that echoed in the church. Kate wiped her eyes dry and stiffened her resolve.

"Yet, we can find hope in our loss. We know that Jenna and Kyle did not experience this world's delights, but they will surely drink of the next world's cup. We now know that there are two wonderful angels who look down on us each day."

An Absence of Faith

Why am I here today? Two kids along with their mother are killed by the man who should have protected them, and for what? Where was God? Walking beside them as their father blew holes in them? Where was God when Jessica Connors got her neck ripped open and her heart pulled out? Kate felt the sadness subside and the rage take over. She unceremoniously dumped the book back onto the shelf in front of her.

"They are with us each day as God is with us. They are with Him now, safe and protected from harm." Please, Kate thought with sarcasm. When she was eleven her dog Candy died. The dog was very old and sick, but Kate loved her very much. Kate had asked her Sunday school teacher if Candy could sit on God's feet and keep them warm like she used to do for her. Kate promised she would pray hard for it. The teacher told her that dogs don't go to heaven, only people do. Kate thought she was a mean bitch and should never have been around kids. She hated her for that, but Kate hated God just a little bit more for not welcoming Candy into Heaven and protecting her.

"Our Father, who art in Heaven, hallowed be Thy name. Thy kingdom come. Thy will be done . . ." Kate avoided muttering the prayer. She reflected on the last time she had said those words. Kate was fourteen when her Nana had died. She became sick very suddenly and Kate had again prayed to God to keep her safe. It was hard for her to speak to Him again, but her mother used to say that God would always help us when we needed him to. She did not want to lose her grandmother. Kate had already lost her mother. The day her Nana died Kate remembered saying to her father that she had tried, but God had not listened.

"on Earth as it is in Heaven. Give us this day our daily bread; and forgive us our trespasses, . . ." Kate couldn't figure it out. How could He not have listened? There was nothing she could do for her mother, her dog, her grandmother. She decided to go to the one man who knew everything and could solve almost any problem, her dad. That was the first time Kate ever saw the man cry. It was the first time her dad couldn't solve her problem or make the hurt go away. He simply said that maybe God didn't hear her.

"as we forgive those who trespass against us; and lead us not into temptation . . ."

If God is all knowing and all seeing, then how could He not hear her? Maybe He wasn't real? Maybe He never existed at all? Maybe He was absent? That had to be it! God was absent sometimes. She was fourteen and it all seemed so logical at the time.

"but deliver us from evil. Amen." As Kate got older she realized that God was absent a lot.

Chapter 8

"We all know that art is not truth. Art is a lie that makes us realize truth, at least the truth that is given us to understand. The artist must know the manner whereby to convince others of the truthfulness of his lies."

Pablo Picasso

As Victor watched the door open he filled with pride at his selection. His date, Sara, wore a tankini knee-length dress that spewed cleavage as if it were a shaken soda.

"Hey, you're on time," Sara chimed in a sing-song voice that wavered between subtle annoyance and sublime satisfaction. "And you brought roses!" she squealed as Victor pulled the bouquet from behind his back. He presented them to her and she gave him a peck on the cheek in gratitude.

She put her face to them and inhaled the aroma of the flowers. They were not the sort of flowers one picked up at a local bodega or grocery store. They were beautiful, full bodied roses. They were perfectly formed, in full bloom and their scent was even more perfect than their shape. The perfume filled her lungs with an exuberance they had not felt in a long while.

Sara left the door ajar and started to walk back into the apartment, heading to the kitchen to put her roses in a vase. Victor didn't enter. He had not been invited to do so. Sara spoke quickly about the various things she needed to do and the reasons she wasn't ready on time as she headed back towards the bathroom. When she realized that Victor had not followed her, Sara giggled at herself and the awkwardness of Victor standing on her tattered welcome rug.

"Come in, Silly," she said curling her finger seductively at him.

Victor stepped over the threshold of the tiny studio and removed his gray pinstriped jacket. As if he had taken her instructions to enter too literally, he remained just inside the door like a stone sentinel. Sara eyed him, making no attempt at hiding it. She looked at his chiseled face, hard cheekbones and stone-blue eyes. She carried her gaze down, following the lines of sinew that showed through his silky bright white shirt. A fancy red tie with grey flecks flowed down like lava and split his chest into two distinct regions. She followed the lines of his muscle across his chest and down his abdominal wall where a tight black leather belt cinched a waistline that looked too small to hold up so thick a frame. A bit lower, her eyes lingered on the bulge in his slick dress pants.

"Please, sit," her voice cracked. She reached her hand out for his and he obliged. Sara led him to the sofa, grabbed the remote and turned the TV on. She rested the remote on his lap, her fingers sliding across his thigh. The gap between his penis and her forefinger reminded him of the spark of life on the Sistine Chapel's ceiling.

Victor smiled widely at Sara. She pretended not to notice, as if she had not deliberately suggested that she was very interested in sleeping with him. Victor considered opening her up right now. He already knew what he would find, or rather, not find. No, he thought. Patience would allow him the safety of the night. Wait, he told himself. She isn't going anywhere. Gregory would not believe if he allowed himself to be caught so quickly. He would misread Victor's desperate excitement for an act of God. Too soon, and Gregory would think an act of God had stopped him, rather than a failure of discipline. No, Victor wanted his lesson to be a slow burn as his had been. One in which his brother prayed and begged God to act and received only silence.

Sara returned to the bathroom to finish putting on her false face. Victor considered all of the effort the female went through to hide the truth. Foundation, eye shadow, lipstick, blush, all to make a man believe they were something other than what they really were. He had tried to understand them once. Why did they lie and deceive at first, and then show the truth and pretend it was there to see all along? His hand squeezed the remote so hard that the battery cover cracked. Calm, he told himself, "Only through patience will Gregory learn that it is all a lie," Victor silently promised himself.

"I'm so sorry. We can go now," Sara said apologetically as she rounded the corner. She did a spin in her dress. On her tip toes she pirouetted and then dropped, holding her arms out to her sides and her head tilted. "Well?" she asked, obviously seeking a compliment for her efforts. She looked little like the woman Victor had met in the diner. Her thick red hair was braided and came down gently over her shoulder, like a river flowing into an ocean of cleavage. The thin wisps of hair at the end of the braid splayed out and tickled at her breast. Her lips were cherry red and the shadowing around her eyes brightened her pupils into a dramatic pop. Did she forget that Victor had known her? He had seen her as something very different at the diner.

Victor rose from the sofa and walked towards her. A lie begets a lie he thought. "You look exquisite," he stated and held his hand to her. Soon, he thought, soon. She beamed at the compliment and took his hand.

Leaning into his shoulder she whispered, "If I forget to say it later, thank you for a wonderful evening," and then planted a kiss on his cheek. Then, they headed out to get a cab.

"Le Bernardin, 155 West 51st Street, please," Victor said after he opened the door and slid Sara across the back seat of the cab.

"I'm sorry I couldn't get off earlier," Sara said as Victor settled in next to her.

"Please, do not worry about it," Victor feigned protest.

"I would have loved to walk the MOMA with you," Sara lamented, taking his hand and pulling it into her lap. She rested her head on his shoulder and asked, "Have you ever been?" Victor chuckled a bit. He had been there, many times. He knew the New York art scene quite well.

"Yes. I am an art and antiquities consultant," he said blandly.

"Really?" Sara leaped up from his shoulder and stared at him. "What exactly does an art and antiquities consultant do?" she asked. Victor took his hand from hers and began to explain.

"I locate, evaluate and obtain fine art and antiquities for interested buyers and sellers. I act as a middle man, of sorts. I provide expert analysis of both the quality and authenticity of a piece as well as give insight into the market value of the item."

Sara smiled quickly and then frowned just as fast. She dropped her head. "Wow, you are way out of my league," she murmured, then quickly followed with, "So, what made you fall in love with art?" so as to avoid the awful truth she had discovered.

Victor ignored her self-conscious weakness and explained, "Most art is deception. In truth, artists are almost always liars. They try to convince us that we live in a world that is beautiful or heroic or some such nonsense. But, every so often, an artist breaks the mold. Sometimes, an artist shows us a profound truth; a truth about ourselves or the world around us. I appreciate the skill of the liars, but I seek out the ones who show us the reality most people would rather not admit to."

~

Le Bernardin, like all things in Victor's life, was art. Sara was stunned by the restaurant. Creamy white tablecloths embellished with ornate dishes, subtle flowers and candles were surrounded by plush chairs of deep amber-brown. The walls and ceiling were an immaculate array of wooden décor mixed with decorative glass, fresh flowers and ocean waves. They were seated immediately by a maître d' that made Sara feel like a princess. She was in awe of everything around her. As the maître d' handed her the menu, she nearly fainted.

"Dear God, Victor, the prices," she tried to keep her voice low as she leaned towards him over the table.

Victor smiled at her naivety, "The cuisine is worth every penny, I assure you. Nevertheless, they are no concern to you."

Victor selected a wine from the more than nine hundred different offerings and ages that originated from a dozen different countries. He selected a French one.

"I always like to pair my wine with the national origin of the food. Seems to me the natives would know best, would you not agree?"

Sara couldn't help but giggle. "I have no idea! The only pairings I make are whether or not to go with coffee or tea with your scrambled eggs," Sara was in a world that she had only seen in movies and the reality of it was difficult for her to process.

"Shall we go with the Chef's tasting?" Victor suggested. Sara looked at the price again and visibly shuttered at it. The cost was more than she made at the diner in three days and that was just for one of them.

"Victor, I can't . . ." she stammered.

He ignored her protests and called the waiter over. He ordered the Chef's Tasting for both of them. The waiter explained that each dish would be paired with a different wine and asked if they still wanted the bottle they had already ordered. Victor assured him they did.

"My pleasure, Sir," the waiter replied. Sara shook her head in stunned silence, trying to process the enormous amount of money Victor was spending.

"Sara, there is no finer dining in Manhattan. Enjoy yourself and do not fret over the cost. I have been to more expensive restaurants that do not compare in quality to Le Bernardin."

They sampled Tairagai raw clam, king fish caviar, lobster, monkfish, tuna, truffles and more. Sara relaxed and enjoyed the explosion of flavors that she had never before experienced. She watched as each dish arrived and Victor studied it. He examined the placement of each item on the dish, how the garnish lay atop or on the side. It was as if he cared more about how the food was displayed than the flavor of it. Sara was shocked at the precise care that was taken to place each delicacy so perfectly on every dish.

"Nobody uses a spatula to flip anything in this place," she observed as Victor studied the s'mores like dessert in front of him. Sara noted that his eyes looked angry. It was as if she had interrupted him in the midst of a delicate scientific experiment. Victor retuned his gaze to the dessert and tilted his head slightly. Several uncomfortable seconds ticked by before he responded.

"No," he stated, "They are careful in how they display their work here. It is one of the reasons I appreciate them so much. If you want to send a message, you must craft it carefully, display it in the manner that will ensure people see only what you want them to." He looked up at her and locked eyes with her. "Appearance matters, would you agree?" Victor queried and glanced down at her heaving chest. Sara nodded her ascent and Victor rose from his seat without touching his dessert. "Shall we go?" he asked. Sara was looking forward to this part. She was going to pay him back in kind for the best meal of her life; she planned on giving him the best sex of his.

Victor handed the waiter a thick wad of one hundred dollar bills and escorted Sara out into the night air.

"Did you enjoy it," he asked. Sara tucked her arm into his and pulled herself close.

"Victor, if I had to have a last meal, that would be what I would want. It was just amazing," Sara said, "thank you," and then drew herself up to his face. She kissed him on the lips and let herself linger. She kissed him again, letting her mouth slip open. Sara ran her hand around his back and pulled him closer. Her breasts pushed against him and then she stopped kissing him. She let her head rest near his chin a moment and then whispered, "I really want to thank you for tonight."

Victor tensed with anticipation. Soon, he would go to work. He would sculpt a masterpiece and deliver it to the world. Most of all, he would present to Gregory further proof that he dedicated his life to a lie. Victor took her hand in his and gestured with his other to walk.

"Well then, shall we retire for the evening?" Sara squeezed his hand gently and grinned.

"This is a perfect evening," she remarked.

"Indeed it is. Indeed it is." Victor replied.

~

Sara would die quickly. Victor had no desire to play with her and so he delivered an explosive head butt the moment she had shed her dress. She had come in for a kiss, pinning Victor against the front door. Instead, Victor had driven his forehead into her nose so forcefully that a fine mist of blood and bone sprayed in every direction. He dragged her naked body over to the faded brown leather sofa and unceremoniously dumped her there. He removed all his clothing and folded each item neatly, stacking them on the kitchen counter. Victor noted several blood stains forming on his grey pinstripe jacket. He regretted its loss but wasn't about to allow that to dampen his spirits in so fine a moment.

He selected two black handled blades from the drawer. The first was a small four-inch boning knife. In cooking, it was used to remove muscle and flesh from the bone while leaving little waste. It was large enough to delve deep but small enough to control. Victor planned to use it exactly as it was intended. The second blade was a fileting knife, used to remove skin from fish and other dishes before cooking. That, too, would be used as envisioned. Satisfied with his selections, he returned to the sofa to work. He never brought his own tools, instead preferring to let fortune rule the day. Sara's blades were sharp. His work would go quickly, he thought somewhat sadly. Victor had rested her head back upon the sofa so it faced the sky. Her breathing was shallow but loud, impeded by the damage to her nostrils.

"Look to your God for salvation. You will find none," he remarked.

He dug the smaller fileting blade into her neck, near the jaw line. Her body convulsed from the pain, but she was unconscious from the earlier trauma. Quickly, with the skill of a man who had studied anatomy for two semesters and was used to working with his hands, he drew the blade around her face. The blade cut deeply as it traced a line from her jaw around her forehead and back again. Using his fingers, he lifted the flesh and slid the blade underneath. Slowly, carefully, he flayed the skin from her face. The shattered nose was the difficult part. That he had to remove with less finesse.

He set her face aside, laying it on the sun dried leather of the sofa. He flicked the blade to the side, splattering blood in a lengthy arced curve. Victor examined the clean edge before making a large incision that cut from her breastplate to her navel. Then he crossed the line as if it were a large letter T, giving Sara the look of a drunken shirtless football fan. He exchanged the fileting blade for the boning knife. With the larger implement in hand, he sunk the four inch blade into her midsection. Her body shuddered and then fell limp. Seemingly oblivious to it, he carved through the muscle wall and then dug his hands into her flesh and pulled her open.

Victor watched the blood pour slowly from her. Her heart no longer beat, so the flow was slowing, only gravity working to draw it out. The blood splattered onto the timeworn oaken panels and swirled delicately around the subtle imperfections in the floor. Gentle undulating waves, like ribbons blowing in a gentle breeze flowed through the forming pool. Here was a truth few artists would ever know and fewer still had the courage to show. This was a sublime emptiness, a black hole of truth no one could deny.

Chapter 9

"You know that when I hate you, it is because I love you to a point of passion that unhinges my soul."

Julie-Jeanne Eleonore de Lepsinasse

Mike flushed the toilet for the third time, the swirling motion making him feel sicker than he already did. His stomach was churning and what had come out of him seemed never ending. He decided that this must be a break in the festivities, at least, and tried to break up his love hate relationship with the porcelain throne. After washing up, he headed out of the bathroom door only to find Kate leaning against the wall, waiting for him.

"You weren't listening in on that, were you?" he moaned holding his stomach.

"Feel better?" Kate asked poking him in the tummy.

"What the Hell was in those things, acid?"

The two headed towards their cubicle desks in silence, not bothering to fight the cacophony of noise in the hallway. They dodged other officers and clerks as they made their way through the crowded department office space. The heavy traffic forced them to wait several moments before they could turn into the cubicle.

"You don't suppose that eating four chili dogs from a Halal truck had anything to do with it?" Kate asked and then the detective in her immediately kicked in, "I don't even know if chili cheese dogs are permissible under Islamic law?"

Mike gave her a guilty look, "I didn't go to the Halal truck you like. I went to that one on the corner, near Starbucks. Muslims can't eat pork and I really wanted a chili cheese dog."

Kate shook her head, "A dog, just one? You had four, you moron! Which one, by the way? Everything in this city is near a

Starbucks." Mike pointed off towards the north and then ran back to the bathroom.

When Mike came back to the desk, he looked a little pale, but otherwise intact.

"Had to be the brownie. Chili cheese dogs have never done that to me," he said, looking at the files on the desk over Kate's shoulder.

She reared back and smacked him hard on his behind, "My brownies do not eat holes in people's stomachs, thank you!"

Mike plopped down hard into his chair and feigned pain, "Careful, careful, I'm in a delicate state right now." Kate growled at Mike and pointed sarcastically to the tray of brownies, two thirds of which were gone.

"I'll have more later," he promised and Kate threw her hands in the air in exacerbation.

"You ready to get to work champ?" Kate asked as she watched Mike rub his tight abdominal wall and silently swallow a burp. "So attractive," she added half meaning it.

He shook his head, over exaggerating the speed. Mike held his hand up, palm facing her and pushed it forward at her as if he was halting traffic. Kate snickered at the antics but waited patiently until he was done. Mike finally mumbled something under his breath, and Kate took that to mean he was ready to review the case file.

"Any leads yet?" she asked cautiously.

"Not much," Mike muttered in frustration as he tossed the file into Kate's lap.

Kate sat back at her desk and opened the manila folder. She shuffled through prints of the crime scene, the medical examiner's report and the sparse witness statements they had collected. Mike pulled a scraped up metal folding chair from the corner, turned it backwards and straddled it. His arms crossed over the top of the chair. Kate stared at the veins that ran to and fro in his forearms. They were thick, powerful arms, not body builder big but big enough to impress upon someone that this was a guy that you didn't want to mess with. Kate remembered those arms lifting her into bed and the thought was damn distracting to her! She told herself it happened because they were drunk; but, somewhere not too deep in the recesses of her brain, she knew that was a total lie. She remembered every second of it and had replayed it in her head fifty times over.

"Manning," Mike queried but got no response. "Hey, Manning, you go to your happy place or something?"

"What kind of background do we have on her?" Kate asked quickly, trying to reengage in the conversation. She felt the heat rushing to her face and was certain that she was blushing. Quickly, she buried her face in the folder and waited for Mike to speak.

Mike knew they were retreading old ground, but he understood this was how Kate liked to work a case.

"The victim graduated from high school, just barely, according to her dad. He was a real pleasure to speak to, by the way. So, thanks for that," Mike said and stuck his tongue out at her. "She was estranged from the family. Ran away and never made contact. Dad wasn't all that surprised that he hadn't received this call sooner. His words, not mine. It didn't help him handle the shock any better though. Lots of guilt and regret. He couldn't give me anything about her life since she left home. Total dead end on that front. The victim's only close friend was the witness who discovered the body. She didn't give us much either. I'm still whittling away at the client list, but all of the best candidates have been cleared. You get anything?"

Kate leaned back in the chair and stared at Mike. She wore her frustration on her face and Mike could see it plainly. He reached across her and took a large chunk from what remained of the brownie tray. Kate watched as an enormous brownie traveled across her face. She shook her head and held in the comments that streamed through her subconscious.

"Nothing that will lead us to a killer. Several of the numbers I traced led to prepaid lines. The others had solid, though sleazy, alibies," Kate said, trying to ignore the trap Mike had set. She knew he was egging her on to say something to him. She wasn't going to give the man-child the satisfaction. "I have a good idea of who Jessica was, but I still can't get a handle on the killer."

Mike held the brownie high in the air and let it fall like a circus acrobat leaping and plummeting into a tiny pool at the bottom. He chomped and chomped, smacking his lips in delight. Lips wide open, masticating for all the world to see.

Kate looked at Mike in feigned disgust as if he were a pig. Then, she glanced at the crime scene photos in the file. "I think I have a good handle on the how, just not the who, or why? Can't figure out the why." Kate tried to remain focused, but Mike had taken his little show on the road and started to chew just inches from her face. "That's gross, you know," Kate finally conceded getting up from her desk to put some space between her and her clown of a partner.

Kate began to pace as Mike dragged the tray of brownies towards him and took another large chunk. One more like that and the tray would be finished. This one received none of the fanfare of its predecessor with Mike simply breaking parts off of it to eat.

"We know that he didn't force his way in. We can assume they knew each other at least somewhat due to the nature and condition of the apartment." Kate padded back and forth tapping a pen against her head. "Why though? What was the motive? Why cut apart a beautiful young woman and take out her heart as a souvenir?" Kate paused, waiting for a response from Mike. Mouth full of brownie, he suddenly remembered his manners and simply shrugged his shoulders.

"Was it vengeance? Did she reject him?" Kate went back to her pacing. She stopped every so often and would go to speak and then stop. Mike was always fascinated by this process. It was how she worked a problem. He had known her for several years now and he still couldn't quite grasp how her mind worked. That was okay by him. He liked the mysterious types.

"No. Rejection isn't enough. There is more to this guy than lust."

Mike shifted in the chair. He needed to refocus himself. His mind had drifted to a very different subject with a much more positive outcome. He reached down and adjusted himself while Kate paced away from him. He wouldn't be able to stand for a few minutes without embarrassment. "Maybe the dude was horny and a little too creative for her tastes?" Mike suggested, knowing that wasn't the case.

"Is it a date? Does he pick her up in a bar? Maybe they sit through dinner or a show? This guy wants something. He's willing to devote time and energy to it too."

Mike was willing to do that too. He wanted to take Kate out. Ask her to dinner and give her a proper date. Now's not the right time, he knew. Still, that didn't change what he wanted. It was becoming harder and harder to work with her and not pounce on her and kiss her. He had considered asking for a transfer but knew how that would look, not just to the department but to Kate as well.

"He arranges the date, sits all the way through dinner and then . . . then what, what?"

Mike chimed in with a smile, "He tries to get some, freaky stuff, and she sends him packing?"

"Maybe," Kate pondered, "but then why not rape her before you cut her up. There were no signs of rape."

Mike had already gamed this all out in his head. Kate had to do her thing. She had to talk it out. He was just her sounding board. He knew his role and had learned long ago to just roll with it and sprinkle in some color commentary on occasion.

"We know all of the violence occurred in the living room. So maybe they were fooling around and she rejected him? I don't know. It doesn't seem to fit."

Kate's speed increased as her mind raced against a problem that she had no answers for.

"The two of them are on the couch, suddenly, she rejects him and he takes a three inch portion of flesh right out of her neck and exposes her jugular? It makes no sense."

"I know where you are headed with this one, Katie. You figure the victim was killed not because of who she was; but, what she was, right?" Mike said to her, predicting her answer.

Kate pointed at him for a moment. "Jessica wasn't killed because she was Jessica. She was a generic target and you know it. Every sign points to it. He's looking for something. Maybe he's a collector?" Mike watched Kate return to her pacing back and forth. He tried to mimic the look on her face as she thought. It was a furrowed brow with a sort of left eye squint. He thought it was adorable and loved watching her this way. She was one of the smartest girls he had ever known. Not facts and figures smart, but quick witted and deductive. She was smoking hot too. He knew. He had seen her naked and that definitely didn't hurt either. Mike really liked her and that sort of scared the crap out of him. He didn't like being scared. That was a problem he was going to have to tackle head on.

Kate walked past the desk and slammed her hand down on it. "I just don't know!" she wailed. The empty brownie tray sailed into the air and landed face down on the floor. Mike stared at it for a moment, lamenting its demise despite the fact that it was empty.

"All I know is that he is still out there. He's still out there, and I don't think he's found what he's looking for yet. That scares the hell out of me."

"Want to go out for dinner?" Mike blurted.

More than a little dumbfounded, Kate contemplated what she had just heard. Did he mean, he's hungry, let's go eat or did he mean, I'd like to take you out to dinner? There was a lengthy mental cartoon-like scream that rattled around in her head as she tried to sort through the wording of the request. The words "go out" made an appearance but he didn't say, "Do you want to go out with me?" Kate wished she could just talk to him! Unfortunately, Mannings were not known for their ability to share emotions. They were more the emotionally frozen types. That was why Kate always joked that her sister Julie had to have been adopted. Finally, Kate mustered the courage to answer in an equally ubiquitous form, "Sure."

~

Food, a few drinks and suddenly they had their tongues in each other's mouths. They never discussed it, either before or after. They just sort of knew it would happen at some point in the evening.

"I'm gonna go," Mike stated, reaching his hand across to her.

"Yeah, it's late," Kate agreed, turning her palm up, offering herself to him.

Then they would start making out in the back of the cab.

Kate liked to be in control. Mike let her take the reins and never fought her over it. The few other guys she had ever been with always wanted to control her. They wanted to set the pace and pick the positions. Mike went with the flow and that made Kate very happy.

They stumbled into his apartment and Kate pushed him towards the bedroom. She tugged at his pants while Mike tossed his shirt. Kate dumped him unceremoniously onto the bed and then undressed as he watched her every move. Then, she mounted him and the two rolled into one. They enjoyed each other's bodies, kissing and caressing each other like long lost-lovers, unexpectedly reunited.

"I'm gonna . . ." Mike started to say but Kate grabbed his head and kissed him aggressively. With her other hand she held his bottom and pulled him closer to her. In seconds, she felt him pulse. It was a seismic tremor that sent shudders through her. Pure ecstasy throbbed in her. She had never done an illegal drug in her life, but she imagined this was what heroin must be like. She had tasted this once before with him and couldn't get it out of her mind since. Kate enjoyed the blissful seconds of his taut body and then felt him relax and collapse on her.

She found herself holding him tightly, not wanting him to roll off of her. But, he did. He kissed her, once passionately and the second a simpler goodnight kiss. His arms wrapped around her and pulled her towards him, deeper into the bed. Kate could feel him, still stiff and erect. She listened to his breathing slow and then fall into a steady rhythm. She wanted to stay but she needed to go. Kate had already complicated things enough the first time they had slept together. Now, allowing it to happen again would only multiply those problems. She couldn't add sleeping over to them. They weren't a couple. They couldn't be a couple. She wondered if a heroin addict regretted shooting up when they came off the high, or did they just want to shoot right back up again?

Kate gently slipped her legs out of the bed and tried to slither out from under Mike's arms. The chill of the air conditioning tried to blow her back into bed, every gentle breeze screaming "Stay . . . stay . . ." She grabbed Mike's shirt that had been discarded at the start of things and had landed near the bed. Throwing it over her head, she left the bed and began quietly searching the room for her clothes.

Mike watched her fumble in the darkness. She was wearing his shirt, a major turn on for him. At first, he hoped she was just heading to the bathroom and that she would come right back. As he watched her try to put on her jeans, he realized that wasn't what she was up to. He leaned up in the bed letting Kate know she had been busted.

"Kate, please stay," Mike said.

It wasn't a demand. It wasn't pleading. Kate struggled to pin down what it was in his voice that scared her so much. God, she wanted to crawl back in the bed with him. He was kind and funny, strong and warm. He was damn near perfect and that just made Kate think of all of her dysfunctions even more. I'll only hurt him worse if I stay, she thought, but that wasn't what she said.

"God, I can't do this," Kate cried and ran from the apartment, tears falling from her eyes. What she had meant to say was, "God, I can't do this to you," but like always, Kate made a mess of her life and the lives of those around her. She couldn't make this work and that crushed her. For Kate, life felt like a sort of eternal damnation of mistakes and missed opportunities. Kate dropped to her haunches on the broken sidewalk and sobbed, alone in a city of millions. Silently, she asked, "What did I ever do to deserve this, huh? Please, God, help me."

Chapter 10

"Man does not control his own fate. The women in his life do that for him."

Groucho Marx

Victor entered the church doors, a carefully wrapped gift box tied together with a single red ribbon rested under his thick arm. He looked like a man headed to a fancy wedding. His suit was perfectly tailored, gray with light pin stripping. A pink shirt with a daring tie died pink-gray brought it all together. Victor could be a walking suit commercial.

An attractive young woman sat in a pew drawing in a notebook. She was probably in her early twenties, long brown hair and a seductive black and yellow flower print sundress. Victor smiled at her and she immediately blushed. She dropped her head into her notebook but used her hand to tuck her hair behind her ear. Victor noticed that she made several quick glances at him.

"Excuse me," Victor said softly. "I am terribly sorry to interrupt your work," he said, holding up his hand in apology. The young lady put her pad down and turned her body towards him. Firm, perfectly sized breasts rose slightly from her dress. Her legs, tightly pressed together held the bottom of the frock from floating up and revealing more of her legs. She was a temptress, like all the rest.

"Oh, no. Please. It's no bother at all," the girl smiled demurely.

"My name is Victor. It is a pleasure to meet you." Victor introduced himself formally though not offering his hand.

"Laura. Laura Moles, nice to meet you too." The young woman offered her hand to shake. Victor took hold of her hand and gently shook it.

"I was looking for Father Gregory. Could you tell me where he might be?" He released her hand and it lingered in the air.

Laura pointed towards a door on the side of the church, "He's in the confessional."

"Laura Moles, it was indeed a pleasure. Thank you," Victor said and bowed slightly to her.

She waved at him, her fingers dancing in the air, "Hope to see you around Victor."

Victor smiled as he left her. You will. I will be the last thing you see, he thought. When he reached the confessional door Victor turned to see if she was still looking at him. He knew she would be and she was. Embarrassed at being caught, she quickly took up her pad again and started shading something with her pencil. They are all the same, he thought and pushed the door open.

Victor sat on the bench and placed the box next to him. He thumbed the button of his jacket, releasing it and sliding it from his shoulders. He cleared his throat and announced himself to his brother.

"Brother Gregory, I have brought you more proof." He let the words linger in the stale air. He knew his brother was listening.

"You are not welcome here. Leave!" Gregory whispered, but with clear anger in his voice. Victor, satisfied with the impact of his arrival, smiled widely.

"Now, Gregory, that is no way to treat a guest in the house of God. After all, the sign does say, welcome to all who enter here." Gregory remained frozen in the same stone-like pose he held when he first heard Victor's voice. If he remained still, maybe the predator would not pounce. Gregory took a deep breath and tried to stop his brother.

"Why have you come to God's house? Are you here to repent? Or are you here to assail His word?"

Victor leaned forward in the confessional and clasped his hands, "I have come to finish a conversation started long ago. I have come here for resolution, not repentance."

Gregory, hidden from his brother's view leaned forward and clasped his hands as well. The two men sat inches from one another. They looked alike, shared the same mannerisms but neither believed they had anything in common. Gregory knew this conversation well. "I am listening," he said.

Victor began, "You know that my search has begun."

Gregory quickly responded, attempting to convince his brother, "You will find nothing; we have already been through this." Gregory had been frustrated by this discussion before though his brother had never gone to such great lengths to prove him wrong. Victor was determined to show Gregory that he was smarter. Gregory, in turn, was as dedicated to the idea that Victor could be convinced that the world wasn't full of what he thought it was.

Victor sighed audibly. He waited to respond to his brother. "You are correct on one point at least Gregory, I have found nothing," Victor paused and looked down at the box beside him. "I will find nothing for it does not exist within them."

Gregory was unmovable on the subject, "What you seek is not of this world. You cannot see it or hear it. A man like you cannot even perceive it." Gregory realized his voice had grown louder and he had stood up in the confessional. He sat himself down and tried to steady himself.

Victor, sensing his brother's increasing tension, escalated the conversation. "Still, you remain faithful to the hypocrisy of religion. How sad," Victor lamented.

Gregory lashed out, succumbing to his rage, "You are a murderer, Victor! That is sad. You kill the children of God in a vain attempt to prove what cannot be proven." Gregory again tried to lower his voice. He took a deep, calming breath. "You must have faith."

Victor laughed heartily. "I am no murderer, I am a liberator if nothing else." Victor clicked his tongue a few times. "If what you believe is true, I do your flock a service by speeding them to their maker."

Gregory refused to accept his brother's explanation, "The body is as sacred as the soul! You are disturbed!" he whispered.

Victor now moved to lay his trap, "Jesus is the Resurrection and the Life; He who believes in Jesus even if he die, shall live; and whoever lives and believes in Jesus, shall never die. Is this not so, Gregory?"

Anger welled within Gregory and he fell for the bait. "Yes. You would do well to heed those words," he stated not realizing where Victor was leading him.

Victor continued to entice his brother into a verbal cage, "Does not God teach you that death frees you all from the earthly body? Death frees you from the very vessel that allows sin."

Gregory foolishly continued to participate, "He does." Victor's opportunity was here. "There is a young woman in one of the pews. Her name is Laura, I believe. I may do God a favor and free her from the vessel of sin He has caged her in."

"You will not!" Gregory screamed. "I promise you Victor, I will turn you in. You will never harm another soul. I won't allow you to touch her, you sick . . ." Gregory trailed off, exacerbated, frustrated, and enraged by his brother.

Victor remained seated, as calm as he was when he arrived. The growing ferocity in his brother's voice was met with a cold, simple statement. "Remember . . . You cannot stop me." Gregory started to pound on the wall of the confessional with his fists. His face seethed with anger.

"I can! I can and I will, you devil!" Gregory screamed.

Victor rose and went towards the door of the confessional. He left the wrapped box on the bench. "Don't forget your present, Gregory," he said tapping the top of it.

Gregory, again, yelled, "I'll stop you!"

Victor turned before he exited, "Remember, Gregory." He opened the door and saw Laura still seated in the pew. He smiled at her, turned to his brother and finished him, "Remember your promises."

He walked confidently across the church. The click of his shoes warned her of his approach and she glanced at him and then pretended not to hope that he was coming to speak to her. Victor saw her nervous smile as he spoke. "I know I would forever regret not asking for the number of so lovely a lady," he said sweetly.

Laura beamed at the compliment. She quickly jotted down her number in her pad and tore it off for him. As he took it from her, she held his hand for just a moment.

"I hope to hear from you soon," she said.

Victor nodded and walked out into the aisle of the church. He slid his hands into his pockets and sauntered down the aisle, his suit jacket under his arm. Victor smiled to himself. As he walked through the doors of the church, he paused and looked back, "Remember your promises to mother, and to God, Gregory."

Gregory remembered his promises all too well. He sat with the decorative box his brother had left him. He did not want to open it. Gregory knew the contents would be the same or worse than the previous one. He would need to open it, though. He would need to know what his brother was doing.

Gregory tugged at the ribbon and let it fall to the tiled floor. He lifted the lid and nearly retched. Hands held to his mouth he stared in horror at the heart in the box. This time Victor had taken her face too. The brittle remains of a woman's skin adorned the bottom of the box as if it were tissue paper. Quickly, he slid the lid back on and put the box aside.

~

Gregory buried the first heart in the garden he tended behind the church. He had excavated the area in his free time when he first arrived at the parish. Over time, he had planted a large collection of roses that bordered a simple gray stone walkway. Gregory had placed a large shaded white arbor at the end of the path. Under it, he included a wooden rocking bench that he visited often. The garden was a sort of memorial to his mother. Gregory had started it as a sort of cathartic exercise and maintaining it allowed him to still feel connected to the woman who had so heavily influenced his life.

Now, he took the second gruesome box under his arm and headed outside. He would bury this one as well. Gregory had ornamented the first victim's remains with a small transplanted rose bush from deeper in the garden. Gregory had planted roses of various colors in the garden for years, though red dominated the spectrum of colors. Parishioners thought it was so that there would be flowers available for funerals or other events, but that wasn't the reason behind his decision. It was a gentle nod to his mother's love of the flower and a way for him to remember and honor her. To Gregory, the fragrance of a rose was his mother. She kept them often in their apartment, wore cheap perfume that attempted to mimic the scent and wore red as often as she could. He could not bury her here. So, he buried her son's victims instead. Here, in this garden, he honored his sacred promise to her.

Gregory had just turned temty-one when his mother had passed, her battle with addiction finally getting the best of her. Gregory had led her away from that life, he thought. He had encouraged her and brought her to church with him. His dedication to God, he believed, had inspired her to get clean. But, she was in too deep. The hole she had dug for herself had crafted tall walls around her, like a prison without windows. Succumbing to temptation, she returned to her old life and the hell it brought. Penniless and seemingly alone in the world, her body was carted off and buried in a potter's field.

Victor had earned a scholarship to UCLA to study and had, Gregory thought, left his troubled life behind him. Gregory had tried to contact him about their mother's death, but could never get in touch. The brothers could never claim to have a close relationship. Victor grew up with Gregory as a pseudo-father figure and resented him for it. Gregory had made a solemn promise to care for his mother and brother. To protect them at all costs, and it had made him overbearing at times. Gregory knew that, nevertheless, he was certain it had to be that way. Victor could easily get himself in trouble if he didn't have anyone looking out for him.

Gregory understood that Victor was an angry child. He didn't have the things his peers had in school. As brothers, they grew up with little and what little they had was often donated. Where Gregory appreciated the generosity of others, Victor resented it. Where Gregory saw the hand of God, Victor only felt emptiness. Gregory had tried to help Victor see but had yet to succeed in his efforts.

As Gregory dug a second hole in the garden to bury the remains of his brother's second victim, his thoughts went to the last time they had spoken before their mother died.

"May God be with you and travel with you always," Gregory said, wishing his brother luck.

"There is no God," Victor muttered, frustrated that his brother could not see the truth of it.

"God is everywhere Victor, whether or not you choose to see Him or not. He is with us and in all of us."

"Shut up, you simpleton," Victor unleashed.

"Victor, I am only trying to help you to . . ."

Victor lunged forward and grabbed his older brother by the neck. "Shut up, I said. I have had enough of you and your blind faith. Speak to me of this again and I will prove to you that God does not exist!"

Gregory wrestled his way free and whispered, "That is not possible."

Victor smiled sadistically and said, "We shall see. We shall see."

Chapter 11

"Miracles are not contrary to nature, but only contrary to what we know about nature."

Saint Augustine

Kate stood in her sister's kitchen with the early morning sun shining in. "It's funny how a person's refrigerator tells a story," she thought. Kate had seen more than her fair share of them. In many ways, they were a great tool of the detective. Some were barren and devoid of life. They were sterile. They spoke of people that had little they valued more in life than order and organization. Then, there were those that were peppered with all manner of photos and drawings; a kaleidoscope of a life well lived. A clean house with neat lines didn't matter. These were the carpe diem sort of folks.

The life she was looking at today was a life that almost never was. The doctors said it was impossible. They had told Julie that she couldn't get pregnant. Her little sister had been heartbroken by the news. She had always dreamed of a family, of children and a life full of noise and toys. Kate thought she was crazy but felt horrible for her. Kate even shocked herself when she offered to be a surrogate for her little sister; but thankfully, that hadn't been necessary. Miraculously, Julie had gotten pregnant. Still, doctors told Julie that the likelihood of her carrying to term was infinitesimally slim. The baby didn't have a prayer. But, every day, Julie grew wider. Every day a little life took root inside her and hope grew brighter and brighter. So, too, did the fear that this little miracle wouldn't come true. Then, when Anna was born it was like someone took the world off of Atlas's shoulders.

Anna was as much a gift to Kate as she was to Julie and Donald. I never knew I could love something so much, Kate thought. She stared at a picture of Anna and her in the park. Anna's face was full of chocolate ice cream, and Kate had joined in the fun and had spread some on her face as well. The two of them smiled wide with chocolate mustaches. Kate remembered the day well. Anna had fallen off the jungle gym and Kate couldn't catch her in time. Kate cried harder than Anna did. Julie had laughed at the two of them, chiding Kate, "She's not a china doll. You don't have to be terrified, Kate." But she was. Kate couldn't understand how Julie could be so calm. Kate worried about that little girl all the time. When Anna first learned to walk, Kate ran around the house with her hands on both sides of the little girl's head. Her knuckles were worn thin as she bashed her hands into things protecting Anna from every corner and turn.

"She's my little miracle," Julie would say. "A gift from God." Kate didn't really believe in God, but she wasn't going to argue with the fact that Anna was indeed a miracle. Before Anna, Kate wanted no part of children. Holding her little sister's baby in the hospital changed everything. Kate could see herself becoming a mother now. The thought terrified her but it was there now where it had never been before. Kate doted on Anna. She adored her and spent time with her as often as possible. Anna also performed one other little miracle no one could have predicted. She had brought Kate and Julie closer together.

"So, you don't have anything to go on yet?" Julie asked. She was pouring coffee into wide brimmed mugs. "Can you grab the milk?" she quickly added.

"No," Kate muttered, then quickly realizing she was asked two questions in quick succession, she added, "No leads." Kate pulled the fridge open, breaking her infatuation with the photos and drawings and grabbed the milk. Kate rested the milk on the counter next to her sister and took hold of the spatula sitting in the pan. Kate moved the eggs about, flipping and stirring, so they would scramble nicely.

"Do you want me to add milk?" she asked.

Julie shook her head quickly, "Already done. That's for the coffee."

Julie was a magician in the kitchen. Kate had tried to be domestic, but it had never taken. Her little sister was the Holly

Homemaker of the family. She had coffee, eggs, pancakes, bagels and bacon all cooking at the same time and managed not to burn a thing. Kate could barely manage a bagel and tea without courting disaster. The two sisters looked nearly identical; nevertheless, they had almost nothing in common. Kate knew that bothered her sister. Julie always wanted to be closer. Kate doubted anyone could be closer to her than her sister. That simply wasn't close enough to satisfy Julie, though.

"So, do you think this guy is going to do it again?" Julie asked coyly, wanting to pry although not wanting to get shot down.

The question had caught Kate with a stolen piece of bacon in her mouth. She smiled, knowing she was busted and said, "Absolutely." Kate finished chewing and then elaborated, knowing Julie wasn't done seeking information. "Mike and I have some ideas as to how he did it, but we're still not sure why," Kate said, picking at another piece of bacon.

"Could you leave some for Donald and Anna, please," Julie reprimanded her while dropping a stack of pancakes on her plate.

"Do you want me to go wake up the Little Banana?" Kate asked. "No. No need. Anna will come running as soon as she smells bacon." Kate smiled. That was something she and the Little Banana had in common, an aggressive love affair with bacon.

"I haven't heard anything on the news about the . . ," Julie struggled to say the words.

Kate understood that Julie didn't want to talk about the fact that a young woman's heart was cut out of her, not far from her own kitchen. "No. They don't know details like that. We don't share those kinds of things with the press," Kate paused and gave Julie a stern stare then continued, "or anyone for that matter because they could impede the investigation." Kate drenched her pancakes in syrup and took a big bite. "You are the only one outside the department who knows. You know the rules on that, right?" Kate mumbled, her mouth half-full of food.

Before Julie could answer the house erupted in the thunderous footsteps of a five-year-old girl who just caught her first whiff of bacon. Julie and Kate looked at each other and started to laugh. Anna burst into the kitchen, her little blonde head swiveling back and forth, looking for bacon. Instead, she found something else she loved just as much.

"Aunt Kate!" she yelled, collapsing into her favorite aunt's arms. A few quick tickles and giggles later, and Anna was loading a plate with bacon.

"Excuse me, Little Miss," Julie said stopping Anna in her tracks. "Pancakes and eggs, too. And, put some of that back!" Anna begrudgingly complied and put her plate next to Kate. She pulled a chair so close Kate could barely move her elbow. Julie looked at Kate and then turned to hide her laugh. Kate had no place to hide hers and had to fight to hold her giggles in. "I love this kid," she thought.

"Good morning, Banana, how have you been?" Kate said with a wide smirk.

Anna let every little event of the last few days come tumbling out of her mouth. In no particular order the little girl discussed her dance class, the new Barbie doll her daddy bought her, how she skinned her knee on the sidewalk when she fell off her bike, even though it had training wheels, and how her mom spilled her coffee in the car. The verbal vomit came so fast it was difficult for Kate to keep straight, much less a straight face! Kate gave an occasional, "That's cool, or no way!" but Anna needed no encouragement.

"Good morning, my lovely ladies," Donald said, announcing his arrival. He kissed Julie, then Anna and then gave Kate a peck on the cheek. He was a good guy, Kate thought. He was the perfect foil for Julie. She was idealistic, a religious dreamer that saw the good in everyone and everything. Julie wore her emotions on her sleeve. Donald was quiet, reserved and difficult to read. You never knew if he was happy or angry. He was consistent and steadfast. Best of all, he loved Julie. He indulged her in ways that everyone who knew them understood were his way of saying, I love you more than words could express. Because of that, Kate loved him too.

"Sorry ladies, I have a morning meeting. Save me some bacon, Little One!" He made the rounds again, kissing everyone goodbye and stealing a piece of bacon off of Anna's plate.

"Bye, Daddy," Anna waved. "An' Kate, are you gonna watch cartoons with me? Please! Please An' Kate!"

Kate loved that she could never really get the aunt part out properly. "You bet I'll watch cartoons with you!" Kate took the little girl into her arms and stood her on her lap. Anna did a little dance on her and Kate laughed out loud.

"Okay there, even the Rockettes need to eat. Finish your breakfast and you and Aunt Kate can go watch cartoons, okay? Grace, first, too." Julie said pointing at the little girl's plate.

"Okay, Mommy," Anna answered brightly. She made the sign of the cross and bowed her head in silent prayer. When she was done, she grabbed her princess fork and stabbed into her pancakes. Anna lifted two entire pancakes into the air and tried to get them high enough to fit her head underneath them.

"Adorable. Simply adorable," Julie said sarcastically.

Kate stared in awe at the effort and then sweetly suggested, Anna, honey, why don't we cut them up first?"

"You sure you are ready for a full day and night of this?" Julie asked, motioning to Anna. Anna excitedly spoke with her mouth full of pancakes. Kate made out pretty much what her niece said, only missing a few words here or there. "You're gonna sleep in my room and we are gonna have ice cream and popcorn and Mommy said she was gonna make shakes and maybe, if I'm good, we can bake cookies together, which will be really fun and then we can watch movies and play Fan-G and dolls together." Kate was stunned that Anna's little lungs had the air to get out a run-on sentence that long.

~

Kate's sleepover last night in Anna's room came with barely any sleep. Kate had expended more energy chasing around a little girl than she had ever spent chasing a perp. She was completely wrecked. "That's what happens when the favorite aunt stays the night," Julie had said. Combined with the monotonous cartoons after breakfast, Kate fell into a deep, slumbering mid-morning nap on the couch. Soon, the LMFAO song that Kate used as a ring tone blared and the light from her iPhone gently lit the room, though Kate couldn't wake as quickly or easily as the technology she relied on. Kate instinctively patted her back pockets but came up empty. The phone continued to screech "Party Rock Anthem" but was nowhere to be found.

"Anna, did you take my phone, honey?" Kate mumbled.

The television was set to some PBS kids show that had Anna glued, "OH, NO! The alphabet has fallen overboard! Come on kids. Help grab all the letters." Kate found herself staring too, just not for the same reasons. "Great Job! Let's put all the letters in order and see if we're missing any!" Kate stuck her hands down into the couch cushions, finding nothing. In frustration, Kate blurted, "Come on!" while the brightly dressed character on the television started singing, "A! B! C! D! E!" Party Rock Anthem ended and Kate still had no phone in hand.

Then, Kate remembered too late that she put her phone on the end table. She grabbed it and looked at the missed call. It was work. It rang again. Groggy and a little queasy, Kate managed to catch the call the second time around now that the phone was firmly in hand. "Hello!" she shouted too loudly, "Manning, here." She pulled herself up off the couch and tossed her hair back. She felt some dried up drool at the corner of her mouth and knew she was a hot mess. "Yes, this is Detective Manning," she said in response to the caller's question. Then Kate went white-faced. "Hold on! Let me get a pen," she said scrambling, trying not to step on Anna or her toys.

Kate headed for the kitchen saying, "Not yet! Give me a sec." She dodged a Barbie doll only to step on a hard plastic pony. By the time she made it into the kitchen she was hopping on one leg and biting her lip so she didn't curse out loud. Kate grabbed the pen that Julie kept on a string on her fridge. "Okay, go," she blurted. As she jotted down the address the caller gave her on a "to do list" pad Kate said, "Yes, okay . . . is Mike there, yet? Don't let anyone in until he or I get there; is that understood? Okay, give me that address again." Kate checked what she had written and then hung up the phone.

Julie stared at her disheveled sister. She put down her cookie dough scooper and wiped her hands on her apron, "What's wrong? Is everything okay?" Kate started to look around for her things. She needed to get dressed, find her keys, but she wasn't home and her routine was totally thrown off.

Julie was concerned and pleaded with her sister, "What is it, Kate?"

"Where are my keys?" Kate demanded.

"In your purse, probably. It's with your clothes in the hall," Julie said, growing more alarmed by the second. "Kate, what's the matter?"

Kate looked at her sister with alarm, messy hair, drool and fatigue dotting her face and blurted, "I have to go. It's happened again."

Chapter 12

"It is a man's own mind, not his enemy or foe, that lures him to evil ways."

Buddha

K ate arrived at the address she was given. Once she had gotten within a half mile of the place, it became obvious where she needed to go. Four police cars and two ambulances were on the scene. Kate's heart sank at seeing so many first responders. Her crime scene was going to be a trampled mess with so many bodies on site. She flipped on her lights and parked next to one of the patrol cars. The area had been taped off nice and wide. That, at least, was a good sign. First rule of crime scenes was always, "wider was better." Well, not the first rule, Kate thought, but an important one.

Civilians crowded the scene like bugs to a deck zapper, gawking at any movement a police officer made. Kate became somewhat of a miniature celebrity upon arrival. She was something new to look at after a seemingly endless supply of nothing at all. She felt all of the eyes drift towards her. Like rubberneckers on the highway, the crowd slowed its movements and stared at her. Kate flashed her badge to an officer lingering at the tape and he waved her through.

"Hey! Detective Manning!" an officer near the front of the apartment complex called to her like a drunk friend at a football game.

"Craig Benjamin, how are you? I haven't seen you in what, three years now?" Kate wanted to hug him but already felt awkward about the happy reunion.

"Good to see you too, Kate," he said, trying to bring the sing-song excitement down a bit in deference to the crowd. "Head on up. It's apartment 6B," he informed her. "It ain't pretty, though," Craig added as a final warning as Kate headed to the stairs.

The two of them had met at an FBI training. He was a brilliant young officer but his wife hated the job. Kate couldn't blame her for that, even though the resentment ruined their fledgling marriage. Craig took up the bottle and crushed his upward mobility within the department. He was a good guy that just had crappy luck. Kate figured that was the case for most people with whom she came in contact. She inhaled quickly and didn't smell booze on him now. She was glad for that and hoped he was turning his life around. They chatted about old times for a few minutes before Kate excused herself.

"Hey, has Detective Cooper arrived on scene yet?" Kate called back as she walked towards the building.

"Not that I've seen. Coulda missed him though," Craig replied.

Kate wanted to wait for Mike but she hadn't been able to get through to him. She had texted him and left two messages and got no reply. Looks like I'm a solo act today, Kate thought.

She headed in, already looking for anything that might be of assistance. Kate looked in corners, in stairwells and elevators for any sign of security cameras. When Mike arrived, he would speak to the super, but Kate guessed that whoever was doing this was careful about the buildings he chose. He wasn't ready to be seen yet. These types were measured, patient killers. She suspected that he would sooner walk away from a victim rather than to risk being filmed.

The officer at the door of the apartment greeted her. "Good morning," Kate replied and introduced herself.

"Well detective, I hope you didn't have a big breakfast," he quipped. She had and it already wasn't sitting well in her stomach.

The door to the apartment read 6B. Gold letters on a dark brown door. They matched the doorknob perfectly. No scratches, dents or dings. No damaged wooden frame. No signs of forced entry again. Two dead girls, at least that Kate and the department were aware of, that both willingly let this man in. She tried to get into his head. He would be charming, probably confident and good looking. She doubted that he would be someone who had been in their life for very long. He would have to be engrossing enough for them to want to bring him home quickly. He would be dangerous, maybe, mesmerizing. He would be exciting to a young woman, though not so scary as to put her off. Every woman knows the type. Usually, they result in a long walk home with disheveled buttons and carrying a pair of high heels in the walk of shame. Not this. Kate snapped on her gloves and turned the knob.

Kate nearly fell over, trying to avoid the unexpected pool of blood at the front door. She managed to side step it and land on a tawny shag carpet to the side. Kate knelt down and examined the macabre pool. Several foot prints tracked through it. A few were the same print but there were at least three different prints that she could make out, some overlaying the others. Her crime scene had been trampled. She thought of Museum and how well the rookie had handled himself, despite blowing chunks. He had followed the rule book to the letter. Confirmed the victim was deceased, ensured there were no signs of the perpetrator and then secured a wide area around the crime scene. He avoided the mistake of trying to investigate himself and most importantly, he stood up to the pressure of letting anyone in before she and Mike had arrived. Kate couldn't say the same for the officers who had arrived on this scene. She knew by the comments they made that both Craig and the officer at the door had been through the scene. She silently cursed them and decided that this was something she would have to discuss with them.

Developing a suspect in this case was difficult enough without trampled crime scenes. It was the lead detective's responsibility to sort through the mountain of evidence collected and determine what should be sent off to the various labs for analysis. When DNA samples were sent to the lab, they were prioritized. This case would fall in the higher end of that spectrum, but the lab usually wanted something to compare the DNA to. In this case, they didn't have a suspect or someone they were trying to rule out as the killer. Nevertheless, Kate was confident that the lab would at least give her a profile to look at.

Kate considered the difference of this scene already. Did she manage to break free? Did she dash for the door only to be pulled back and killed? Kate glanced at the rest of the apartment. She scanned for signs of struggle but saw none. No, she didn't escape him, Kate decided. He had attacked her first, right here at the door. Why? Why the sudden urgency? Could he not wait until he was allowed deeper into the apartment? Maybe he wasn't going to be allowed, Kate considered. Maybe this girl had second thoughts and she wasn't going to let him in. Maybe that wasn't it at all. This guy had had a taste of it already; maybe he was excited. Wanted to get to it quickly and couldn't control his urges. That didn't strike Kate as plausible. This was a man who had some very disturbing urges that he had controlled for a very long time. He was too controlled, too measured in his efforts, Kate thought. Kate envisioned him like a snake; something that lay hidden and still, then, moved with lightning speed once he decided to strike. A woman wouldn't even know she was in danger until it was too late. But, this time he struck at the door. That was different.

Kate followed a single set of foot prints to the kitchen. Big feet, probably twelves or thirteens, she thought, measuring them against her own demure little Asics. They would reveal a great deal about the killer; his height, maybe even his weight, where he might shop. Kate carefully walked aside the prints making sure not to disturb the evidence. The stride was long. She felt his steps would have been quick, even urgent. They traverse from the living room to the kitchen and fade, as the blood is spent on each print, until two washed-out partial prints remain in front of the kitchen counter. Kate stood next to them. She looked slightly to her side, taking in what he would be looking at. So he never brings his own, she thought. Kate gently glides the drawer open that sits right in front of the two partial prints. A small assortment of knives, spatulas and serving spoons. Not at all a typical man. He cleans up after himself, Kate mused. Even puts things back in their proper place. Which would he have chosen, Kate pondered. The big, butcher knife? No. He would want something he could take his time with. Something he could manipulate and work with. He was a perfectionist. He would want clean lines and proper depth. No, Kate thought, he won't select a large knife. He wants a knife to carve with. Kate couldn't tell the difference between a carving knife or a boning one or one used to filet. She figured he would want one he could manipulate to his will, just like he would have done to his victim. Guided her, without resistance, right to where he wanted her. He is looking for a tool to fulfil his purpose.

Kate turned quickly and returned to the apartment door. He is satisfied with his selection and returns to the front door where . . ., Kate thinks as she looks around for evidence of her suspicions. Kate can see that the blood of the victim is smeared and moves away in the direction opposite the kitchen. He dragged her away from here. Kate considered the timetable. He strikes her at the door. There is a good amount of blood but not enough to suggest the victim is dead. He then leaves her. Walks to the kitchen and selects a knife. He doesn't stab her where she lies. There is no blood evidence for that. He drags her away from the door, deeper into the apartment.

Kate rose and followed the trail of smeared blood into the apartment. Towards the living room again, Kate mulled over what she was seeing. Why? Why not the bedroom, or kitchen, or even the bathroom? Why does it have to happen on the couch? Kate glanced up from the prints on the rug. An old TV and part of a brown leather couch came into view. She smiled, knowing her suspicion was correct. What is the connection to the living room? Does he watch TV while he works, maybe using the volume or the radio to cover any sound? Kate thought there had to be more to it than that.

She moved around the corner and into the living room. The boxy TV faced her. It was off. A long worn out leather couch blocked the path. The victim's body was propped up on the couch, just as the last victim's body was. He staged her, Kate thought. The room was dark now. She looked up for overhead lighting and found none. Kate wondered if he did his work in the dark or turned on the lights. She noticed two pole lamps and one on the end table. Kate figured the intricacy of his work required lighting and looked to see if there was any blood evidence on the toggles and switches. Nothing was visible.

There was more than enough visible on the couch and floor though. Blood leaked out from underneath the back of the couch. Kate looked at the parts of the couch that weren't stained in blood. It was dry and peeling, like a body left out in the desert and picked apart by vultures. So much of the room looked secondhand. A quick glance would make someone think it was perfect though anything more than a cursory look would tell a very different story.

Kate moved towards the window. A single window was shaded by mahogany red curtains. "Did he draw them closed?" she wondered. She glanced outside and saw that there was no hope of witnesses in this direction. The window looked out onto the brick façade of a neighboring structure.

Kate returned to her walk through of the crime. "He moved the victims into the living room and placed them," she said aloud to herself. "He opens them up . . ."

Kate returned to the center of the room and moved around the edge of the couch. She looked at the blood amassed in front of the couch. She could see one of the victim's legs clearly now. Kate's eyes began to scan upwards.

". . . and removes the organs from inside his victim. He removes what he is looking for and then . . ."

Kate's eyes started at the bottom. She examined every inch of the victim as she worked her way up. Kate reached the victim's lap and her own stomach tossed like a washing machine. The woman's hands were neatly cupped on her thighs with her palms towards the sky. Her internal organs rested in her lap, atop her hands. A single red rose stood amongst the carnage. Kate's stomach was on a long, heavy-duty rinse cycle. She rubbed her belly and ordered it to chill out.

". . . he stages the victim on the couch and places the organs into her lap."

Kate knew that she didn't have to wonder what he was after this time. Her monologue became an inner voice. "He takes his victim's heart. Why? Are you a jilted lover? No," Kate doubted that these women knew their killer well. Plus, that theory wouldn't explain the cross. This was a religious experience for this pyscho, she thought. What was religious about carving up a girl you barely knew? That was the question Kate couldn't answer.

"Finally, he paints a cross in blood on the victim's forehead."

Kate had not seen it yet but she knew in her soul that it was there, just like the last time. "What the hell? Once he has what he came for why stage the victim? He's saying something, but what? Who is he talking to?"

The body of the victim was seated on the couch. She was in the exact same position that the first victim was placed in. Kate sat crouched like a catcher in front of the body looking up at it, waiting for a pitch that wouldn't come. Kate spoke aloud, into the empty room, "What do you want to tell me? Why are you doing this, huh?"

Kate rose from her crouched position and looked over at a picture hung on the wall. She continued to talk to herself, musing, "Who made you into this . . . monster? Why pick these girls to butcher?" She walked over and took the picture off the wall and looked at it. Kate recognized the scene instantly. A woman, probably the victim, playing with a little girl on the jungle gym in the very same park that Kate and her niece, Anna played in. Her stomach hit high heat, speed wash. Kate turned from the wall, trying to avoid the volcanic uprising within her. She still held the picture in her hand. Wondering, Kate asked, "Who were you? How did you get involved with this guy?"

Kate looked now for the first time at the victim's face. She wanted to compare the girl in the picture. "OH, JESUS!" Kate blurted as the picture crashed to the floor and shattered. Kate was aghast. Standing amidst the broken glass of the frame, Kate stared at the disfigured face of the victim. A bloody cross was indeed on the forehead, just as Kate had suspected. The victim's head was slung over the back of the couch and tilted slightly backwards. The victim was staged almost identically to the last one. Except . . .

Kate swallowed down the first wave of vomit that had crested over the edge.

The woman's face was shredded. Her nose had been smashed, her eyes a black-red pulp. The flesh of her face had been removed, exposing a ghastly mix of sinew, muscle and bone. At her forehead the search went deeper, carving down to the bone. There, a small, deep cross was carved into the forehead of her skull.

Then, Pompeii.

Kate knelt among shards of shattered glass and chunks of vomit. She clutched her belly, waiting for a third or fourth round. She had never thrown up at a crime scene before. This wasn't just once. She was retching now. She had expended everything she had and her body still wasn't satisfied. Then, it just got worse.

"She was a pretty girl, wasn't she?" Mike said sadly. Of course, he would have to arrive now, Kate cursed. Mike crouched down near the picture on the floor and shuffled some tiny pieces of glass off of it. Kate sat on the floor still holding her stomach, unable to even move. Mike handed her a tissue. It took Kate far longer than she had wanted to admit to even reach for it. She wiped her mouth but stayed crumpled into the ball her body had brought her to.

Mike knelt next to her and rubbed her back gently. He waited a few moments and then whispered, "You feeling better yet?"

Kate couldn't look at him. Shame, embarrassment, confusion and anger fought a war for dominance in her empty stomach. She kept her head facing the wall and muttered, "I've never gotten sick on a crime scene before, not ever."

Mike put his arm around her. He tugged her towards him and let out a soft laugh. "It's okay. Happens to all of us, sometimes," Mike said and something in his voice suggested that it had really happened to him, too. That somehow, this tough Marine had lost his cookies too, once. Kate warmed to him; to his touch and his gentle hand, to his kind words and his softness. Then, Mike patted her on the bottom like a football player and popped up, "Though, maybe next time you shouldn't have so many . . . pancakes, is it?" as he moved chunks of her vomit around with the tip of his sneaker.

Kate gave Mike a playful punch in the leg and said, "I am never going to eat again."

Chapter 13

"For every good reason there is to lie, there is a better reason to tell the truth."

Bo Bennett

Father Gregory sat at the dining room table and forced a smile. Julie had broken out the fine china from their wedding registry and the table had been adorned with a thick table cloth and the fresh flowers Donald had brought home for her. It was a beautiful display, though not one Gregory needed. He had yet to grow accustomed to these dinner invitations where parishioners felt the need to impress. He genuinely liked Julie and was hoping for something more relaxed. Nevertheless, his mind was decidedly elsewhere.

"Siblings! Ugh, they don't make it easy, do they," Julie grumbled, looking at her watch. "Would you like some wine, Father?" Gregory had jumped at the word siblings and wasn't paying attention to her. "Father? Are you okay?" Julie asked.

"Yes. Fine. Thank you," Gregory recovered. "Wine would be wonderful," he finished.

Julie grabbed the bottle from the center of the table and poured him a glass. "I'm very sorry about this. My sister is usually very punctual," Julie said, straightening the silverware on the table. Donald was in the kitchen helping. Normally, she didn't need or want his help, but Julie was determined to put on a show tonight and panic had set in.

Gregory tried to console her, "Please don't worry yourself over it, Julie. I'm just thankful for the dinner invitation. Are you sure there isn't anything I can do for you?" She smiled and shook her head.

Donald brought in a basket of freshly cut bread and gave her a peck on the cheek. Julie gave him a look of death that he blew off like any experienced husband would. "Gotta follow orders," he said to Father Gregory, pointing to Julie's "Kiss the Cook" apron. Gregory smiled politely and offered his assistance to Donald who dismissed it with the wave of his hand. "You just relax and try not to starve to death while we wait for Kate. If she doesn't show in fifteen minutes, I'll see if I can convince Julie to serve dinner without her," Donald said, winking at him.

"I will not!" Julie scolded him as she ran back into the kitchen.

Gregory lifted his wine glass and watched the red liquid swirl as he circled his hand. "I look forward to meeting her. What did you say she did for a living again?" Gregory asked, sipping his wine.

"Oh, you'll love her," Julie called from the kitchen. "She's a detective with the NYPD." Donald glanced into the kitchen with a sarcastically shocked look. There was no way Father Gregory and Kate were going to get along and he couldn't have been more certain of anything in his life. So much so that he had bet his wife a week's worth of laundry and dishes that this was going to be a disaster. While Donald stared at his wife, he missed the terrified look on Gregory's face. A detective was the last thing he wanted to encounter right now. Gregory's hand shook visibly. He put his wine down on the table and it spilled. Quickly, he grabbed a cloth napkin and dabbed the table. A dark red stain appeared on the pure white cloth.

"A detective, huh. That must be an . . . interesting line of work," Gregory said, still trying to repair the stain. No matter how hard he tried, it wasn't coming up. He put his napkin over it and hid it. He'd have to tell Julie about it later. Just not right now.

~

Kate was indeed stuck in traffic. Forty minutes and she had crawled only a few miles. These are the times every cop is tempted to throw on the sirens and flashers, she thought. Kate had a strong sense that even if she did, it wouldn't have helped. After all, sirens and lights don't create spare lanes and people would ignore the sirens anyway. There was simply no place to go. Kate tapped her fingers on the steering wheel in tune to the music of Meghan Trainor's "All About That Bass" while she waited for the construction to clear. As she craned her head to look at how close she was to a break in the traffic her view was blocked by a large electronic traffic sign that read, "Obey speed limit. Strictly enforced." The irony was the only thing that made her laugh at the situation.

~

Thirty minutes later than she wanted to, Kate was ringing her sister's doorbell. "An' Kate, you're late," Anna said as she opened the door to let her in. She had been sitting near the front door patiently waiting her arrival.

"Yeah, well, you're short!" Kate joked back as she tousled the little girl's hair.

"I'm only five," Anna said, defending herself from the accusation. "Everyone is in the living room and Mommy says we can't play upstairs tonight," Anna moped as she took Kate's hand and led her into the house. Kate thought it was odd. No playing upstairs, and Anna had said everyone. Plus, the munchkin was in a dress. Who was everyone? Kate wondered.

"Couldn't you move to Manhattan or something?" Kate joked.

"Ever hear of the subway?" Julie joked back. "I told you they never pick up that construction on time. Donald has gotten caught in it a few times." Kate noticed that Julie had a dress on underneath her apron. She took Anna into her arms and feigned a look of shock.

"You are getting sooooo heavy! Quit growing so fast!" As Kate spun Anna in her arms she noticed the fine tablecloth and fancy china. Something was up. She turned to Julie and stared at her, "Oh, I'm sorry. I didn't realize you had company." The tone was unmistakable. Kate thought that her sister set her up on some sort of date. Too late! Kate could see the man's shadow enter the kitchen.

"Hello, you must be Kate," Gregory said, introducing himself. "I've heard a great deal about you, all good!" he added quickly. "My name is Father Gregory Sloan," he said, reaching out his hand to shake.

Kate let Anna slide down her side and then shook his hand. The look of confusion must have been obvious. "It's . . . uh, it's nice to meet you," Kate replied rather quizzically. Julie guided Father Gregory back to the dining room so dinner could be served.

"I'm not dating any guy she sets me up with and sure as hell not a priest," Kate whispered to Donald as they walked into the dining room.

He laughed and threw his arm around her, "Come on. I'm starving."

Dinner was a cordial affair. Everyone was hungry, so little conversation of any depth occurred between bites. Julie, as always, was an excellent cook and the chicken caprese she made was phenomenal. When the guests had eaten their fill and the utensils finally given rest, Anna was the first to jump ship.

"Mommy, can I go watch cartoons now?" she asked sweetly.

Julie smiled, satisfied with the outstanding behavior of her five-year old daughter at a fancy dinner party. "Sure sweetie. Let's go get you cleaned up and in your pj's first, though."

As Julie took Anna upstairs, Gregory and Kate almost simultaneously said, "She sure is cute." The choral sound of it made them both chuckle a bit and went far to breaking the awkward silence.

Donald began clearing dishes. When Kate and Gregory joined in, he flicked them away and told them to sit. The silence returned and Kate could not abide it. She decided it was best to be blunt, "So, if you don't mind me asking, what made you want to become a priest?"

Gregory laughed and replied, "Julie did say you were very forward, but, no, I don't mind you asking. I felt I owed God for all He had done for me. How about you? What made you want to become a detective?"

Kate scooped up her wine glass and leaned back into her chair as if she could slide right off of it. She took a long, slow sip of wine and considered her glass for a moment before responding, "I loved Law and Order as a kid."

Gregory was surprised by such a simple answer. "Really," he said, shocked, "Law and Order?"

Kate tried to explain herself, "Yup. You know, the TV show. They were the greatest detectives in the world. There wasn't a crime they couldn't solve. I wanted to be like them, to help people I guess. So, what made you feel like you had to dedicate the whole of your life to a guy you've never even seen?"

Gregory mimicked the body language of Kate, dropping back in his chair. Instead of holding his wine glass though he folded his arms. He suspected her answer wasn't altogether truthful, but he wasn't going to push. His response was an awful truth and he figured it might shake her into honesty later on. "My mother was a heroin addict who needed all the help she could get. One day my brother and I came home from school and found her strung out on the couch. I asked God for help and He granted it. I felt that I should return the favor," he said with far less gravitas than the story deserved. "So, you became a detective to help people?"

Kate still sat back in her chair holding her wine glass. She was surprised by his forthright reply. She hadn't considered a priest could have a dope addict for a mother. Kate gave in a bit. "I think there's a tremendous amount of injustice in the world. I figure I'm out there to try and right it. If I can't right it; then, maybe I can avenge it, you know what I mean?"

Gregory nodded and then got right to the point, "Julie tells me your father was a cop, wasn't he?"

Julie walked back into the room holding a cake. Kate glared at her. It was indeed a setup. Just not the kind Kate had thought. Julie shook off the evil look from her sister. "Father Gregory, Kate is the eternal pessimist of the family. Donald says she could find evil in a newborn if you give her enough time. Would either of you like coffee or tea?" Julie looked at Kate, a victorious smile on her face.

"Tea," Kate replied, an edge in her voice.

Father Gregory requested, "Coffee, please."

Gregory accepted the coffee and poured some milk in it. "Is that true, Kate?" he asked. "Do you think everything in the world is prone to evil?"

Kate replied with her head down, stirring sugar into her tea, "No, let's just say that God and I don't see eye to eye on how things should run on earth."

Gregory leaned forward and sipped his coffee, curious now about the real purpose of the dinner invitation. "I see," he mumbled.

"Kate gave up on God when our grandmother died. She doesn't believe in Him," Julie added as she cut large sections of cake and doled them onto plates. Gregory reached his hand out and rested it on Kate's wrist. She didn't withdraw, still, her fingers tensed visibly.

Gregory tried to restore Kate's faith, "There are so many miracles in the world. What about Anna? Who could have brought life to such a wonderful little girl? Kate, have faith that there is a greater plan than we can know. We cannot stay on this earth forever."

There was the preachy pain in the ass she had expected. Kate retorted with a stubborn, "I don't like death; it's unjust and often times indiscriminant. That doesn't strike me as a grand plan."

She rose from the table, slipping her hand from his.

Gregory looked hurt, "Kate, the body is nothing more than a temple, a tent that our eternal soul resides in. It's temporary housing until our permanent home in heaven is ready for us." He spoke quickly, trying to reach her before she ran, "I understand it is hard to lose a loved one, but think of the better world they have gone to."

"What did you just say," Kate demanded. Julie's face grew nervous. Her dinner party was about to explode. Donald came into the dining room with a dish towel on his shoulder and holding a wet plate. He figured he was about to win his bet. But, Kate didn't look angry. She looked perplexed. "What did you say?" she asked again.

Gregory repeated his statement, somewhat confused by Kate's reaction. "The body is simply a vessel for the soul that resides within us all. Its loss is sad to those left behind, but it does not mean that the spirit dies with it."

Julie looked at her sister with concern, "Are you okay, Kate? You look a little white? Kate?" Julie went to her sister's side ready to catch her if she fainted.

Kate smiled and said, "Son of a bitch!" Julie was shocked and went to chastise her sister for her utter lack of manners but didn't have time. Kate bent over and kissed the Father on the cheek. Donald looked at Julie and they both could not have been more confused. Overjoyed, Kate blurted, "Father Gregory, thank you very much. Thank your boss for me, too!" Kate kissed the priest again on the cheek and then added a slap to the shoulder for good measure. "Julie, I've got to run. Thank you for dinner," Kate said as she dashed from the room. "Thanks again, Father!" she called as the door slammed behind her and Julie rushed out after her.

Donald, stunned by the loss of his bet, blurted, "I did not see that coming!"

Chapter 14

"I remember my mother's prayers and they have always followed me. They have clung to me all my life."

Abraham Lincoln

"Oh, come on!" the cute receptionist blurted at the flat screen TV in the foyer of the gym. "Same old Mets," she muttered in frustration. Athletic and in her early twenties, she was clearly passionate about her team. Her long brown hair streamed out of the back of a faded blue Mets cap. She had on a requisite company t-shirt, advertising the very place where only members who had already paid could see it on her. Her resentment towards her uniform could be seen in how she wore it. The neck had been cut and skillfully sewed into a women's cut. The bottom of the shirt had been cut into strips and then tied into a frilly pattern. Her bracelets, as well as a simply adorned chain, complimented the color scheme that had been forced upon her. She had taken something that was ugly and dull and bedazzled it. Regrettably, the effort had caught the attention of one of the newer members.

"Excuse me," Victor said, vying to gain the receptionist's attention.

She waited a moment to watch the delivery of the next pitch. The batter struck out looking, retiring the side. She huffed under her breath and turned to greet him.

"Hi. How can I help you?" she asked brightly as if serving him was a relief from the pain of watching another Mets' loss.

"Good afternoon. I am looking for one of those energy bars. It was in a red and black package. I cannot remember the name of it," Victor said, holding his hands up to suggest the size of the energy bar.

She smiled at the silly gesture. Clearly, she had a pretty good idea of the size and shape of an energy bar.

"I know just what you are looking for," she said as she came around from behind the counter. "It's called a Nitro-fuel bar." She took a few quick steps towards a glass sales case and then squatted like a catcher in front of it. A thin silk line stretched across her lower back as her tight black yoga pants exposed the top of her barely-there underwear.

"Sorry. No luck," she said, popping up from her position and heading around the counter. "Let me take a look and see if we have a new case."

"Thank you. That is quite kind of you," Victor replied, watching her every move. She dressed the part, but as of yet, did not act the part of the temptress. So, he acted. She would be easy enough to ensnare. After all, her kind wanted this. "The bullpen gives us a real shot this year."

"Huh?" she said, confused.

"They have not been this good since '86," Victor said, pointing to the TV.

"I sort of have a love-hate relationship with them," she quipped and handed Victor an assortment of Nitro-fuel bars. "Wasn't sure what your tastes ran to."

"Thank you. These are fine. What do I owe you?"

"Sixteen." The sound of the bat cracking on the TV distracted the receptionist again. "Oh boy, that does not look good."

A deep outfield hit bounced several feet away from the right fielder and rolled towards the wall. The man on second had already reached third by the time the ball had been fielded.

"What was it that you were saying about the bullpen?" she asked sarcastically as the runner rounded third and headed home. The two of them stared unbelievingly at the TV as a walk off double ended the game for the Mets. The receptionist gave Victor a gentle, but firm punch in the arm.

"That's what you get for jinxing them!" she muttered in frustration. "You know, my grandfather was in the hospital and had slipped into a coma. We used to leave the TV on for him, keep him company, you know?" She added the phrase, "you know," at almost every juncture. "Well, once, we thought it was close to the end. Game is on. The guy comes out of the coma and his first words are, "same old Mets!" This team is like heroin, you know? They make you believe and then crush your dreams!" She dumped her face into her palms and shook like she was about to cry. When her face reappeared she was laughing.

"What is it that is so amusing?" Victor asked.

"Oh, just that I punched a guy and I don't even know him. See what the Mets do to an otherwise stable and sane person?"

Victor smiled. "Shall we rectify that?" he asked, holding out his hand to her.

She took it and shook. "My name is Alison. Alison Gaines. Nice to meet you."

Her grip was a strong, confident one.

"Victor Sloan. Pleased to meet a fellow masochist," he said motioning up towards the TV. He gave her a quick wink and released her hand.

"Listen Victor, you better be careful in this gym. This is pretty much Yankee's territory in here, you know? It's me and one of the custodians, but other than that, all these people bleed pinstripes."

Victor noticed the lean-in over the counter, the subtle change in demeanor she exhibited. How her elbows closed tightly under her breasts, pushing them up and out towards him. She preened and displayed herself, tempting him. It took so little to get them to show themselves. A word here, a simply gesture there and suddenly the camouflage fell and they stood before the world as they were, whores and temptresses.

"Not that I think a guy in your shape needs to worry," she added giving him a quick look over and returning the wink she had received earlier.

Victor smiled widely. He had found his third example. Gregory would still not understand. He would have to take one from his own flock before Gregory would concede that he was right, but Victor wanted to build to that. He wanted Gregory to squirm a bit. Victor wanted his brother to have time to speak to his supposed god and beg for help only to get none. Then, and only then, would Victor take one close to Gregory. He would take as many as he needed to prove to his brother how wrong he had been. Not yet though. This one will be a fine offering to the stupidity of Gregory and his faith.

"Thanks for the help, and the warning. See you around, Alison," Victor said as he started to head out of the gym.

"You bet you will, handsome," she replied loudly. She lowered her voice and told herself, "I plan on seeing a great deal of you, Mr. Hunk!"

Alison then went directly to the computer and looked up Victor Sloan's membership. He was a recent add. Just joining two days ago and only for the month. Alison jotted down his name, address, and phone number. Then, she clicked open Internet Explorer and Googled him. His name popped up in several places. He was an arts and antiquities consultant. He worked with auction houses that Alison had heard of though never had cause to visit. These were big time wealthy places. She noted that he had attended and graduated from UCLA. No warrants. No articles detailing an arrest or involvement in strange political or environmental stuff. Plus, Cheaterville, Don't Date Him Girl and none of the other sites popped with his name either. This guy seemed clean, handsome, wealthy, and best of all, a legit Mets fan.

John, one of the other employees spooked her when he asked, "What are you up to?"

"Stop sneaking up on me!" she yelled at the young man. A pen flew at his head and she returned to her computer. "You know, I may have just found the future Mr. Alison Gaines," she mused.

"What number does this make him?" John quipped and faked ducking as if she would throw something larger this time.

Alison clicked off the Internet and turned to her colleague. She leaned against the counter and pushed out her chest towards him. "Don't be so jealous, John. You weren't the one, that's nothing to be ashamed of." Alison turned down her lips as if she were sad and held up her fingers, measuring something minute in size between her thumb and forefinger.

"Screw you!" John said and walked away in a huff.

"Been there, done that, was disappointed," she fired back sarcastically.

~

The following day, Victor returned. He smiled at her as he entered and used her name in greeting. Alison was aglow that he remembered her name. She made it a point to find reasons to be near where he was lifting. Exchanging towels, inspecting equipment or helping other members with technique, Alison was never more than ten feet from him. It was impossible for Victor not to notice.

Alison worked with a middle-aged woman on a big blue exercise ball. She was telling the woman to focus on her abdominal region but Alison was focusing on something else entirely. She watched as Victor alternated from the bench press to doing free standing head stands. As Victor went into the headstand and then started to do pushups within it, his entire body tensed with power. Alison had seen gymnasts do the move but very few others could do it with the fluidity and consistency that she was watching now.

Slowly, a crowd began to gather and watch as Victor pushed the limits of endurance and finally collapsed. Several onlookers clapped and Victor demurred, waving them away embarrassingly. He sat on the bench and wiped himself with a towel. He smiled at Alison, acknowledging that he knew she was watching. Over her head was a TV that blared "Breaking News" in large text. The obnoxious text was accompanied by a deep booming voice declaring the same information the text had done. Victor sat and watched while many members of the gym had paused to see if the breaking news was worth their attention.

The text was replaced by a plastic looking news anchor that looked as if she had slept her way into the position. She fumbled with some papers and acted shocked that the camera was on her. Everything about her timing was just off.

"CTS news has just learned that the New York Police Department has discovered a second young woman murdered in Queens this week." The anchor made the statement while flashing an overly bright white smile as an image appeared at the corner of the screen. It showed a clearly photo-shopped corpse covered in a white sheet and crossed by yellow police tape.

Several people in the gym returned to their workout, clearly thinking the death of the woman was insufficient to spend their time on.

"Sources close to CTS news have confirmed that the murders were almost identical in nature." Again, the anchor flashed her pearly whites. Quickly, she seemed to realize the smile didn't fit the story. The smile faded and she faked a solemn tone as she continued the report.

Victor studied the gym. Only a remote few had decided to watch the segment. He noted that Alison was one of them.

"Police refuse to comment on the investigation only saying that it is ongoing. Several police officers were willing to speak to this CTS reporter on the condition of anonymity. They confirm that the murders were identical in nature yet refused to disclose any details."

Victor no longer watched the TV, rather eyeing Alison intently. He was going to give her fame. Fleeting, but fame, nonetheless.

"One officer stated and I quote," the anchor emphasized the statement, "We've got no leads and this guy's gonna keep tearing girls apart until we stop him."

Again, the talentless anchor emphasized, "End quote."

Victor thought he could see an almost imperceptible shudder go through Alison.

"Another officer, when asked if he thought this was the work of a serial killer stated, and I quote, 'Absolutely,' end quote." The same strange verbal stress points were included on the statement. She was a perfect representation of everything Victor despised about them. He rose from the bench and touched Alison's shoulder gently. She turned nervously then relaxed when she realized it was him.

"I apologize for interrupting you," Victor said quietly. She shook her head and he continued. "I realize this may be somewhat forward," Victor said, pausing to seem somewhat uncomfortable with himself. "I was wondering if you would be interested in going to the

Subway Series game with me on Wednesday evening?" He watched as her eyes lit up at the proposition.

"That's so kind of you," Alison gleamed, "but we are not allowed to date members," she added sadly, glancing around the gym to ensure that anyone who might have heard his offer would have heard her rejection as well. She nudged her head towards an empty corner, suggesting they talk over there. Victor followed.

"I'd love to!" Alison gushed. "I just can't be seen saying yes to you. I really need this job, you know?" she said as her eyes darted around making certain no one was watching.

Victor gave her an out that he knew she would not take. "I understand. Please, I withdraw the offer if it risks your employment."

Alison was quick to ensure that wasn't what she wanted. "No. Please don't." Her head tilted down slightly. "I'll give you my number when you leave. Don't forget to come see me," she pleaded and then dashed off towards the reception area.

Victor would take her someplace very public. He would be the last to be seen with her before her death. Still, they wouldn't find him before he had a chance to destroy his brother's faith. This would end only when he wanted it to.

He glanced one more time at the TV. The anchor announced her guest. "Here now with us is our resident criminal psychologist Dr. Fredrick Murphy. Dr. Murphy, could you shed some light on just what goes through the mind of a serial killer . . ."

Chapter 15

"You never really understand a person until you consider things from his point of view."

Harper Lee

Mike didn't understand them. Standing in the middle of his apartment he wondered, did anyone really. He listened to the message again, trying to decipher meaning from it.

"Hey, Mike, Mike, Mike!" Kate fired quickly and excitedly into the phone, repeating his name in rapid succession.

It was a happy excited, not a scared or angry one, he was certain about that.

"We have to talk."

Usually, those words were followed with an obligatory, "It's not you, it's me," break up. The kind that makes everyone really uncomfortable because both sides know the other is lying and it would almost be easier to just say the truth. Like, man, I just find you boring or you have no talent in the sack. Sometimes, the harder people worked to preserve your feelings, the more they stomped on them.

But, they weren't dating. They weren't anything really. Partners, friends, but not the kind of thing Mike wanted them to be. Mike pushed the thoughts of being dumped out of his head. In order to be dumped, you have to have dated, he argued to himself. Plus, her tone of voice was too happy. The word "have" got the emphasis rather than the "we" or the "talk." That seemed to suggest good news to him.

"Call me as soon as you get this."

Here, the stress was on the word "soon." A lengthening of the word to suggest urgency. What was so urgent? Did she decide that walking out on him, no, running out on him might not have been the smoothest move? Did she realize that she should have stayed? Did she decide that she was madly in love with him and wanted to shout it out to the world? Mike's mind went wild with a million different alternate realities.

He listened to it again.

"Hey, Mike, Mike, Mike! We have to talk. Call me as soon as you get this."

That was the fourth time he had listened to it. He was starting to feel like a chick, and so he tossed his phone into the worn out couch, narrowly missing a slumbering Labrador sprawled out across it. The phone slid neatly between the cushions and Mike heard it ping like a pinball until it hit the floor underneath the couch. Then he heard it ring.

Mike didn't want to even look at it. He wasn't ready to talk to Kate yet. He stubbornly stood sentinel over the couch, like a guard in front of Buckingham Palace. He waited until the ringing stopped before he dove in and searched for the phone. His face was pressed against the couch as he reached for the phone. He felt a long wet lick slobber his cheek as he grabbed the device. When he stood back up, Spanky had not even woken from his nap. "Seriously, man, is it just in the programming?" Mike asked the snoozing drool factory.

He wiped his cheek and checked the recent calls. It wasn't Kate. It was the other woman in his life. Mike dialed the phone and waited.

"Hi, Mom. What's up?"

His mom made all the typical inquires about her son. She asked how work was, whether he was eating well, if he was steering clear from the seedier aspects of the big city. Mike patiently assured her that he was being a good boy and not doing anything that would bring shame to the family name.

"How's Kate?" she asked, transitioning to her favorite topic.

Mike took a deep breath and sighed. That gave him away to his mom as certain as having his hand caught in the cookie jar. She waited, however, until he spoke so as not to shut him down. When he was a child, Mike never spoke about his feelings. His mother used to describe him as Atlas, carrying the weight of the world on his shoulders and not letting anyone help him with the burden. Secretly, she was always a little fearful that the childhood version of him would return. With all that he had been through, she feared that would be the end of him. She decided to change the topic to one that would signal a need to talk out his emotions.

"Mrs. Rainer called yesterday," she said simply. Mike wouldn't be able to ignore the name.

"Is she okay?" her son asked gently. "Does she need anything?"

"She just called to check in. On you, specifically, to see how you were," his mom told him.

"I'll call her," Mike said regretfully. "I've been meaning to call her." He looked at the photograph on the end table in his living room. Two Marines in the field, proud and strong.

"She understands, Michael. You don't have to feel guilty all the time."

Mike picked up the picture and went silent for a few moments before he responded. "We've been through this, Mom," he said, frustrated.

"Yes, we have Michael. Yes, we have. He died. You came home. That doesn't mean you have to live as if you died too. You don't owe him or the world anything other than to live and be happy."

Mike disagreed. His therapist had told him the same things and at some stage, Mike had realized that you just needed to tell them the same types of things they told you. Mike had never drunk the Kool-aid they were serving him. He just pretended to and spat it back out at them like a well-trained parrot.

Mike did owe Rainer something; his life. His best friend had knocked him aside just before an IED blew up. Rainer saw it and took the blast full force. Mike had walked away with a few deep gashes and an enormous hole in his life. One woman's son came home. Another woman got a neatly folded triangular flag that she could display on her mantle. His mom assured him he would have done the same had he seen it. Problem was, he didn't see it. He never had the chance to save him. He was too slow and because of that he came home and his brother didn't. That was what Rainer was, a brother. His mom understood that. She was just saying what she had to say to help him through it.

It happened seven years ago. Mike wasn't going to get over it. It wasn't something that was ever going to go away. He was alive, his friend was dead. He watched parts of him fly through the air as his body exploded like a water balloon. He saw it in his nightmares every night. Every night he was too slow. Some nights, in the depths of darkness, Mike shoved him forward or dove to the side, letting Rainer take the blast for him. Those were the toughest for him. The sweat and panic that lingered into the early morning.

"I am happy, Mom," Mike lied.

She wanted to chastise him for lying to her. When he came home, she had witnessed the nightmares, the oppressive guilt that sat like a stone on his chest. Instead, she struck right at the subject that she figured was at the heart of her son's mood. "Well then, how is Kate?" she asked with a bit of an edge in her voice.

So, Mike told her. He left out certain unmentionables that were not for his mother's ears, dancing around the particulars. He didn't dance well enough to hide the truth from his mother though.

"Michael, you have to be honest with the girl," she instructed.

"Mom, I'm trying," Mike pleaded with her as if he was trying to stay out of trouble.

"Did you tell her that you loved her?" his mom asked bluntly.

"No," Mike conceded and didn't argue over the word love.

"Then you haven't tried and you haven't been honest with her."

His mom was a human lie detector. She was also known as the queen of bluntness. If something difficult needed to be said, just tell her and she would say it with all the tenderness of ripping a Band-Aid off.

"Where is all that crap about courage and which way would you run stuff? Come on, you are a United States Marine! Be brave and tell the girl how you feel. If nothing else, at least you'll know," his mom let him have it, hitting him where it would do the most good.

"Former Marine, mom."

"Once a Marine, always a Marine," she responded, not letting him run or hide. "Tell her. Soon."

"I will," Mike lied again.

"Michael, if you pretend like something isn't there long enough, chances are, it won't be there when you want it. If she is important to you, she's worth the risk."

"Thanks, Mom. Love you," Mike ended the call wondering if it would have been easier to talk to Kate. He dialed Kate right away but got her voice mail. "Hey Kate, it's Mike. Just calling you back," he said awkwardly. "I'm gonna go down to Patties tonight if you want to meet up and talk. Maybe we can have a few drinks. Anyway, let me know or I'll just see you there."

~

Mike hadn't heard from her all afternoon. He sat atop a barstool milking a beer for the better part of an hour before she had shown up. "Hey, Puppy Dog!" she called out. The nickname was one Kate had unsuccessfully tried to hang on him one day after hearing him called Devil Dog by another Marine at the station. Every so often she would dust it off, usually when she was feigning happiness, but it never stuck.

She looked pretty; then again, he always thought she looked pretty. Kate was casual, a blouse and jeans that fit snuggly and showed how trim and athletic she was. Her hair was tied back in a low pony tail that trailed behind her as she approached him.

"Hey," Mike said as he stood up to greet her. He wasn't sure if he should kiss her, hug her, or fist-pump her. So, paralyzed, he just stood there. "Want a drink?"

Kate ordered a beer and when it arrived she grabbed his and moved the two of them to an empty booth in the corner. She took a big swig and sat triumphantly back in her seat. Mike thought she might be waiting for him to ask what was going on. So, he took a deep breath and steeled himself for what he was about to say.

"I know," Kate said cryptically.

She knew what, exactly? That he loved her? That he was mad at her? What? Mike looked questioningly at her.

"I know. I know what he's looking for!" Kate said injecting excitement into her voice.

Mike slumped in his seat feeling dejected.

"Whoop-de-do!" Mike muttered sarcastically.

Kate didn't even notice. She pushed forward, a juggernaut of apparent excitement.

"He's looking for their souls!" Kate beamed at the sudden break in the case. "This is a religious experience for him. That explains the cross, the staging of the victims in the same place, why he opens them up and takes their hearts," Kate rambled, spewing forth every little detail that she felt was explained away by the revelation. It was what little good she was able to salvage from her night. Especially, after the blow up she had with her sister on the front stoop.

Mike pretended to listen. He had never really felt like this before. He had been sad. He had been angry. This was new to him. A mix of sadness and anger like he had never known. He wanted to yell at her and at the same time he wanted her to hug him.

"What are you moping about," Kate said suddenly as if she had finally seen him for the first time. She felt like she had more justification to sulk about than anyone tonight. She wanted to talk to him about what just happened between her and Julie, but she didn't know how to say, "I need help." Instead, she just went on the offensive and made a face at him, mimicking his misery.

"What?" Mike feigned.

"You. You're brooding. What gives?" Kate seemed offended that he didn't celebrate her informational coup.

"Nice job," Mike muttered, "It fits, but it doesn't put us any closer to the perp."

"Okay, seriously Mike, what's up with you tonight?" Kate asked, letting a bit of her anger show.

"That's all you wanted to talk about?" Mike asked barely above a whisper.

It wasn't, but this also wasn't the Mike she expected to see. Kate felt like it was destiny for her to fight with everyone in her life today.

"Shit, I thought you'd be excited!" Kate threw her hands up in frustration.

"Good night, Kate," Mike said and slid out of the booth without looking at her.

Mike walked away from Kate, more hurt than anything else. He had gotten his hopes up. Kate hadn't dashed them because she hadn't even recognized them. If you pretend like something isn't there long enough, chances are, it won't be there when you want it. That's what his mother had said. Wise words, but he was beginning to realize that he wasn't the one who needed to hear them. Kate didn't think about the future. In the Corps, Mike would have referred to her as mission oriented, focused on the goal and ignoring the environment around her. She didn't see, couldn't see, and Mike didn't know how to make her.

Kate sat alone with her beer and her thoughts. That was the second person she cared about who stormed off on her tonight. She thought about the fight with Julie and wished it could have been different. Kate wished so much that she could have been better. She reviewed it again and again in her head.

"Where are you storming off to?" Julie screeched, as Kate had rocketed out of the front door.

Kate was ecstatic that she might have put a part of the case together, but her sister's sinister tone dragged her down. Whenever Julie got testy, Kate never hesitated to shoot back.

"So, what's the deal with the dinner guest tonight?" Kate asked with sarcasm, answering Julie's query with one of her own.

Julie, realizing her tone had set off her sister, tried to retreat. She timidly replied, "Oh, Father Gregory. Sorry about that. I had asked him over for dinner, so we could go over the details for the children's party at the church."

Kate dripped with sarcasm, "I'm sure you totally forgot that you invited him to dinner when you asked me over. Why do you keep pushing me all the time?"

Julie was pissed off now and yelled at her, "Why don't you at least try to be a part of the church, huh? You are so negative all the time. All you ever see is the bad in things. I'm sick of it!"

Kate ripped into Julie, "I'm sick of you being so naïve. Nobody was there to help those kids! Where the hell is He every day I go to work? I don't see Him taking a hand in saving these girls. Where is He, huh, where? I am so tired of hearing this. Just mind your own business and leave me alone!"

Julie battled back with, "You don't see God anywhere, do you? Everything bad in the world is just another piece of evidence to you that He doesn't exist. What about everything good in the world? How do you explain that evidence, Detective Manning? Can you catalog and quantify that? No! No, you can't! You just refuse to see it. There are miracles in this world that defy lo . . ." Julie stopped mid-word and stared at her sister for a moment. Then, in a huff, she turned and stomped back into the house and slammed the door.

Kate sipped her beer and choked back tears as she reflected on a night that had seen the two most important people in her life walk away from her.

Chapter 16

"The pure and simple truth is rarely pure and never simple."

Oscar Wilde

When Victor was a young child, he used to watch his mother put on her costume. Sitting on the floor of the bathroom, he would observe the intricacies of her routine. She would exit the shower with a towel wrapped tightly around her and stand in front of a foggy mirror, ensconced with rusty edges. First, she would pick at her face with tweezers, removing tiny hairs that no one but her would notice. This could take an hour or more and she never seemed satisfied with the job. There was always something more she needed to remove or something more to hide.

She followed that with her teeth. Brushing alone wasn't enough. Here, too, she combed over things with floss. Sometimes, she would brush three or four times in between flossing. His mother would push at her teeth, trying to straighten crooks that had long since settled into a comfortable place.

Admittedly, Victor was always most fascinated by the application of her makeup. Here, his mother's guise became readily apparent. The young boy would watch as a spent and strung-out woman would become a carefully crafted image. The subtle layer of rouge giving color to gaunt cheeks, a bright lipstick to mask waif-like lips, and thick layers of eye shadow to hide the emptiness within combined to create someone who wasn't really there.

Sometimes a client would arrive at the door and Victor would note his mother's reactions. Where once there had been a cranky, tired, selfish woman, now suddenly there would appear this geisha. She would dote on the man, ensuring his comfort was complete. Pleasantries were not enough in these cases. Victor would watch as his mother giggled and flipped her hair to and fro. She would use proximity to suggest intimacy where none really existed. It was at times like these that Victor realized that a tawdry costume wasn't enough to sell the lie.

Victor was an astute child. Despite the fact that Gregory thought what his mother was doing was beyond his comprehension, it was very much understood by him. Through his mother, Victor learned many things by observation and study. While his family ignored him, pretended he was ignorant or oblivious, Victor watched and learned. If they had taught him anything, it was the value of the lie.

Victor stood naked in front of a large bathroom mirror now. The glass that reflected his image back at him was lined in thickly fluted molding, with expensive vanity lighting adorning it on the top and sides. To its side, the mirror had a second, smaller reflective surface, a lighted halo on a pole arm that jutted out towards him. Victor leaned into it and examined every inch of his face.

It was beautiful. The mirror, or for that matter, anything Victor allowed into his life, wasn't worn or battered as his mother's had been. He wasn't either, he observed. Where she had sold herself, allowed herself to be used and discarded, Victor had ensured that he would not be consumed by lies. He was young, strong and virile. He flexed his muscles in his chest and then his arms, observing their size and noting how vascular they were.

Victor was not vain; quite the contrary, in fact. He cared little about his looks or appearance. His size and strength were necessary to his mission. His fancy suits were merely a uniform to him, in a war he intended on fighting as long as was required. Just as his mother's makeup and clothes had been to her, Victor's suits did not tell the truth of him. His flexing was a kicking of the tires of sorts. An assessment of the tools required to achieve his objective. His mother used tools of a different sort, but tools nonetheless.

This he understood from her; in order to destroy a liar, you must deceive them first. One must show as though the lie has been believed. Then they grow comfortable in their deception. They drop their guard and allow you into their enormous falsehood. Then, and only then, will the deceiver realize that they have been exposed. Victor hated the ruse, but understood the necessity of it. The best place to root out an evil, he believed, was from within.

Gregory had lied to him once. He had told Victor that mother was sick and that she would get better with God's help. Two lies wrapped in one, Victor thought. Mother was never sick nor would God save her. Gregory was too naïve to see the truth. He always thought that some great power guided him and watched over him. He attributed everything to a force unforseen in the universe.

Victor saw the world rather differently. All of man's actions were within his power to control. The game pieces were set, but how the game was played was up to the players. Where Gregory saw some enormous tapestry painted by a divine hand; Victor understood that the canvas was his on which to paint and that only he could choose the colors, lighting, and subject matter of his canvas. How he used his life was entirely up to him.

Church bells rang out in the distance. Victor dressed for the evening. Tonight's auction would net him somewhere in the vicinity of three-quarters of a million dollars. That would be more than enough for him to continue his artistic pursuits indefinitetly. But, that wasn't what he wanted. If he could, he would have educated Gregory differently. His brother had left him little choice in the matter though. Victor had tried and failed to get Gregory to see certain universal truths.

Victor couldn't really recall when he had realized it. His mother had contributed greatly to his view, no doubt, but Victor couldn't be sure he knew it for certain before he left her. He thought how the Greeks viewed women as the source of emotion while men were bastions of logic. He considered the legends of Pandora, of Eve, and original sin. Even those of Norse mythology, where Loki, the trickster takes on the form of a serpent or a woman to deceive the pantheon of gods. That women were the origin of sin and the vessels that contained it, Victor had long been convinced. The evidence before his eyes abounded with all the proof he had needed.

He remembered confronting Gregory on the issue while he was in the seminary. As always, he found Gregory's understanding of the subject questionable at best.

"Is it not Eve that tempts Adam?" Victor asked his brother.

Gregory shifted in his seat and pulled a long sip of soda through his straw. "Well, it's a bit more complicated than that," he answered, fearful of where his brother would take the conversation. Gregory had grown increasingly alarmed at Victor's viewpoints on religion.

"And does not Paul teach us that sin is death?" Victor continued.

Gregory nodded and waited to see where this path would lead.

"Yet, that which is dead is freed from sin?" Victor mused.

Gregory and Victor had talked late into the evening on the subject of sin. Gregory had little clue that he was integral in helping his brother solidify his views on the subject. Women were the source of sin. They were temptresses and deceivers, emotional and illogical. In legend after legend, they brought evil into the world.

Victor walked out into his expansive living room and sat on an antique upholstered chair. It was his favorite. Solid and hand crafted, ornate, like the throne of some king. It imbued within him a sense of power and purpose.

From his chair, he admired the painting on the wall in front of him. The piece was difficult to procure but worth the effort. It was an oil on canvas painting of Pandora peeking into the box gifted to her by Zeus. The artist, Waterhouse, had given the viewer just a hint of what would be unleashed on the world as the box crept open. It was one of his favorite works, and it had taken a massive effort to purchase it from a private collector.

He had only one other like it. A piece by Odilon Redon, entitled Pandora. That one, however, was a reproduction as the original hung in the National Gallery of Art in Washington, DC.

Victor's walls were adorned with numerous pieces of art, both original and reproductions. Titian's Adam and Eve, aptly titled Fall of Man, was a reproduction with which he had never been fully satisfied. It showed Adam reaching towards Eve's breast as Eve reached for the forbidden fruit.   A tapestry of Lucas Cranach the Elder's vision of original sin hung next to the reproduced work of Titian. Here, the artist showed the next step, where Eve handed the forbidden fruit to Adam. The tapestry was several hundred years old and one of the priciest pieces in his personal collection. They were the centerpieces of a voluminous collection of both antique and contemporary works on the subject. His walls were covered in reminders of the deception and lies that stemmed from females.

Victor loved to go to comic book conventions and commission artists to draw various interpretations of Pandora, or Eve, or Loki. He had a favorite pencil and ink piece done of Loki as a female. It hung in a mahogany frame that seemed to close in on the piece. In it, Loki was beautifully rendered as a female, seducing her unwitting brother, Thor. The rendering was powerful enough, yet the frame gave the audience the sense that the trap Loki was setting would soon snap shut. Comic artists often saw women as Victor did. They were buxom and curvy, using all the visual weapons they had at their disposal to lure their prey into taking a bite.

Alison Gaines was a deceiver. She was Eve's and Pandora's decendant. A trickster. A vessel of sin and death. He could not be trapped by her. Victor intended on ensuring that her sin was exposed and that her sin became death. She was a souless creature, just as his mother had been. She, like his mother, was not sick, just empty. Devoid of a soul, full of sin, and waiting for death. Victor would speed her on her way.

He slipped into his shoes and walked out of the apartment and into the elevator. He greeted an older woman who was traveling from a previous floor as social mores dictated and quickly took out his phone to avoid any further need to feign interest in her. Luckily, she quickly got the frigid message and gave up her attempts at warmth.

He called Alison.   With each ring the pace of his blood quickened. When the call went to voicemail, he cleared his throat and prepared himself. "Hello, Alison, I was hoping to reach you. I wanted to offer you dinner before the Subway Series tomorrow evening. I do hope you can make it," his formal air and deliberate pattern of speech was as carefully crafted as the rest of the façade he chose to show the world. "Please call me back. I look forward to hearing from you," he said, allowing a measure of need to creep into his voice. "My apologies. This is Victor, by the way. I should not have been so presumptious as to expect you to recognize my voice," he added, suggesting that he didn't see himself as perfect. Arrogance was off putting, he realized. Confidence however, now that was something that had served him well.

"How sweet," the old lady complimented, trying once more to engage him in pleasant conversation. Victor couldn't help but smile at her. Alison would call back. She would call back and he would punish her for it.

Chapter 17

"You don't choose your family. They are God's gift to you, as you are to them."

Desmond Tutu

The air conditioner of the black Dodge Charger pumped a cool breeze as Kate hopped in the passenger seat. Mike watched her slide her legs in before she dropped into the seat. He didn't say anything to her as he pulled away from the curb and headed west towards Manhattan. Contrary to popular belief, they had more than one case to work and they were going to make an arrest today in a fatal shooting that had occurred last month. Two marked cars would meet them at the store where the man worked and make the arrest but they wanted to be there to ensure it all went smoothly.

Kate closed her eyes and let the cool air wash over her. Mike glanced at her and watched a droplet of perspiration disappear into her light purple blouse. He swerved a bit and decided it was better if he focused on the road. He was still angry at her but that didn't change how he felt. Cold shoulder aside, if she had offered herself to him at this moment he wouldn't have turned her down.

Kate looked at him as he stared at the road. Mike was laser focused and didn't give her any indication that he would break the silence. She was still mad at him for storming off at the bar. Kate had decided that she wasn't about to be the one to speak first. Stubbornly, she took out her cell phone and used it to avoid any social interaction with him. Kate saw there were three new messages. She put her phone on speaker as she usually did, most messages for her were work related and it saved the step of having to play it again for Mike to hear. She pressed the first one. It was the M.E.'s office calling, "Detective Manning, this is Javier, with the Medical Examiner's office. Please call back when you get a chance. Thank you." They never left anything on a message. Kate understood it was out of a preponderance of caution but sometimes it frustrated her. The second message was from Mike.

"Kate. Mike. Call me." So, he had broken the silence. He continued to be cold, though. Kate didn't understand it and she didn't like it.

After a few long moments, Kate spoke, though her voice was a little shaky, "You are a wordsmith. A real poet." Kate looked at him and gave him an ugly face, with a turned up lip and tongue out, desperately trying to lighten the mood between them.

"Is that really how I sound?" he asked, ignoring her contorted face and leaving his eyes on the growing traffic before them.

The final message was from her sister.

"Hey, Kate. It's Jules. Donald and I are going to take Anna to the Dutchess County Fair on Saturday. You should come." Up to that point, Kate had not regretted having her phone on speaker. It was more efficient and she preferred it, so she didn't have the cell phone on her ear. She still wasn't convinced that cellular devices were not going to give everyone brain cancer. "Oh, and you should bring Mike." Kate tried to quickly thumb the speakerphone button but in her panic she dropped the phone. Jules' voice continued, unabated, "I know you are sooooo into him." Kate ducked down, trying to catch the fallen phone and instead hit her head on the dash. Undeterred, she used both hands to probe the floor of the car. She scoured the gray carpet to no avail as her sister's voice continued to lay out Kate's feelings for Mike like a teacher who had just confiscated a seventh grader's love note. She could feel her face was getting flush already. Then, Julie finished off the message with immature, fake kissing sounds. It was too late. Mike had heard the whole thing. Kate stared straight ahead and tried to tamp down the embarrassment. Her face was awash in crimson. Kate decided to play a game of church mouse, hoping it would go on into eternity. Mike let the embarrassment linger a few moments, enjoying every second of it.

"I'm free Saturday. What time do you want me to pick you up?" This time, there was real warmth in his voice.

~

"I don't know who is more mature," Julie laughed as Mike sat carefully shading Blueberry Muffin in Anna's *Strawberry Shortcake* coloring book.

"No bumps!" Mike chided as Donald took the car up the Taconic State Parkway and into Rhinebeck.

"Does he color often?" Julie questioned Kate. She shrugged her shoulders and looked at him curiously. Mike ignored the condemnation and turned his masterpiece towards Anna.

"Like that?" he asked her.

Anna beamed a great big grin at him and shook her head so fast she looked like a bobble head. "Uh-huh, and she has green and white stripes on her socks," Anna instructed and then returned to her own coloring.

"I like her yellow hair," Mike said charmingly to her.

"She's Lemon Meringue. She's my favorite!" Anna said without taking her eyes off of her own work.

"She's pretty. She looks like you, too," Mike said, complimenting her subtlety and sweetly.

Kate warmed at the thought of Anna and Mike getting along so well. She wasn't sure why exactly, but it was important to her. She pushed the thought aside and queried, "I didn't know you were so good with kids."

Mike grinned and held up his finished Blueberry Muffin coloring, "I'm still a kid, so I know exactly how to get along with my own kind. Look! Cows!" Kate laughed as Mike and Anna's heads pivoted to the side window and began staring at the cows.

"You are too cute," she said. Julie gave a knowing smile, understanding that Kate did not mean that for just Anna.

~

"What's everyone's pleasure?" Donald asked as they entered the gate of the fairgrounds.

"Strawberry, please, Hon," Julie said without hesitation.

Kate shook her head in mock disgust, "Seriously Jules, it's barely past ten in the morning and you are going for shakes."

Mike had taken Anna and walked up a small hill to the first in a series of barn like structures that housed cows in open stalls. "Chocolate for Anna and me!" he yelled and then whispered something to the little girl who firmly held his hand. In unison, they both yelled, "Thank you!" Donald was standing on the line that was growing faster than Kate could imagine. At ten minutes after ten in the morning there were sixteen people on line for 4H shakes, and a steady stream of others were on their way.

Julie put her arm through Kate's and rested her head on her big sister's shoulder. "Katie, when something is this good in life, you don't wait for the right time, you just go for it." As Julie looked at Anna and Mike in the cow barn, Kate considered how smart her little sister was.

"Vanilla, please," Kate conceded.

"That's a good girl. In life, you need to learn to take risks," Julie quoted their dad and poked Kate in the side just as he would have done. Julie walked off to join her husband, leaving Kate alone with her thoughts.

Kate pretended to look at a display that challenged visitors to identify different types of trees. She had no interest in tree differentiation and no idea that there were so many. The small pavilion did allow her to stare at Mike and Anna without being spotted though. She watched as Mike lifted Anna under her shoulders, so she could pet a black and white cow that looked like it had been taken right from the side of a milk container. Anna's feet were already running before they touched the ground, so she could reach the next stall and pet another cow. Mike walked behind her and lifted her each time, pointing things out to her, talking sweetly to her, keeping her safe and happy.

"Oh, God, Kate, sleep with him already!" Julie said a bit too loud while she stuffed a vanilla shake into her hands. Julie swigged down her strawberry and then sampled Donald's chocolate, while Kate stood red faced and embarrassed.

"She already has," Donald said matter-of-factly.

Kate wanted to run and hide behind a massive yellow farm machine with five-foot tall tires parked just next to them but knew it wouldn't help. Julie looked her sister over. She wore a pair of silver and black open-toed flats. Her toenails were done with a cherry red high gloss, matching her hands. She wore a pleated black skirt that was four inches above the knee and a lacey black and silver tank top that brought it all together. Julie noticed there was only one strap. Kate had gone with a strapless bra. She looked hot. Julie slapped her sister's arm, "You did, you little slut! Worse, you didn't tell me!" Julie then hugged Kate like a little kid who was just informed they would be getting the toy of their dreams. "Way to go, Katie!"

"Wow, you weren't kidding that she likes shakes, huh," Mike said, assuming Julie's little celebration was over ice cream.

Kate and Julie looked at Mike, both embarrassed and unable to answer. Donald laughed heartily, "If you only knew, if you only knew."

Julie carried Anna's shake for her and every so often stuck the straw out for her to take a sip. She also didn't hesitate to take a few sips of her own, too. They walked through the barns and saw all manner of farm creatures. There were tons of ducks, chickens and other birds. Anna liked the fuzzy ones the best. Most looked like no chicken Kate had ever seen in her life. Not that she had seen much beyond a cock fighting bust, but these things looked more like poufy house pets than egg producers. As they moved through each barn, Anna's excitement ebbed and flowed based on what she could touch and what she could not. So, when they reached the goats, Anna started to quiver in enthusiasm. The little girl dashed from goat to goat, petting, rubbing and carrying on conversations with them all. Mike and Donald stayed close to her as they chatted about the upcoming football season, they celebrated the miserable season the Yankees were having and pondered whether anyone in their right mind could be a Met fan. They were both Mets fans and only Mets fans understood how painful that experience can be.

Julie and Kate lingered behind, watching Anna as well. "Dish," Julie demanded. Kate looked at her shocked and motioned with her eyes towards the two men. "They aren't paying any attention to us," Julie said with a *"don't be ridiculous"* look on her face. "When? How? Who started it? How many times? Was it good? Where?" Julie blurted questions out faster than a carnival water gun. Kate went to pet a brown goat that was being pushed out of the way by a larger spotted one.

"Ssssshhhh!" she chided.

"Details! Now!" Julie demanded as she grabbed Kate's arm and dragged her backwards, away from the men.

Kate caved and told her sister everything. It was a conversation only sisters could have. Subtle details, where he put his hand, how he undressed her, the walk of shame, everything was shared, willingly or not. For Kate, it was a weight lifted from her. She was a private person who shared little or nothing of her personal life. Truth was, there wasn't much to share in that department. It felt good to talk about it.

Julie hugged Kate tightly, "I'm so happy for the two of you."

Kate pushed her sister back and shook her head.

"No. We aren't a couple or anything. It's . . . complicated."

Julie frowned at her and took her hand. "Then stop complicating it," she said.

"Ladies, we should head to the pig races," Donald called to them. Rosaire's Pig Races was a sort of tradition in Donald's family that he carried on into his own.

"I can't believe you survived twenty-two years in a place like this, Donald," Kate said sarcastically.

He laughed at her turned up nose, "You think this smells weird and I think the city smells weird. It's all relative, Kate." Donald chuckled to himself a bit and then looked at Julie. Like they had some form of telepathic communication, they both eyed one another intently.

"Go ahead. Tell her," Julie grumbled.

Kate looked confused but Donald quickly acted to clear things up.

"The first time I took your sister here she complained the entire time about how bad it smelled. Then, she starts yelling, "I stepped in shit! I stepped in shit!" Like there was an emergency. There was an emergency; over her shoes! Who wears high heels to a county fair?" Donald laughed at the telling of his own story as if it had just happened.

They walked to an area with aluminum benches and a twenty five-foot raceway, covered in wood shavings and surrounded by rope lines. A loud, auctioneer-type voice, boomed on the microphone that the pig races were about to begin. Anna didn't like it. She had to pass a petting zoo without petting any of the animals and the sound blaring from the speakers was too loud. The crowd cheered in hopes of being selected as a pig "rooter", but Anna didn't even try to get selected. Instead, she squirmed and whined until they let the first pigs into the starting gates. Corny names like *Britney Spare Rib* and *Shakin' Bacon* ruled the day and won their respective races. Giant pot-bellied pigs raced too, though not very quickly. *Tyrone the Terrible* lost that day. He was distracted by something, and the Oreos used to bait the pigs around the track were long gone by the time he crossed the finish line. Mike giggled and laughed the whole way through the show. Best of all, Anna stopped moping and laughed right along with him.

"Seriously?" Kate looked at him condescendingly.

"You really need to lighten up, Manning. Be silly for once in your life, would you?"

Kate wouldn't admit that the races were really fun. "You need to grow up," Kate fired back.

"Never!" Mike yelled and then followed Anna into the petting zoo.

As promised, Anna got to feed an array of animals. Goats who acted as if they were eating for the first time in weeks, little horses, and a few animals Kate wasn't even sure of.

"I thought those things were mythical," Kate joked as she pointed at an animal with large thick curling horns.

Anna burned through every quarter the adults dug from their pockets or purses to buy animal feed. Half of it never even made it to the animals and just dropped to the ground as Anna ran back and forth. Mike took to holding the food for her and giving her small bits as she selected animals. He also ran interference for her so goats she had already fed didn't steal another helping. Kate found herself laughing at

Anna and Mike. Soon, she was participating in the craziness while Donald filmed it and Julie encouraged Anna's high jinx.

"Hey Kate, look at this one," Mike called. It was a little black goat with a white goatee beard. Big eyes, along with its small size and adorable markings made him hard to resist.

Kate let out an, "Aaawww," and reached in to feed him. Then, suddenly, she felt a large furry creature bump the side of her head and give it a big lick. Kate withdrew, dropping her feed, the goat dashing to grab it. "Oh, gross!" Kate yelled as she realized that a large camel from the center of the paddock had reached out and kissed her. Drips of camel spit dripped down her cheek as Mike and Anna giggled and pointed.

"Please tell me you got that on film?" Julie screeched.

"Oh, I did! I got the whole thing!" Donald said, joining in the laughter.

"You set me up!" Kate yelled at Mike, but she couldn't help but join them in laughing.

"Here, let me help," Mike offered, as he put his foot on the pump under the wash sink used at the exit of the petting zoo. The blue pump sink with soap dispensers required a bit of coordination to wash your hands, but washing a face was a special challenge.

"Are you going to spray me now?" Kate asked with a smile.

Mike chuckled and put his hands into the water to wet them. He took a bit of soap and rubbed it on his palms. "Stand still," he said and began to gently rub the soap on her face.

At first she withdrew slightly, nervous at the gesture but she calmed down quickly. The cool water felt nice on her face. His warm hands felt better.

"Sorry about that," Mike offered.

Kate smirked a bit, "I'll get you back."

Mike returned his hands to the water and rinsed them. He left them wet and returned to Kate's face to rinse off the soap.

"You don't really wear any makeup, huh?" he observed.

Kate felt his touch linger longer than it needed to. She broke away and tried to ruin the moment. "You smell like goat," she said.

"You seem to like goat," Mike said back without hesitating.

Kate started to walk away, thinking, he was right about that.

It was past lunch time when they decided to get something to eat. "I like the way this part of the fair smells much better," Mike said inhaling deep breaths and pointing his nose in different directions as he did. "Roast beef, corn dogs, nachos, where do I go first?" he asked no one in particular.

Donald slapped him on the shoulder and said, "Follow me, my friend."

They met up behind the food trucks in a grassy area with some picnic tables. All of the tables were taken and so they sat on a ledge near a wooden retaining wall. Anna wolfed down French fries and ketchup from a dog bowl shaped dish. Kate and Julie had settled on pulled pork sandwiches and sodas. Mike and Donald returned with both hands full. Neither man had bought a drink. They came up the ridge like conquerors displaying the spoils of their victory. Roast beef sandwiches, bacon wrapped corn dogs, cheese soaked French fries, calzones and even a slice of pizza. Julie didn't even react. She had seen this before. Kate was stunned.

"What are you going to do with all that?" she asked in shock.

Mike took a bite of his corn dog and said, "I wanted to try upstate pizza." He silently offered a bite of corn dog to Kate and then asked, "Can I have a sip of your soda?"

"Gee, I guess we are on a date now," she joked, shoving the soda at him.

"Eeeww, diet. Unnecessary, Manning. You look hot."

Kate looked away quickly so he didn't see her smile.

After lunch, they headed into the buildings and went shopping. Anna was having none of it. As Julie looked at everything from nail files to tie-dye sweatshirts, Donald looked at Australian leather hats and carved wooden airplanes; Anna grew more bored by the second.

"Hey, Julie?" Mike said, pulling her aside for a minute. "You mind if Kate and I take the munchkin to the rides? That way the two of you can shop in peace, maybe find a private corner or something."

Julie gave him a jolt to the arm. "I wish! That sounds great. Let me give you some money," Julie offered, but Mike was already three steps away.

He took one of Anna's hands and Kate the other. Julie and Donald watched as Anna was lifted from the ground and swung back and forth as they walked off to the rides.

"Well, Baby, do you wanna shop or go find that private corner?" Donald asked, his eyebrows raised in false hope.

"Shop first. Then maybe a private corner."

Donald knew it wouldn't happen, though it was nice to dream.

~

The first ride was a dragon coaster. It was a kiddie one with a few dips, but nothing crazy.

"I'm scared," Kate said to Anna, feigning fear.

"Maybe Mike can hold your hand?" Anna said innocently.

"I'll do it for you, Anna," Mike said. He pushed on the bar to make sure it was secure and then took Kate's hand.

Kate had no idea how many varieties of the color red there were in the world. She thought of the names of the Crayola crayons from the car and thought there had to be way more than that. Kate could feel her face bursting with an array of colors, all red! They rode the coaster around the loop. Anna laughed and squealed, her hands up in the air the whole ride. Kate's hand, however, never left her lap. Her fingers interlocked with his, she stared down at the sight of it. She watched as his thumb caressed the top of her hand. It felt like a cool summer breeze coming off the ocean. Kate's heart fluttered. It was so loud, so insistent that she thought for sure Mike would be able to hear it.

By the time Julie and Donald had returned from their shopping, Anna had gone on more than a dozen rides, played countless carnival games and had bled both Kate and Mike dry of money and tickets. Tucked under his arm, Mike had Anna's stash. He handed Donald an enormous Rastafarian banana, a little bear-shaped sand art, and a stuffed pink unicorn; the same kind from the *Despicable Me* movie. Clearly, the marksman skills of two cops were too much for carnival games.

"Here's her winnings. They're so fluffy!" he said mimicking the film. Kate held a three-foot tall pink teddy bear with a red-heart nose under her arm. Donald and Julie looked at it and at the two of them. They were holding hands and the big, pink teddy bear was clearly Kate's, not Anna's.

Julie beamed an enormous smile, "Well, it looks like the three of you had a lot of fun. Did you say thank you?" Anna bounced up and down as she told the story of each ride and stuffed animal victory. Julie tried to focus on her daughter, but, she kept glancing at her big, tough sister, who never let anyone in. It felt like Christmas to her.

It was time to go. They stuffed the winnings into the back of the car. Anna, cranky and struggling, was strapped tightly in her car seat for the ride home. Mike elected to take the middle seat, in between Anna and Kate. Anna fell asleep in minutes and her head rested on Mike's shoulder. Kate's head rested on the other. Mike had slipped his hand into her's the moment the car door had closed. Kate held tightly to her bear, while their fingers remained entwined, resting gently on her bare thigh. The quiet hum of the car and the rhythm of the tires bumping along the road put the ladies to sleep. Mike sat alone with his thoughts while Donald drove the two-plus hours home. As the parkway ended, and the stop and go of local traffic emerged, so too, did Kate.

"Where are we?" she asked, barely above a whisper.

Mike brushed her hair from her face and smiled at her, "We'll be to your place in a few minutes."

Kate nuzzled into his shoulder and tightened her grip on his hand. She took a deep breath, taking in the scent of him. Then, before her courage could leave her, she took one last leap for the day, "Stay with me."

~

They made love that night. It was different though. Kate had held his hand as they walked up the two flights of stairs. They did not talk. The two of them understood what was about to happen. When they had sex in the past, it was drunken passion or out of a frustrated emotional need. Tonight wasn't any of those things.

Kate opened the door and dropped her purse and keys on the shelf. She turned and faced him. Taking both his hands in hers, she began to walk backwards towards the bedroom, never taking her eyes from his. Once they reached the bedroom, Kate's plan faltered. She seemed not to know how to begin. Mike caressed her check with his hand and then cupped her chin. He kissed her forehead, her nose, her cheeks and then placed a single kiss softly on her lips. His hand ran down her neck, and danced along her shoulder, gently carrying her black strap down her arm. Kate could feel her knees buckling. She nudged her head up to his, kissing his lips. She tugged at his lower lip and her mouth opened, their tongues intertwining together.

Kate felt her tank top slide off her shoulders. Mike's one hand held her tightly around the small of her back while the other skillfully unhooked her bra. Kate felt the black and purple night-sky bra with small, glittering starry flecks fall to the ground. She had selected the matching set last night in preparation for this. Somehow though, what was happening felt completely unexpected. Mike unzipped the back of her skirt and it too dropped to the floor. Kate felt his hands slide down her hips, slipping her panties down her thighs. His tongue quickened with passion, then suddenly broke contact as Kate fell back onto the deep purple comforter. She was completely naked now, lying on her bed in front of him. She had never allowed him to see her this way. Kate had never exposed herself so much. Mike stood at the edge of the bed and drank in the sight of her. He didn't hide his widening smile at all. Somehow, Kate felt embarrassed and pleased all at once. She slid off the bed, dropping to her knees in front of him.

"Kate, you don't have to . . ." Mike said, nervous that his standing there had sent the wrong message. Kate smiled up at him and began undressing him.

They made love that night in a way they had never done before. Kate pleasured him, drinking in his joyful groans. Mike wrestled with her, making certain that she too would have the chance to simply enjoy herself. Their passion wasn't an urgent need. It was volcanic. Deep, hot and unquenchable. The kind that would only cool when the world had given up all hope. Depleted of all energy, the two lovers fell into an exhausted sleep, seemingly tied together in purple sheets.

~

Kate awoke, still interwoven in the arms of Mike. She thought about extricating herself and then decided there was no need. This was her bedroom after all, where was she going to run to? Kate felt the warmth of him, the comfort of his arms and legs. She felt something else too and smiled at the thought of it. It was just like the movies, she thought. Except that she had to pee and her breath smelt like yesterday's fairgrounds. Her stomach was playing games with her again, too. She hadn't thrown up since the crime scene but she didn't feel right, either. Kate slipped out from his arms and dashed to the bathroom. When she returned, bladder empty and breath refreshingly minty, she stood, naked, staring at him. Kate was giddy with happiness.

On a whim, Kate grabbed the phone next to the bed. She sat on the edge, inches away from his hands and dialed. "Hey Jules," Kate semi-whispered into the phone, "Sorry to call so early, I just . . ." Kate tossed her hair back over her head and rubbed her temples. Kate wasn't sure how to summarize all of her emotion efficiently. She didn't consider herself a robot, but emotion didn't come naturally to her either. Despite that, she had to admit that she was learning some things about herself. She may not show her emotions; however, that didn't mean she didn't have them. If last night was any indication, she could no longer control them.

"Sign me up, okay?" Kate said quickly before she lost her nerve.

"Wha?" Julie mumbled, too early in the morning to comprehend anything, especially before her coffee.

"Sign me up." Kate repeated, feeling a bit light-headed at the changes coming over her. "For the church picnic-thing you talked about. I'm in. And, boy, do I have something to tell you!"

She looked at Mike in her bed, sleeping peacefully, and reflected on her feelings for him, for Julie, for Anna. She loved Jules. She was her little sister. She protected her, fought with her, laughed with her. Anna was a miracle. She was an innocent little slice of Heaven on Earth. So, what was Mike? Kate knelt before him and stared penetratingly at him. A good man. Funny. Sweet. Strong. Caring. My best friend. My lover. That thought sent a big, guilty grin across her face. Butterflies floated in her stomach. Big, with bold, bright colors, flapping their wings and flying high on a summer breeze. Kate wondered if that was why her stomach had felt odd lately. She decided it must be. That these were the kind of butterflies that were unmistakably, undoubtedly love.

Chapter 18

"Even the smallest person can change the course of the future"

J.R.R. Tolkien, *The Lord of the Rings*

"I'll get it!" Julie yelled, half-dressed as she scampered towards the front door of her family's two-story walk up in Woodside, Queens. Kate's call to her had still not really sunk in. She had always wanted a closer relationship to her sister, but never felt successful. Sure, Julie would call Kate to go shopping or to come to dinner; it was just that she never felt like Kate needed her in her life as much as she needed Kate. Since they were young, Kate was independent and willing to go it alone. Julie liked company; being in a group felt comfortable to her. Naturally, she wanted her big sister to be a part of that group.

As Julie approached the front door she tried to neaten her bed head hair. She could see her sister through the storm door screen. Kate's hair was tied back in a tight pony tail and a tall cup of Starbuck's coffee was in her hand held high near her face. It was a face that didn't even bother trying to hide its disdain. Julie took a deep breath and promised herself to be patient. "First times are rarely easy times," she said to herself, repeating a mantra their father used to say to his two daughters.

"Good morning, Sunshine." Julie was never a morning person. Kate never let her live that down. Kate swung the storm door open with a bit more force than was required. "Why do you have the screen in and why is this door unlocked?" Kate chided her little sister like a mother would her disobedient child. "Seriously, Julie? Are you asking for something bad to happen?" Kate looked at her in exasperation, like a frustrated pre-school teacher who has told a child ten times not to touch something. Kate handed the tall coffee off to Julie and walked down the hallway saying as she did, "Where's my Little Banana?"

Julie smelled the cup, drinking in the aroma like a true addict. She smiled at the coffee her sister had bought for her and thought, same old Kate. "She's upstairs, lying in wait to pounce on you."

Kate headed up the wooden stairs and allowed every creak and stomp to exaggerate themselves. "Anna Banana! I'm coming to get you!" she threatened, smiling as she did. Her frustration with her sister was gone; only her incalculable love for her niece remaining. As Kate reached the top of the stairs, she saw Anna's eyes peer around the bathroom door. Playing along, Kate instead headed into Anna's bedroom. Pouncing like a great cat on the back of a zebra, Kate leaped onto Anna's bed and messed the sheets as if she were in the fight of her life. "I got you little one! There's no escape from the tickle monster!" Anna charged headlong into the bedroom and jumped onto Kate's head. The little girl wrestled and hugged her aunt and the two let out a long carefree giggle.

"An' Kate," Anna began, saying it so fast that, as usual, the word Aunt never made an appearance. "Would you like to shop at Fan-G?"

Kate knew the store well. She had spent a great deal of time and money at her niece's make-believe store. Fan-G stood for Fancy Girl and Anna worked diligently to recreate a shopping experience for her customers that included a toy register, gift cards, discounts, and wrapping paper. The only thing Anna wouldn't replicate was speed. Once this girl got you into Fan-G, you were not coming out for a long while. After all, there were lots of bargains when you were the favorite relative.

"Did you get any new items in?" Kate asked, feigning excitement.

Anna was nearly bubbling over with joy. "We got a new seal. Wanna see him?"

It must be a new stuffed animal addition to the already large collection of pink unicorns and Rastafarian bananas that came home from their adventures together, Kate thought. This one came from the Central Park Zoo. Kate had been invited, though she couldn't make it because of work. Julie always invited her; always included her in her family.

"Sure, kiddo. I hope it's not too expensive."

Anna's little hand slipped into Kate's and off they went to shop.

~

"Hey, up there! We have to go!" Julie yelled up the stairs, as she pulled on her shoes.

Kate had no idea how long she had been shopping, but she knew her purchases had piled up. Kate had purchased the small stuffed seal that Anna had suggested, along with a decorative glass slipper from Anna's dresser and two inappropriately dressed Barbie dolls with tangled hair all for the bargain price of fifteen dollars.

"Could you wrap these up for me?" Kate asked.

"Oh, yes. Would you like them in a box, too?" Anna asked in her playful voice that was most decidedly a British accent.

Kate found herself mirroring the "*across the pond*" style, "Why thank you, my dear."

"Fan-G?" Julie asked as Kate made her way down the stairs. "How much did she take you for this time?"

"Fifteen," Kate mumbled and then turned the volume up to ten so Anna could hear the second part, "There are some really great buys today."

"Sucker," Julie shook her head. "Nice hair, by the way."

Kate looked at herself in the reflective glass of one of the family photos on the wall. Her hair was a disaster. The pony tail had held but escapees were running everywhere. She had hair going in at least seven directions. Kate pulled out the hair tie and patted her hair down before redoing her pony tail.

"Want a brush?" Julie offered and Kate declined. "Bye Sweetie!" Julie yelled up the stairs. She knew better than to go up and get roped into Fan-G when it was time to leave. "You ready for this?" Julie asked. Kate gave her sister a great big, "are you shitting me look" and walked down the stairs. Donald met them in the foyer and gave Julie a kiss on the cheek. "You girls be good now," he said sarcastically and ushered them out. "No candy," Julie warned him with a waving finger, but Donald just let the door close without a word.

"Thank you for doing this," Julie said, not hiding her excitement at the fact that her sister had finally agreed to volunteer with her.

"What's this like? Do we all hold hands and read the Bible and hope Jesus does the cooking?" Kate said in a snarky tone.

Julie didn't take the bait. Kate's sarcasm defense mechanism had gotten her many times in the past, but not today. "You'll see. Mostly, it's just exorcisms and arranged marriages," Julie shot back with a smile.

Kate was surprised at all of the activity in the park. It was packed full of people of every conceivable ethnic group. They sat on blankets, kids were playing football and Frisbee and four large tents were set up, full of tables, chairs and coolers. Several grills were already filling the air with the smells of summer. A few of the adults had already popped some beers and were enjoying lounging in the sun. The atmosphere was relaxed and happy. It reminded Kate of tailgating at a Jet's game, only on grass. It was classic Woodside to her. The melting pot of America could not be better represented then right here in Queens; Asians, Irish, Muslims, Dominicans and all the rest, just doing what people do. This was not at all what Kate expected from a Roman Catholic Church function. Then again, not everyone in the park was here for the picnic.

"Kate, may I introduce Ms. Laura Moles," Julie motioned to a pretty young woman behind the grill. Her long brown hair was tied back, but a piece of it had escaped and fell in front of her chestnut eyes. Laura blew it out of her face and smiled brightly at Kate.

"Nice to meet you, Kate." Laura already made a good impression on Kate. She always liked when a person used a new acquaintance's name. "I'd shake your hand but I'm afraid it might get bitten off," Laura joked as she motioned to the crowd of kids with plates, buns, and assorted other foods gyroscopically moving to and fro. Laura served a few hot dogs to the front of the crowd and then motioned them away. "Go on! Other kids need to eat, too. Come back after you finished that one."

Kate smiled as one of the boys, probably about eight years old moved his hot dog off his plate and behind his back. He held his plate high like little orphan Oliver asking for more. Laura let out a sweet little giggle, "Who's the one behind your back for, huh? You got a girlfriend I don't know about, kiddo?"

With that the boy uttered a disgusted, "Yuck!" and moved on without a second helping.

"Kate is here to give you a hand, if you'd like." Julie informed Laura.

"I'll take every hand I can get, and if the Health Department allowed it I'd even take a few feet!" Laura handed off a spatula to Kate.

Kate looked creepily at her little sister and whined, "This is NOT what I signed on for!"

As she walked off, Julie didn't even turn around as she answered, "It's for a good cause so just smile and do it. Oh, and this IS what you signed on for!"

Kate fired back, "I have no recollection of that statement, your honor!"

Julie threw up her hands and kept walking. She knew her sister would moan and groan but secretly enjoy herself.

Hamburgers began to flip and Kate was officially a church volunteer. As Kate's burgers sizzled and the smell of charred beef wafted through the air, she too, found herself surrounded by hungry little vultures.

"Well, how does everyone like their's cooked?" Kate asked the hungry crowd. As twenty-five squeaky voices rang out demanding different degrees of temperature and at least a few requesting cheese or bacon, Kate could here Laura laughing behind her.

"Clearly, your first rodeo," Laura chided sarcastically. She reached behind Kate and grabbed a stack of cheese and started flinging slices onto the burgers like rocks skimming across a pond. "They'll eat anything they can get their hands on. Go for medium-well and about two-thirds cheeseburgers to one-third hamburgers."

Kate used her elbow to brush her hair back and smiled at Laura. "Thanks. This is harder than it looks." Kate looked at her newfound friend and asked, "Ever hear of entrapment?"

Laura gave out a chuckle and shot back, "Do you complain this much at work too?"

Kate laughed. Laura was funny, friendly, and wasn't going to put up with Kate's moaning.

"Now, you, I can work with!" Kate said and the two chatted the day away as they worked to feed a hungry crowd.

By the time Kate had a chance to look at her phone, three and a half hours had passed and neither she nor Laura had stopped. The two ladies had served up countless burgers and hot dogs and showed the signs of weariness across their faces.

"You look exhausted," Laura quipped as she used a napkin to wipe the sweat from her own brow. Kate gave a chuckle as she collapsed back into a camping chair that was blissfully unoccupied at the moment.

"Julie is gonna pay for this one," Kate blurted and let out a long sigh. Laura pulled open the top to a long, blue cooler and reached in.

"Want a beer?"

"I love you right now. You know that, right?" Kate joked as she held her hand out and took the cold Bud Light bottle from Laura.

Laura took a seat on top of the cooler and popped open her beer. "Well, I am single, you just aren't really my type. Then again, late twenties and starting to get desperate, so you never know."

Kate laughed and took a long draught of her beer. Then Laura asked the question that Kate dreaded.

"How about you? Is there a Mr. Kate Manning?"

Kate's shoulders shrugged a bit and she didn't respond beyond that.

Laura quickly tried to withdraw the question. "Sorry. Didn't mean to pry," she said apologetically.

"No. It's okay," Kate said quickly, realizing it was her, not Laura at fault here. "It's complicated."

"Isn't it always," Laura replied and handed Kate another beer.

~

"Ladies, can I really believe mine eyes?" It was the distinct song-bird voice of Father Gregory with a "*this is not happening sort of tone.*" Laura nearly dropped her beer, but Kate gave no outward indication of guilt whatsoever.

"Hello, Father," Laura stuttered, "Great turnout this year."

Gregory smiled and looked around, "Indeed. Thank you for all your hard work; but, I'm still a little upset with you."

Laura stood up and put the beer behind her as if hiding it now was enough to make him forget about it. Maybe she forgot about the dozen or so empties strewn on the lawn around them. She tried to mumble an apology or an explanation, Kate couldn't tell which it was. Man, she has a guilty conscience, Kate thought, giggling. Gregory seemed so amused by Laura's drunken ramblings that he might have just burst out laughing. He tried to butt in a few times; but, Laura was so busy trying to back pedal that she wouldn't let him.

Finally, Gregory held up his hand and firmly said, "Laura, stop." She obeyed like any good Catholic school girl would. Kate half thought she was going to get a rap on the knuckles for this. Gregory looked down at the cooler and back to Laura. "You have any Heineken?"

Kate burst out laughing at the dumbfounded look on the poor girl's face.

"Uh, no, um sorry, Father," Laura muttered. "I have some Sam's Summer Ale, if you want that?" Laura asked timidly.

"Please! I really need a cold one," Gregory said appreciatively as he took a seat on the ground next to Kate. Laura opened the bottle for him and handed it to him. Gregory clanked his Sam's Summer Ale against Kate's nearly empty Bud Light, "To happy kids and the great people who put the smile on their faces," and with that he took a long swig that emptied half the bottle.

Laura, clearly flustered and uncomfortable began moving off and cleaning up. She was in full on social avoidance mode.

"I made her uncomfortable," he lamented. "She's always so nervous around me. I was just trying to joke with her. Lighten her up a bit," he explained.

Kate smirked, "She makes a mean hot dog, though."

Gregory laughed at that and rose to grab another beer from the cooler. "Want one?" he asked.

Kate shook her head and simultaneously held up her hand, "No. Thank you."

"Come on. You aren't going to make me drink alone, are you?" Gregory asked while slapping another beer into Kate's hand.

"Am I going to go to Hell for this?" Kate asked sarcastically.

Gregory sat on top of the cooler and opened his beer. He drank and considered the label a bit before he responded. "I get the sense that you don't like me very much, Kate."

That one made Kate feel pretty small. Red-faced and more than a little embarrassed, Kate tried to ease the tension she had created.

"No. It's not that."

"I don't get to decide who goes to Hell, you know. That's above my pay grade." Gregory said matter-of-factly. "Though, I doubt drinking alcohol with a priest is a cardinal offense. We, Catholics, have a long history with good booze."

Kate gave an apologetic smile to him. He was a nice guy. She had to give him that at least. He didn't preach down to you, he just talked to you. She didn't want to like him, but he made that very difficult.

"Thank you for coming today," he said. "I know it meant a great deal to your sister." He took another drink and continued, "Big help to Laura, too." There it was again. That nice, normal guy approach that disarmed her. Kate hated feeling disarmed. It made her feel vulnerable.

"Can I ask you something?" Kate said.

"Open book. What do you want to know?" Gregory leaned forward, ready for anything.

"Do you believe all of it?" Kate queried with an edge in her voice.

"By all of it, do you mean the Bible?" Gregory asked without a hint of anger.

"Yeah. The Bible. Adam and Eve, original sin. Noah, the whole boat," Kate listed them out.

"Can I tell you a secret?" Gregory asked. Kate nodded as if she didn't particularly care about the secret, but wasn't going to stop him if he shared. "The Bible was written and compiled by men. Men that believed what they were writing was the word of God, but still, men. Men are flawed. We make mistakes, lots of them," Gregory shook his empty bottle as if to exemplify his point. "I don't believe every word the Bible says. There is room for interpretation, debate, even disagreement. What I believe in, is this," Gregory motioned to the surrounding park, the people. "People. God's children. That's what I believe in. People are inspired by God. They do great things in His name."

Kate listened and wasn't prepared for him to concede the veracity of the Bible so easily. Again, she found herself surprisingly disarmed by him. "People do some pretty horrible things in His name too, don't you think?" Kate retorted. "Come on. 9/11, the Crusades, the Inquisition," Kate trailed off.

"The Inquisition! What a show! The Inquisition! Here we go!" Gregory started singing the tune from Mel Brook's *History of the World*. He let out an ironic chuckle and formed his response. "Kate, you are right. But, can't you see that so am I? Yes, people do horrible things in the name of God, but that's like blaming ole Sam Adams here for drunk driving. He made it, but it's what we choose to do with it that counts."

Kate felt like she couldn't win the argument and so shifted gears to another. "Don't you ever get tired of lying to these people about Heaven? Please, rapture and the end of days, that's so Y2K," Kate said, ratcheting up the sarcasm to ten.

Gregory smiled a knowing smile. "Is that what you think I do? Lie to them? I give them hope. Hope that their work will be rewarded.

Hope that they will see their loved ones again. Hope that the pain and suffering they feel will be alleviated and that comfort is coming."

Kate tried to interject, "But . . ."

"I don't know any more than you do about what happens after we die. I believe in Heaven. I believe in God. I have hope, Kate. In that hope I have happiness. What do you have? Pessimism and a gun. You do good work here on earth. You try to help people. Protect them. Why work so hard to do the right thing if you don't believe that doing the right thing matters in the end?"

Gregory rose from his seat on the cooler and opened a mini bag of M&M's from the picnic table. He held a single yellow M&M in between his thumb and forefinger, examining it. "No, Kate. I don't believe this hard candy shell for a minute. You want to wear this thick coat of disdain for religion but inside of you is a woman who believes in hope and love. There's something sweet under that shell for sure." He popped a piece of candy in his mouth and with that, Gregory walked off to be amongst his flock and left Kate to consider the prospect that she may not know herself as well as she would like.

Chapter 19

"If an injury must be done to a man it should be so severe that his vengeance need not be feared."

Niccolo Machiavelli (1469-1527)

The man in the recliner chair quivered with emotion, ". . . that I loved her. You know, people just don't say it often enough and then, well, you know. I should have told her every day and now I can't. That son of bitch took her from me. He took her."

He held a photograph in a white frame in his hands. His arms shook. His right wrist was tattooed with the eagle, globe, and anchor of the USMC. Kate knew it well. Mike had one strikingly similar on his shoulder. Once a Marine, always a Marine, they said. The photo was of his daughter from her prom. She had a long, formal purple gown and a small lavender flower in her hair. She was strikingly good-looking. So much so, that Kate thought she could have been a model.

Mike and Kate sat on the couch opposite the man. Kate had realized within minutes that this interview would be yet another dead end in a long string of dead ends. The man was in agony. He needed to vent his sadness and rage, though none of that was going to help them catch a killer. Kate had a pad and pen in her hand, but had put them down on the couch. She was frustrated that no one could give them a viable lead.

Mike tried to ease the man's pain, "I'm sure your daughter knew how much you cared for her, Mr. Curtin."

He was a good dad and by rights, he was close to his daughter. They talked once a week or more. She was a waitress in a diner, working the job on the side for spending money while she was at York College in Jamaica, Queens. She was studying biology. She wanted to go into bio-tech. None of this was helping find her killer. She didn't frequent the coffee shop where Jessica worked. They shared no history at all. Never traveled in the same circles. There was no connection whatsoever between the two victims. Well, other than their killer, Kate thought.

The man wept and buried his head in his hands. Mike knelt beside him and put his hand on the man's shoulder. Kate remained seated, tapping her foot in frustration.

"Mr. Curtin, Sir, I want to get this guy. I want to stop him from ever doing this again and my partner and I think you can help us. Can you do that?" Mike asked. He always knew how to get people to do what he wanted. The bereaved father looked up and took his head out from his hands. His face was stressed and full of anguish. He stared into Mike's eyes.

Suddenly, Mr. Curtin lashed out like a cobra, spitting venom, "When you get him promise me you'll kill him." The man grabbed Mike by the shoulders and held large tufts of his shirt, squeezing them in his hands. "Promise me, he won't get away with this. He has to pay for what he did. Please . . ." Then, as suddenly as he struck, he retreated, collapsing back into the folds of the reclining chair. Hopeless sobs echoed in the room.

Mike looked at Kate and furrowed his brow. She understood what he was getting at, but lacked the patience to care. She wanted to catch this guy and playing grief counselor wasn't getting them any closer to doing it.

"Thank you for your time, Sir," Kate said, rising to her feet.

Mike whipped his head around and snapped at her, "We're not done here, Detective!"

His voice was stone cold, shocking in its ferocity. Kate collapsed back onto the couch without a word. She had never seen Mike like this.

Mike stood in front of the broken man. He looked around at the walls of the living room; at the pictures of a life cut short. Coldly, Mike swore an oath, "I won't let him walk away from this. I promise you that."

An Absence of Faith

The drive back was marred by silence. When they had left the house, Kate had expected an apology. She got none. She had expected some measure of warmth and all she got was silence and a thousand-yard stare. She knew he was upset and she wanted to reach out and hold his hand, but she was terrified that he might pull away. What should she say? She hadn't the words, and expressions of emotion were not really in her wheelhouse. She was angry about this, too. She was frustrated, too. Would that work, she wondered. Should she share her feelings with him? Should she tell Mike how she felt about him? This didn't seem the time to say such important words. The uncertainty was maddening! Kate was like a duck on a pond, steady on the surface and churning away underneath.

Mike drove back to the precinct. His eyes were laser beams, never leaving the road. He didn't glance at her like usual. Kate was used to him stealing looks at her legs or her cleavage. Lately, she had been deliberately selecting a wardrobe to encourage it. Today's ensemble included tight low-waist jeans and a pretty red blouse with frills that drew the eye to just the right place. It was as sexy as work attire could possibly be and it wasn't working.

As the drive continued, Kate started to get mad. If he doesn't look at me, then what, I'm not really here, she pondered. He's the stubborn ass that wanted to go to the house in the first place. He's the one that was wasting our time. He's the one that made a stupid promise he knows he can't keep. He's the one acting like a child! Over and over again in her head Kate railed against him. By the time they were five minutes out from the precinct, Kate decided it was time to break the silence.

"What the hell were you thinking?" she fired at him.

Mike looked at her for the first time since they had left the house, but said nothing. He returned his eyes to the road as if her question wasn't worth answering. Ugh! How he infuriated her sometimes!

"Damn it, Mike, don't make promises you can't keep," she yelled making sure she could not be ignored again. The volume was worse than she had intended it to be. It pinged around in the car like a bullet bouncing around inside a tank. She could see his hand pull tighter around the steering wheel.

"What do you want?" Mike asked with ice in his voice. "This guy will cop an insanity plea and never see a day behind bars."

Kate wanted to argue the point, she just couldn't. Mike was probably right. She looked at his hand as it tightened its vice grip on the wheel. He was controlling a rage she had never known in him. Would he hit her? The thought left as soon as she had it. That just wasn't even something he could ever do. He was too honorable. He was too gentle and caring. It's why she fell in love with him.

"Marines take care of their own," he stated flatly as if that explained everything. "When we find him, he's a dead man," Mike said, ending the discussion abruptly.

"Mike, I . . . I don't want," Kate muttered, confused about how to handle all these emotions. She was afraid for him. She was also mad at him. Kate wanted to hold him, to feel his warmth around her. She wanted to scream! Then, suddenly she couldn't control it any longer. The old her took over. Sarcasm flew from her mouth, "Is this some stupid Marine brotherhood macho thing?" As soon as the words escaped her lips she knew she would regret them.

Mike slammed the car into park and got out of the door. "You're not my girlfriend so drop it, alright!" With that, he slammed the door and walked into the building.

That wounded her. As Mike stormed off, Kate sat in the car and wondered why. Why did she care so much? Why did she fight so hard? And, most importantly, why did that last statement cut so deephurt so much?

Chapter 20

"A stiff apology is a second insult . . . The injured party does not want to be compensated because he has been wronged; he wants to be healed because he has been hurt."

Gilbert K. Chesterton

Victor stood naked and sharpened the steel blade, dragging it back and forth across the stone. He eyed the edge and saw the glint of light reflect off of it. Satisfied, he placed it down on the white linen towel folded neatly at the edge of the sink. He picked up the shaving brush and dabbed shaving cream on his face. Once his face was covered in foaming soap, he took up the straight razor he had just sharpened and gently flicked down his face. He had always shaved with a straight razor. Nothing gave a closer shave.

Victor was a man of strict tastes and stricter habits. His grooming was a sort of choreographed dance in front of the mirror. A step by step process; he didn't deviate from it, ever, just like his mother.

He dabbed his face clean with the towel and pointed his chin towards the mirror. Satisfied with his work, he moved on. He took out a pair of tweezers and tugged a few stray hairs above the line he had marked as absolute north. He yanked a few others from the gap between his eye brow. His hair was lightly gelled and taken just off center as he preferred it. Cologne sprayed, but not rubbed in. His teeth were flossed, brushed and vigorously swished with mouthwash. Every detail was attended to.

If an outsider had ever observed the process they might liken it to a religious ceremony. Victor did not allow for noise or distraction. He folded his towels in just such a way, never with a hint of variation. His attention to cleanliness and order was obsessive. His clothing was dry cleaned when it could be and destroyed and replaced when it could not be.

He chose a more casual outfit for this evening, though still one that suggested wealth and refinement. He wore gray slacks and a fitted blue and gray collared shirt from Armani. He would look as if he had just come from work on a casual Friday. That was the image he wanted to convey.

Victor finished dressing and headed into the living room. He sat and slipped on a pair of stylish black Mezlan shoes. He took his prepaid, disposable phone from his pocket and turned it on speaker. He listened to the message from Alison again.

"Hey, Victor!" she said in a flirtatious sort of voice that suggested she had been a member of a slutty college sorority. "I'd love to go to the game with you. It's so sweet of you to offer." Victor could almost hear her biting her lower lip as she said it. "Call me and let me know when you want to pick me up." She went on to include her address which Victor had already memorized, but now confirmed with a second listening.

He looked at his watch and made certain he would arrive on time. He gathered his wallet, the tickets and both his phones, and slid them into his pockets. He glanced at the images on the wall of Pandora and Eve and smiled. With that, he walked out the door and headed off to end Alison's life.

~

The massive white and orange lettering above the jumbo-tron scoreboard read CitiField. There on the kiss cam was Victor being mauled by an inebriated Alison. The back of his head appeared on screen as Alison's hands held his face and kissed him deeply. Had Victor known even a part of him had appeared there, it might have saved the woman's life.

It was the ninth inning and the score was four to two in favor of the home team. The screen was surrounded by beer and soda advertisements. The entire place seemed to Victor to be a marketing agent's dream. A captive audience, half drunk and almost all with their blood up. The outfield reminded him more of Times Square than of a ball field but he wasn't really a sports aficionado anyway.

"I thought I would miss Shea but this stadium is really beautiful, you know?" Alison said, repeating the annoying habit of including the "you know" at the start or end of nearly every other sentence.

She wore her long brown hair down for dinner but tucked it in her ball cap outside the stadium. She sported a comfortable, flowing blue skirt and white blouse with an orange infinity scarf. Mets colors had been strategically blended into her outfit ensuring that her blue and orange hat would not clash.

"Shea was all blue outside. This place just feels classier, you know," she remarked and sipped her near ten dollar beer. Victor cared little about the money; but, it seemed to bother Alison the first two times he had purchased them. Now, it didn't seem to faze her at all.

"Come on!" Alison stood as she yelled, her beer sloshing in her inebriated hand. Apparently, she had not been alone in her frustration over a call by the home-plate umpire. Clearly, a stadium full of fans could see the pitch was a strike when he could not.

Victor watched Alison react to the subtleties of the game much as his mother had. She got lost in the throes of passion and lost sight of the things going on around her. To them, there was the game and nothing could draw their attention away. Somehow, what was going on in that stadium, on that field, was more important than anything else in the world. Their jobs, their families, none of it mattered, especially when the game was close.

"Alison," Victor said. He repeated her name two more times before he gave up, realizing she was no better than his mother. The thought did not surprise him, but somehow it made him angrier than he normally was. He would enjoy tonight immensely.

The batter knocked a fly ball just behind third base and the infielder caught it easily. The crowd roared. Alison turned and waited for Victor to give her a high five. She realized he was looking at her and suddenly she felt a little awkward. Victor smiled and returned his attention to the game.

Sports fans are an odd sort of creature Victor mused. He watched as Alison sat down next to him. She clasped her hands in prayer and shook them vigorously, muttering, 'Come on God, come on," as she did so. Her fingers were wrapped so tight, Victor could see the whites of her knuckles.

They call upon their God for the most trivial of matters, he thought. A curve ball missed the outside edge of the plate. The umpire signaled ball one. Victor watched as her head bent low as if further supplication might enjoin God to intervene.

The batter swung and missed and the count was one and one. Her eyes peered slightly over her hands, fixated on the plate. The batter let the next pitch pass undisturbed. A called strike and the crowd roared. Alison released her hands to clap and then grabbed Victor's and held it tightly to her chest.

The batter dug in and watched a fastball blow past, inches from his chest. The count was two and two, and the crowd began to stand intermittently around the stadium. Alison tugged Victor up with her.

Suddenly, the crowd thundered as the ball dribbled from the bat and slunk towards third base. The infielder rifled the ball to first base and nobody even waited for the umpire to make the call. The game was over. Alison leapt into the air in joyous excitement.

"Thank you, God," she yelled and then kissed her fist and jutted it high into the air.

When fate gives them what they wished for, they see it as divine intervention; Victor ruminated on the paradox of it all.

Alison hugged and kissed him, her beer spilled at their feet. She tasted like a bar, nevertheless, Victor didn't stop her. Soon, he would be through with her and he was a patient man. In the end, he would rule the day and that was enough for him. Fans high-fived random strangers and congratulated one another on their victory. Did they ever wonder, how God picks who wins and who loses if people on both sides pray for victory? Victor wondered. Their hubris amused him.

~

They walked out of the stadium, members of a gallant and jubilant parade. People yelled joyously at one another, screaming obscenities and slapping each other's backs. Alison joined in the foray, yelling "Break out the Broom! Can you say sweep?" Victor had to grab her as she tumbled to the side, almost knocking over a pretzel stand.

Alison smiled appreciatively at him and yelled over the din of the crowd, "I can't wait until Monday morning . . ." She stopped mid-thought and had to collect herself. The high volume of alcohol now taking its toll on her faculties. "You know, I'm gonna give it to those guys at the gym," she swore, slurring her speech a bit.

The crowd poured out into a gated area outside the stadium. Vendors sold t-shirts, hats and the last remnants of food. A man offered them a ten dollar t-shirt that Victor unceremoniously shoved away. Alison leaned heavily on him, her head on his shoulder and her two hands holding his bicep and the bend of his elbow.

Alison continued, repeating herself for the fourth or fifth time, " . . . those guys at the gym are gonna here it from us, huh?" He was growing tired of her and the time was fast approaching where he would no longer need to pretend. Victor grinned at the thought. "They'll be in tears when I'm through with them," he said suggestively.

Alison glanced up at him and smiled. "Thank you for inviting me tonight. I had an amazing time and the seats were awesome. The best I've ever had." She leaned in and kissed him, sliding her tongue into his mouth with all the grace of a charging rhinoceros.

~

Victor strode into the apartment building with confidence. He had already reconnoitered the building when he had picked Alison up. There were no security cameras, though there was a dummy one in the corner when people first entered. It was a cheap piece of plastic that hung limply from the graying ceiling. It had been broken, probably by a child throwing something at it and had never been replaced. Thus, the illusion of security wasn't even maintained here.

Alison clung to his right arm, still drunk and now tired. In the other, he held a single long stemmed crimson rose. She had gushed when he had stopped to buy it. He told her what he had told all of them. "A single rose to symbolize the future." Strange how two individuals could see a thing so differently. To the woman, she saw a future filled with romance and love. Victor meant that the rose was already dead. Beautiful still, but soon it would be rotting and forgotten.

They walked up the narrow, dark stairwell. Alison stumbled in the darkness and Victor had to pull her up more than once. She giggled the first two times, then swore in frustration.

They reached her floor and Alison leaned against the wall outside of her apartment door. Victor waited for her to get her keys, but she didn't even make a move for them. Instead, she reached out and grabbed the center of his shirt. Pulling him towards her, Alison planted a sloppy kiss on him that missed his mouth by several inches.

She giggled again and took the rose from his hand. She put the flower to her nose and inhaled it. Then she rubbed it on her face and his. Victor was trying not to show his impatience. He took her hand and held it against the wall, the rose lingering high above them. He kissed her and then withdrew backwards, letting her hand go. Alison took the opportunity to reverse their positions and pushed Victor against the wall.

Unbeknownst to either of them, they were being watched. A little old lady had paused several stairs down to watch the scene unfolding. She probably had hoped to avoid detection by waiting them out. Maybe they would head into the apartment and then she could go about her business. Or, maybe she was curious about the whole thing.

Regardless, the bags she lugged had grown heavy for her and the couple outside the apartment gave no indication they would be heading indoors anytime soon.

"Hu! Huh! Huff!" she exaggerated the sounds as she moved up the stairs. The warning signals seemed not to dampen the spirits of the two of them.

"Now, where are those keys?" she fumbled through her oversized purse, glancing often at her neighbor and her new man. "Heaven help me, when will I ever learn," she muttered. Then, her purse dumped out onto the floor.

The little old lady was struck by the steely, grey-blue eyes of the man who was making out with her neighbor. His eyes were open despite the fact that he was supposedly in the throes of passion. He stared blankly at the ceiling, disinterested in what was happening. She watched as Alison rubbed herself all over him and he stood coldly against the wall and looked off into some unknown distance. It was extremely unnatural. The man seemed oblivious to all that was happening around him, as if he was in another world.

She gathered her belongings into a pile and dumped them in her bag only to need to search for her keys again. She frantically pushed her way into the apartment and felt a wave of relief at not having to look at those eyes. She closed the door behind her, but left a tiny crack so that she could keep tabs on what was going on out there.

The little old lady peered through the crack in between the door and the jam. Alison stopped kissing Victor for a moment.

"I'm drunk. You know I'm a sure thing, right?" she said, stating the obvious. As Alison led Victor into her apartment, the two fell into shadow and out of reach of prying eyes.

Alison shuffled her feet as she moved into the apartment. She pointed Victor towards the couch as she tossed her hat across the room. She turned on some music and swayed towards him, her hips rocking to the beat of the song. Now, standing in front of him, Alison kissed him a few times in quick succession. She gave him a forceful shove that knocked him off balance and plopped him onto the couch.

She seemed to register that Victor wasn't happy at the manhandling he received. Comforting him a bit she said, "Don't worry, Baby. I'll take care of everything."

Alison moved her hips and slithered her hands around her body as if she were making love to herself. Her hands glided over her, up and down then taking hold of the bottom of her shirt. She peeled it upwards, slowly, all the while watching his reaction. His stone cold demeanor made her want to warm it any way she could. The harder he was, the sexier she would be.

Her shirt sprang from her fingers like a sling shot. She took her hands and cupped the sides of her bra. Forcing her breasts upwards she bent low and pushed them into Victor's face. She rubbed them and then pulled back, simultaneously unhooking the bra and letting it drop to the floor.

"You like what you see?" she asked suggestively.

Victor smiled a bit and waited until she moved closer to him before he struck. When she did, his hand grabbed her neck and squeezed. Alison's face went white with shock.

"Too . . . way too . . . rough," she muttered, clawing helplessly at his powerful fingers.

Victor rose from the couch and stood, his height and size suddenly loomed large over her. Alison was lifted from the couch and could feel her feet leaving the floor.

"You are a whore. That is all any of you have ever been. A delicately decorated deception," Victor dripped with quiet anger as he spit out the words.

Victor held her, his arm straight and parallel to the floor. He slapped her across the face as if she were a cartoon character suspended in midair. His grip tightened further around her neck as his hand impacted across her face.

A small whimper emanated from Alison and her hands held tightly to his wrist, digging her nails into it. She was desperately trying to free herself. Desperate for air.

She managed to swing her leg enough to connect with him. The first blow was blunted by her surprise, but the second came with all the force she could muster. A year's worth of karate her parents had signed her up for had come in handy. Alison planted a solid front kick into Victor's chest and his grip slackened.

She didn't hesitate now. Her feet firmly on the floor she struck forward with her elbow and landed a glancing blow on her attacker's face. She tried to throw another, but Victor stepped back from it, easily avoiding her.

Alison's drunken stupor seemed all but a memory as the adrenaline kicked in. She managed to eke out, "Screw . . . you . . . psycho!"

Victor shook his head, as if to say he was anything but insane. Alison looked around the apartment for anything she could use as a weapon. Her throat was agonizingly pained. She tried to scream but it came out as a whimper. Stumbling backwards Alison became frantic. "Get out!" she ordered as if he would actually leave.

Victor came towards her with incredible agility and smashed his fist into her face.

She dropped to the floor in agony, dazed and on the verge of unconsciousness. Alison tried to bring her hands to her face to assess the damage, but couldn't manage the coordination that was required.

Victor grabbed her by the hair and brought his face close to hers. His breath stung as it wafted over her wounds. He smiled and asked quietly, "Will you not ask your God to save you?"

Alison lashed out in total desperation. Her hands swung wildly, hoping to make contact with something vital on him. Her nails gouged into the side of his neck, tearing skin and drawing blood. It was a victory, though a fleeting one.

Victor pulled away and brought his hand to the wound she had given him. Alison tried to scurry across the floor.

"Get away from me!" she bleated weakly.

Victor looked at the blood on his hand, considering it for a long moment. He touched the tip of his finger to his tongue and swallowed. Then he gave Alison a swift and powerful kick to the mid-section. All of the air came rushing out of her, wailing like a balloon that had been impaled with a pin.

He reached down and wrapped his fingers around her neck again. Lifting her limp frame into the air, Victor began to use his other fist to pummel her. Over and over, his fist crashed into her face, shattering bone and mangling tissue. His wrath rained down on her long after she was gone.

~

Victor stared into the mirror in the bathroom of Alison's apartment. There were three gashes on his neck where her nails had dug into him. He had washed them out and found some gauze and medical tape to put over them along with some antibiotic ointment. He had cleaned up as best he could. There were blood splatters on his shirt and pants that would show if he were seen, but he doubted anyone would see him as he left at this time of night.

He had been angry. Truthfully, he was always angry but tonight he allowed it to conquer him. He would have to be more careful in the future if he were to convince Gregory. Gregory will be angry, he thought. He will make idle threats. His temper will grow with each gift that is brought to him. Victor smiled triumphantly at the thought of that.

Victor finished washing the blood from is hands and dried them on the towel. He didn't concern himself with DNA evidence. Once he was caught, if he was caught, he would be linked to every one of the deaths. He knew his mission was a temporary one.

Victor stared deeply into the mirror again. "But Gregory will not see the truth of it," he thought. He splashed his face with cold water and dabbed it with the towel. "And he will not stop me."

Victor picked up the small plastic bag he left on the counter that contained Alison's heart and walked towards the door.

"I must cull one from his flock. Then he will see the imprudence of his loyalty to a God of lies."

Victor walked calmly from the apartment, quietly pulling the door closed behind him. He glanced over at the doorway of the old lady who had seen him. He didn't think much of her ability to identify him. It was dark and she couldn't have seen much of his face if any at all. So, with bag in hand, he strutted down the stairs and headed home to wrap his new present for his brother.

Yet, as Victor moved down the stairs a pair of eyes followed him. The little old lady allowed the door to open first by centimeters and then by meters. She stepped out onto the landing and watched him walk away, never quite able to shake the feeling that something was very wrong with that one. She decided to speak to Alison in the morning about him. With that, she headed off to try and sleep.

~

An Absence of Faith

Mike sat on his tattered leather couch with Spanky sprawled across his lap. The two were engrossed in the Subway Series game, though they showed their excitement in very different ways. Mike stared at the screen, an anticipatory smile stretching across his face while Spanky eyed something else with desire. Several empty beer bottles stood sentinel around a half-eaten bag of Doritos. The pizza box had just three slices remaining and if truth be told, Mike had not eaten all of those that were missing. A small stream of drool hung at the side of the dog's mouth.

The jarring sound of the phone ringing had shaken the dog. His head whipped towards the unexpected noise and the stream of drool shot into the air and landed on his head. The burst of moisture further confused him and he looked skyward for the culprit. Mike grabbed the phone and looked at the caller ID. It was Kate.

"Can't talk. Game!" he said curtly and hung up the phone. He was still mad.

When the phone rang a second time he didn't hesitate. "Can't talk. Game," he said again and hung up.

The phone rang again. Mike ignored it and Spanky used his paw to wipe his head clean of drool.

"Mike. It's Kate. Pick up," Kate pleaded. There was a long pause before she spoke again. "Talk to me." Again a long pause, then, "Please."

Mike stared at the phone, tempted to pick up; nevertheless, he held firm. He heard the click and then the machine hang up.

"Crap," he muttered and Spanky gave him a big wet lick across his arm and then rested his head on his lap, returning to his vigilant stakeout of the pizza box. It all felt hopeless to them. Mike stared dejected at the game; Spanky, with puppy dog eyes at the cheesy triangles. Neither had much hope of getting what they wanted.

The Mets won four to two in a pitcher's duel. Mike should have been ecstatic. They had a better record than their cross town rivals. They had taken the first three of a four game series and had a strong chance of sweeping the whole thing. He should have been leaping around the apartment and texting his Yankee friends insults. Instead, he sat staring at the post game show, not hearing anything they had to say. "Women!" he thought angrily. He kicked at the coffee table with more force than he had thought. The beer bottles tumbled like dominos and the pizza box flipped up into the air. Spanky moved as if he had struck gold. Mike went to push him away and then thought better of it. "Enjoy it, man. At least one of us will have a good night," Mike moped.

Then the doorbell rang. At first, Mike wasn't even sure what the sound had been. He couldn't think of a time when someone had rung his doorbell without the buzzer downstairs going off. Usually, people arrived with him or he left the door open whenever he expected company, which was rare. He stepped over Spanky who paid him no mind and walked to the door.

"Hi," Kate said as Mike pulled the door open.

He stared at her in silence. She was in a white button up dress with green and orange flowers. Colorful but serene. She reminded him of one of those gorgeous girls in the beer commercials, sitting on the beach, kicking back in paradise. Her hair was pony tailed but had a hint of curls at the bottom. He had never seen her hair in curls before.

Spanky barreled past him and rubbed himself against Kate. She grabbed his ears and tousled them around, scratching his head and chin. "Hi, there, Buddy, at least you're still talking to me," Kate said and looked at Mike, waiting for him to cave.

He left the door open and walked back into the apartment. Kate followed him with Spanky at her side.

"What happened in here? This takes bachelor pad cleanliness to a new level you know," Kate said, trying to break the ice. She wanted to apologize but those words never came easy in her family. She was mad at him about the way he handled the interview. She was furious about the promises he made. Still, she knew she had taken it too far. She didn't want him mad at her. It sucked; like a black hole had formed inside her level of suckiness.

"Minor accident," Mike said, careful to use as few words as possible.

Kate felt the frigid welcome she was getting and a part of her wanted to go on the defensive. She pushed down those feelings, knowing they would only lead to hurt. She sat down on the couch and asked, "Is the game over?"

Mike nodded and walked into the kitchen. He opened the fridge and pulled out another beer and held it up to her in offering. Kate shook her head no so Mike opened it and drank some himself. He leaned on the counter and stared at her, waiting.

Kate wanted to talk to him. She wanted to explain how she was feeling. How her insides churned. She wanted to tell him that she loved him. That she was scared to lose him. That was why she reacted that way. There were so many things she wanted to say, but it felt like they came flooding towards her mouth only to pile up like traffic on the BQE.

Kate couldn't handle his cold stare anymore and looked down. Her hands were folded in her lap and she fiddled with the lower button of her dress. The silence was oppressive. She fiddled more and then the button came undone. Kate decided to undo another, then another. Within a few seconds, she had unbuttoned her dress and stood up in front of him. She dared not look at his face for fear of rejection.

He didn't want to want her so much. He wanted her to apologize, but he knew she wouldn't. She never did. It didn't matter. Mike walked towards her like a moth to the flame. Like he wasn't in control of his own actions, he reached out his hands and slipped them between her body and her dress. Kate timidly brought her arms up to his shoulders. He slid his hands upwards, caressing her and then gently nudging her dress from her shoulders. He pulled her tightly to him and Kate hugged him like it was the last thing she would ever do in her life.

Chapter 21

"Youth is a wonderful thing. What a crime to waste it on children."

George Bernard Shaw

It was easy to grow cold and detached, Kate thought. See enough horror, enough death and destruction, and you have to. A defense mechanism of sorts, she supposed, but something every cop needed to survive. Ever since the domestic, something wasn't right. Joanna, Jenna, and Kyle Wilki had touched a nerve in her and it was one that remained extremely sensitive. Kate was having a hard time hiding her feelings. She seemed to switch on and off, randomly, going from being cold to near bursting into tears for the loss. Usually capable of controlling her emotions; Kate was now at the mercy of them.

Her name was Alison Gaines. Now, she is a number; three, to be exact, in an ever growing list of victims to a serial killer of which the NYPD had few real leads. Kate kept imagining the *True Crime* series or a Lifetime movie special where Alison would be no more than a sixty second character, if at all. Her life would be boiled down to one simple reality. She was one of his victims. As the credits rolled and got shrunk to make space for a commercial, Alison would be listed as victim #3 in stark white print of the tiniest font, probably not even earning her name in the credits. Her name would be forever owned by this sicko and there was not one thing Kate could do to change that now. All she could do was stop some other woman's name from becoming a part of him.

Alison was a pretty young woman. The "was" in that statement gave Kate a shudder as she considered it. Alison wasn't alive anymore and she wasn't pretty anymore either.

Each of the three scenes they had investigated had clear similarities. The victim in each case was an attractive female in her twenties. In every case, they were totally nude, not even a sock left on them. The bodies were staged on a couch in the living room, hands splayed out to the side, palms up. The head was always tilted backwards over the cushions looking skyward. Each time, they had been opened like a deer in the woods, their hearts removed and taken away to where and for what, Kate did not know. She remembered the movie *Snow White* from her childhood but quickly dismissed any notion of a connection. After all, the huntsman took pity on her. Kate made a mental note that she would need to watch it with Anna though.

The killer was meticulous in these details. Alison Gaines was identical to the first two victims. Jessica Mathers and Sara Knoll, Kate chided herself for referring to them as numbers. They were people, not some notch in the belt of a madman. Mad, he was though. Each scene could be replaced easily by the previous one in photographs. The color of the couch, the wall décor would be different, but the positioning of the body was perfect, right down to the position of the fingers. They had recognized the staging at the second scene, though Kate hadn't noticed just how meticulous it was until now. Kate was certain of it. He was recreating a scene from his past. There was no better explanation. This was an event that was very important to him. It had to be just impeccable in every way.

"If you can ignore the horror show, kinda looks like an OD, right?" Mike posited tilting his head like a puppy; a really adorable cuddly puppy. He wore a red Flash t-shirt with blue jeans. The color scheme made Kate think not of the fastest man alive but of Superman. The red, yellow and blue made her swoon. People who were not in this business would judge her harshly for the distraction if they knew. Sadly, detectives grew accustomed to these scenes and tried hard not to let them interfere with their lives. A coping mechanism most of the world would react with abhorrence to, but one that was necessary to survive the job.

Kate could feel a faucet turn on somewhere south of the border and she tightened her thighs and tried to refocus. "Mmmm," Kate replied and walked around behind Alison, trying to distance herself from him while showing off her outfit at the same time. She had chosen a frilly tank top with thin straps that dipped in the center just a bit. A pair of low waisted jeans that hugged her bottom just tightly enough to suggest the lack of underwear lines that Kate hoped would make him wonder. Bringing it all together was a pair of the most impractical shoes she owned; a pair of strappy summer pumps that lengthened her legs a tad. She strutted away from him, trying not to fall.

He was spot on though. Kate bent over and looked for track marks. She examined the fingernails, looking for bruising. There was no sign of a heroin addiction.

"He's not killing them because they are drug addicts," Kate said still hanging over Alison's body.

Mike had been enjoying the view of her cleavage as her shirt parted from her body and swung loosely under her. The bra was pink and purple, swirls that looked like seventies tie dye. It made him feel like he was a stoner, flying high. All he needed was some Marvin Gaye playing in the background. He started to wonder if Kate owned any undergarments that didn't have a hint of purple in them. That was an investigation he could spend a lifetime on. He smiled and then realized he had been caught.

"Mike, thoughts?" Kate asked as she lifted her head and pulled her shirt up with her thumb and forefinger pinching each strap and hiking her breasts up.

"No. It's not drug related. Toxicology showed alcohol in the first two victims and some weed in the first, but otherwise they were clean." Mike felt his face flush with embarrassment. He had seen her naked. Why did peeking a hint at her breasts embarrass him? "That's not the angle I think we should play."

"I'm open to ideas," Kate huffed, frustrated that they had so little to go on.

Though each victim's position was carefully crafted by the killer, they also had differences that were as terrifying as the scenes themselves. Since Jessica Mathers was the first victim they compared each scene to hers. It had been the worst one Kate had ever been involved with. Never before had she seen such gore done in so purposeful a way. So, when they had arrived on scene at Sara Knoll's apartment, Kate had thought she was prepared for it.

Mike had not said a word about her vomiting and she wasn't about to bring it up. Lately, she had been feeling very queasy, but she wasn't about to admit that to anyone, especially him. Kate knew that he would strike when she least expected it, a torrent of jokes overflowing from a broken dam.

Alison's face had not been removed like Sara's had been. Instead, it had been pummeled. It had been mashed in with a violence that spoke of pure rage. Her eyes were gone, either hidden amongst the stew or blended into it. Several teeth were visible, floating like bits of pasta in too much gravy. Kate could make out the line of her lower jaw and the circumference of her skull but otherwise there was little in the way of forms that remained recognizable.

It had reminded Kate of the first horrible car accident she had ever responded to. A teenage boy, driving too fast, had wrapped himself around the corner of a building. The kid had been ejected from the vehicle and had slid, face first, across the pavement for sixty or seventy feet. Kate had turned him over to confirm he was gone. That he was. Everything that had been in his skull had oozed out onto the ground in front of her eyes.

That was what Alison Gaines had been reduced to. Her killer had kept all of his trademarks though; the staging, the cross on the forehead, the removal of the heart and the single long stem rose that seemingly flourished among the horror. All of that had been done to Alison, as well. But, for some reason, he unleashed his fury on her.

"He hates," Kate whispered as she stared into the abyss that had been Alison's face.

The tech team started to arrive, and began fanning out across the apartment. Kate offered up a few suggested items she thought might be of value but otherwise left them alone. She was confident the team knew what she wanted since they were pretty much the same group she had worked with at the last two scenes. Kate stepped aside and left the techs to their grim work.

Mike was going over every inch of the victim like a hound dog following a scent. So, Kate decided to start marking her territory and started her more detailed examination of the apartment as a whole.

It was small, typical of a city apartment. The place consisted of a bedroom, kitchen/dining room/living room sort of open concept design that could fit all of twelve people standing up. The appliances were old, and the sounds of their creaking and humming combined with street noise were part of the charm of the place.

The apartment was well-kept. Alison was clearly a bit of a neat freak. All the signs of a person addicted to Staples or Office Depot were here if a person chose to see. Desk organizers, stackable bins, and hanging white boards and caulk boards could be found throughout. A note board was hung on the side of the refrigerator, another at the front door and a third near Alison's phone next to her bed. The place spoke of a responsible young woman.

Kate read every note, examined every photo and receipt that Alison had written or pinned around her home. She hoped that something would give her a name or phone number of the man she had seen last. Some clue as to who her killer was. There were notes about groceries, another one to call her mom. Kate hoped that she had. Then Kate noticed something. There were two different notes about Mrs. Kraus. The first had just been the name. The second, near the front door was to check with her before she went shopping. Kate crossed her fingers and hoped that maybe she was a neighbor. Maybe, just maybe she would know a name or have seen someone.

Kate dashed across the apartment and swung the door open. She looked at the door across the hall and hoped it would be Mrs. Kraus. Suddenly, Kate saw a hunched frame sitting on the stairs. It was an elderly woman, probably deep into her eighties in a flower-print house dress. Her head bobbed up and down and Kate couldn't help but notice that the woman was crying uncontrollably.

Without a thought or a word, Kate wrapped her arm around the elderly woman and held her as she sobbed. The little old lady's body heaved and rocked and Kate felt like she was trying to hold onto a piece of flotsam in the middle of the ocean. As the waves subsided and the woman's body calmed; Kate took her arm from her and moved down the stairs so that she kneeled in front of her. Kate looked up into her gray eyes that had been reddened with sorrow and introduced herself as gently as she could.

"My name is Kate," she said as if she were talking to one of Anna's friends in the park.

The old lady sniffled a bit and took a deep breath.

"You seem like a sweet girl," she began, "There's no need for you to wear things like that to get a boy's attention, you know," she castigated her new friend gently as she lifted her eyebrows and motioned towards Kate's exposed cleavage.

Suddenly, Kate felt like a teenager again being reprimanded by her English teacher. Her voice rang in Kate's head, "Have some respect for yourself, Katherine. If you won't, the boys surely won't." She quickly pulled at her straps and tried to look demure, but it only came off as guilty. She really was trying to get a boy's attention.

"I used to tell Alison that all the time. She was a good girl, just didn't see herself as worthwhile," the woman said as if she was her grandmother, then broke into tears again.

Kate took her hands into her own and squeezed them gently. "My name is Kate Manning. I'm a detective with the NYPD. I want to catch the man who did this," Kate steadied herself and tried to sound professional. "Do you think you can help us?"

Nodding assent, the silver-haired lady sniffled again and tightened her grip on Kate's hands, making sure she couldn't let go this time. Kate remained, feeling awkward as the woman found solace in her uncooperative affection.

"We have not been properly introduced yet?" Kate suggested.

"I'm old, Sweetie, not stupid," she had suddenly become indignant.

This is why Mike handled the witnesses, Kate thought, feeling a sudden swell of impatience.

"May I ask your name," Kate muttered, feeling like whatever she did was going to be condemned.

"Dottie Kraus," she said quickly.

Kate's heart leaped! "Nice to meet you. May I introduce you to my partner?" Kate asked, hoping to pawn her off on the far more patient Mike. Hopefully, she would be able to give them something to go on.

"Of course," she smiled.

Kate rose and yelled into the apartment, "Mike! Get out here!"

"Ugh! Dear, that isn't the way to behave at all. Rather unladylike, wouldn't you say?" Mrs. Kraus shook her head giving Kate a healthy dose of tsk-tsk-tsk.

Mike's response was nearly identical, "Kate! Get in here!"

He was kneeling next to the victim, refusing to move for fear that the evidence he discovered might disappear if he took his eyes off of it. He stared at an outstretched arm, particularly the hand, studying it. When Kate did not materialize, he muttered in frustration, "God dammit, Kate . . ." and rose to go get her.

Kate stood next to Mrs. Kraus who was still seated on the stairs. Her hand was gently resting on the old lady's curled shoulder as if she might run away if Kate did not keep contact with her. Kate mirrored her partner's feelings, "God dammit, Mike . . ." and began to stomp towards the door.

Kate and Mike slammed into each other in the doorway of the apartment. "Come on . . ." and "Oooofff!" mixed in the air as they bounced off of one another. Kate and Mike stared at each other with embarrassed looks on their faces. If looks could speak, they both thought that they were bumbling this investigation a bit. They were unfocused, distracted. Their gaze lingered too long on one another only proving their silent point.

"I think I've got something . . .," they both blurted simultaneously.

Mike stopped speaking and looked wholeheartedly embarrassed.

Kate stopped as well, but put her hands on her hips and shifted her weight, looking annoyed. Put off and having had enough of the silliness, Kate ordered, "You first . . . but make it quick."

Sheepishly, Mike replied, "Inside."

He led Kate to Alison's body and dropped to one knee next to her. The M.E. had spread out a body bag on the floor and Kate walked around it so she could look over her partner's shoulder. She put her hands back on her hips and waited impatiently.

Mike took the pen he had tucked in his ear and used it as a pointer, "Looks like Alison here put up a fight. Take a look." He pushed the pen towards her middle finger and then to her index finger and back again.

Kate leaned in and put her hands on his shoulders to see. Her breasts pushed against his back and she felt his hand slide down to her leg. Kate wondered if he was just trying to steady her or if he was showing affection. Why did everything have to be so complicated? She thought and then pushed herself harder against him. The hand that Mike had pointed her towards was palm up, but Kate couldn't see what she was looking for. The fingernails pointed towards her and she needed to see underneath them.

Kate pushed off of him and circled the room to position herself in such a way that she could see the underside of Alison's nails. She stood, staring at them and saw exactly what Mike had discovered. There, tucked under her two nails was a set of almost imperceptible piles of flesh. She had scratched her attacker.

As he watched her eyes gain recognition of the find, Mike triumphantly stated, "We've got DNA, girl!"

She was happy about that. It would definitely link the killer to multiple victims, but DNA evidence wasn't much good for tracking a killer unless he or she was already in a database somewhere. This guy wasn't, she was certain of that fact. Still, it was a good find and it would be useful if a court date ever materialized.

"That's good . . . but I'll do you one better," Kate offered. She smiled smugly and took a long wistful look over her shoulder.

"A witness?" Mike's jaw dropped in astonishment. He correctly guessed Kate's bombshell.

"I've got a witness," she said with a wide smile confirming his guess.

Kate snickered a bit at the role reversal. It was usually Mike who dealt with the witnesses and Kate that did the detailed search. She was changing. Her life was changing. Mike grabbed her and hugged her, a spontaneous display of happiness and of the blossoming relationship between them. It scared her. It excited her. Most of all, she was just really confused about how not to mess it up.

Chapter 22

*"Sometimes it is the person closest to us who must travel the
furthest distance to be our friend."*

Robert Brault

Kate and Mike stood in the hallway outside Alison's
apartment. Kate pointed proudly toward the elderly
woman who still sat on the stairs.

She spoke gently to her, "Mrs. Kraus? . . . Mrs. Kraus?"

Mike waited patiently as Kate tried to gain the woman's
attention. After several attempts, Mike leaned in and rested his chin on
Kate's shoulder, placing his lips close to her ear. Her heart quickened
and the faucet turned back on.

Mike whispered, "Good job, Manning. You found us one of the
Golden Girls for a witness." She felt his breath caress her earlobe and
she thought of it dancing softly over other areas of her body. He lifted
his chin and Kate could feel her body lean towards him as if to stay
connected a few seconds more.

Mike approached the hunched over woman while he took an
exaggerated deep breath, like he was preparing to blow out birthday
candles.

"M R S . K R A U S ?" he said, ridiculously slow and loud.

There was no answer. The old lady didn't even move, not even a
twitch. Mike turned to Kate and let loose his surprised face. Even he
didn't think she would actually fail that test. He held his hands up in
mock submission, and then Kate watched as he nearly jumped out of his
own sneakers.

"I'm not deaf you know," Mrs. Kraus scolded him from behind
as she patted him hard on the behind and then walked past him towards
Kate.

Mike looked totally dumbfounded, and Kate had to admit that she was enjoying every second of his discomfort. She threw her hands up and shrugged her shoulders, feigning confusion. Then, she lost control and burst out laughing. Mike gave her a dirty look and stuck his tongue out at her. Kate gave him a snide look in return as if to say, "Very mature."

Mike decided to try and fix his rather poor first impression with Mrs. Kraus. He took her gently by the arm and walked with her towards her apartment door like a boy scout helping her cross the road.

"I'm sorry, Mrs. Kraus. We didn't mean to keep you waiting," Mike apologized profusely but didn't mention the sarcastic hearing test he had been burned on.

"Please come in," Mrs. Kraus said waving her hand frantically.

Mike and Kate entered and were immediately shuttled to a pair of seats at the kitchen table. Mike focused on Mrs. Kraus while Kate took the place in. The décor hadn't changed since the late sixties or early seventies. There were several pictures of Mrs. Kraus with an elderly man on the walls and on end tables. A triangular flag in a dark wood display case with a large photograph of the same gentleman was on a shelf where a TV would have been. Kate didn't see pictures of children or grandchildren anywhere though. The refrigerator had a couple of pictures on it. Two of which were of Alison Gaines.

Both Mike and Kate took small pads and pens from their pockets and laid them on the table in front of them. Mrs. Kraus scurried about the kitchen, taking out a long metal baking tray, a mixing bowl and a whisk. Mike smiled and hopped from his seat moving towards the counter.

"So, what are we baking?" he asked, taking the heavy mixing bowl from her hand. Mrs. Kraus tried to shuffle him out of the kitchen, but Mike would have none of it. It was like watching a grown man dote on a favorite grandmother. Kate found it both amusing and adorable. She put her elbow on the table and cupped her chin in her palm, smiling lovingly at the scene unfolding before her.

An Absence of Faith

Mrs. Kraus gathered items from her cupboard and Mike snapped them from her just as soon as she laid a hand on them. When the two of them had an array of baking goods and dishes strewn on the counter, Mrs. Kraus suddenly stopped in her tracks. Kate could see her face reflected in the window she was staring out of. Mrs. Kraus was crying again and it was more than a little heartbreaking to witness. Mike must have seen it or sensed it as well. He put his arm around her and pulled her head onto his shoulder. Mike seemed to understand that what she was doing was cathartic; a distraction from the pain she was feeling.

"Ali didn't deserve that," she whispered through her tears. After a moment, Mrs. Kraus collected herself and pulled away from Mike. Quickly, she started to fill a clear mixing bowl with sugar. "Now, I'm not saying she was an angel and all; but nobody deserves that." Granulated sugar, brown sugar, and butter were added. She added eggs, a hint of vanilla and oddly enough, poured in powdered vanilla pudding mix as well. "Sweet kid, really," she said, combining the flour, baking soda and salt in another bowl and then joined the two mixtures. Chocolate chips tumbled into the bowl in massive numbers and she handed the bowl to Mike so he could mix it. Mrs. Kraus grabbed a teapot and filled it, then put it on the stovetop. "Can I get the two of you anything?"

Kate started to reply, "No thank you, Ma'am," but Mike fired a look at her that made her feel like she just spoiled Christmas.

Mike replied, "We would love some tea, thank you," while Kate dropped her head. "Is the vanilla pudding mix your secret ingredient?" Mike asked as if he were prying nuclear documents from a suspected spy, but she just smiled at him and ignored his question. All Mike needed was a "Kiss the Cook" apron like Julie's and a few puffs of flour on his face and Kate would utterly melt. He was kind, caring, and interested in people. He was hot, muscular and great in bed. Now, he cooked and cared for little old ladies. God had broken the mold when He made him, Kate thought.

Mike stood, stirring the dough, "Would it be all right if we asked you a few questions?"

Mrs. Kraus seemed not to hear him and instead asked a question of her own. She poured the tea and put the first batch of cookies Mike had doled out on the tray into the oven. "So, how long have you two kids known Alison," Mrs. Kraus asked as she stirred honey into her tea.

Mike and Kate stared at each other for a long moment. Their telepathy told them that Mike was going to have to answer that question carefully.

"Mrs. Kraus, we were just curious if you could tell us a little about what might have happened to Alison?" Mike asked, testing the limits of her senility.

"You two are really an adorable couple. He's quite a catch," Mrs. Kraus said suggestively as she motioned towards Mike.

Mike set up a second tray of cookies and left them on the counter. "Would you excuse us for just a minute?" he asked politely.

They walked to the front door and stepped outside. A uniformed officer stood guard at the victim's door. He smiled at them from across the hall and they nodded back. Mike put his arm high on the wall and leaned into Kate, pinning her tightly between. She watched as the muscles flexed to hold his weight back and felt her body shiver with excitement.

"So, what are we supposed to do with Eleanor Roosevelt in there, huh? She's like my great grandmother with a screaming case of A.D.D.!" he said quietly but clearly frustrated. Then his tone went soft again. "My heart breaks for her. She's a lonely old lady and clearly her neighbor took care of her. Now, she's gone."

"Listen, she's a lead and we have got to follow up on it."

Mike folded his arms and turned his back to Kate. Frustrated, Mike muttered under his breath, "Waste of time. You know it and I know it. No way she can keep things straight."

When he turned around, Kate tossed her hair over her shoulder and leaned back against the wall. Mike stared at her as she pondered their situation. His eyes drifted down to her shoulder as one strap fell from the cliff of her shoulder. Kate felt his eyes tracking it and smiled.

"Wanna bet?" Kate proffered suggestively.

Mike let his eyes linger too long at Kate who looked perfect to him.

"My call?" he choked on his words a bit.

"Your call," Kate surrendered too easily.

Mike leaned in uncomfortably close. The uniformed officer looked away, trying not to watch what was soon to become a massive public display of affection.

When Mike spoke, Kate was stunned by his bet.

"A real date! Dinner . . . and a movie!" he said in a clear, firm voice.

With a little, but satisfied, grin Kate whispered, "Deal." She started to bounce uncontrollably on her tip toes.

Mike noticed she didn't counter offer with something she would win. He stood and shifted his weight to one side, counting things off on his fingers as if they had done this type of thing a hundred times before. Kate waited patiently for the terms and conditions. Never before had the stakes been so high though.

Mike rattled off a list on his fingers, "Okay. I want an accurate physical description: My height. My weight, hair, eyes, clothes . . . distinguishing features . . ."

Kate nodded once and said, "Deal."

Mike pointed at Kate as they moved back towards the apartment door. He hadn't finished, "Jewelry, I want to know what jewelry I'm wearing!"

Without turning around Kate cut him off, "You're pushing it."

They returned and stood next to the kitchen table. Mike leaned into Kate a bit and whispered, "No chance."

Mrs. Kraus paid them no heed. She continued to flitter around the kitchen as if they did not exist.

Mike figured he had already won, "I know a great steak place up in Riverdale you can take me. Little pricey though."

Kate ignored him. She approached Mrs. Kraus and gently put her arm around her.

"Mrs. Kraus, I need you to do a favor for me," Kate said softly.

Mrs. Kraus replied sweetly, "What is it, Dear?"

Kate spoke steadily to Mrs. Kraus, "Without turning around I need you to tell me everything you can about my partner's appearance. Can you do that for me?"

Mrs. Kraus didn't answer. She just rattled off every last detail of Mike's appearance, "Well, he's a good looking man in his early thirties. Green eyes, blonde hair, about six feet two inches tall, a nice sturdy two hundred pounds or so. Tight little red t-shirt with a lightning bolt that shows off his chest. The best part is those jeans though. What a cute little bottom he has. Don't you think, Dear?"

Kate was bent over in hysterical laughter as Mike turned several shades of red.

As Kate laughed Mrs. Kraus felt the need to justify herself, "I'm old Sweetie, not dead."

Kate walked back towards her very amazed partner and swaggered a bit in celebration as she did.

"How do you feel about romantic comedies, Detective Cooper?" Kate gloated.

Mike buried his head in his hands as Kate put her arm on his shoulder and leaned into him.

"You are an amazing lady," Mike said.

"I saw him," Mrs. Kraus said, suddenly sad. "I saw the man who hurt Alison," she uttered trailing off at the end.

"Do you think you can work with one of our artists? Maybe work up a good sketch of the man you saw last night?" Kate asked.

Mrs. Kraus replied suddenly happy again, "Be happy to, Dear."

They spent the next fifteen minutes combing over the details of the previous night. What she saw, where she was and what she heard. There was little of value that Mrs. Kraus could provide in those areas, but if she could provide a description, that could potentially break the case wide open.

Kate offered her appreciation to Mrs. Kraus, "Thank you for the tea. We'll be in touch. Soon. I promise."

"But the cookies," she pleaded.

Mike went over and hugged the little old lady. "There is a police officer outside. If I know him, he would love some cookies."

As Mike left, Mrs. Kraus grabbed Kate and hugged her. She whispered in her ear, "Be brave, girl. You'd regret his loss your whole life. Trust me, I know."

Chapter 23

"There is no revenge so complete as forgiveness."

Josh Billings (1818-1885)

Kate stood at the bottom of the slate stairs and stared up with an impending sense of dread. "You will do this Katherine Dorothy Manning," she whispered looking upwards at the church she stood in front of. I can't do this, she thought. Kate turned to walk away from the church and a hot dog vendor on the corner grinned at her from ten feet away.

"Been a while?" he asked, still smiling at her. Apparently, her "Should I stay or should I go?" antics had garnered a following of one.

"Indeed," Kate said as she walked towards his truck. "Such a chicken. I can't believe I'm such a wimp. Suck it up girl," Kate scolded herself aloud.

"Hey now, that's not the way to encourage yourself. Keep it positive!" he said forcefully, like a coach giving a player a pep talk after an on the field failure.

"I'll take one, please," Kate requested. "Just ketchup. Lots of ketchup," she added with a smile.

Kate walked back to the church stairs, hot dog in hand. Mike always says, "It's easier to do almost anything on a full stomach; except swimming of course." She mused.

She sat in front of the church and munched on her hot dog. When it was done, she tossed her napkin in the trash and headed up the steps.

She read the sign above the church door. "Welcome to all who enter here." Kate couldn't help but laugh to herself. Everybody's welcome, huh? I guess no lightning strikes for me then, she thought. Kate stepped with trepidation over the threshold and felt a powerful desire to run away that she had to fight off. As she entered the church she considered her next step. Should she dip her hand in holy water and complete the sign of the cross? She had plotted out getting to the church; beyond the arrival, Kate had not thought about what she was really going to accomplish here.

Kate was surprised by all of the activity she saw. She had expected a quiet place of reflection. She had also hoped to be able to slide in and out without being noticed. There were some twenty to thirty people inside the church praying, talking, taking pictures, and drawing. Her shock at this came spewing forth, "Holy . . ." Kate said, forgetting herself.

A voice from above cut her off, "I wouldn't finish that if I were you."

Kate looked above her and could see nothing but buttresses and spires. She took a step forward and saw Father Gregory above her, hanging over the railing. He waved politely at her and smiled. He held a small collection of books under his arm.

"Come in! Come in," he urged her.

Kate said, "Oh . . . Sorry Father. It's just that, well, I . . . I've never been in a church when a ceremony wasn't going on."

Gregory bounded down the stairs and replied, "Didn't expect all this activity, did you? Walk with me?"

Kate walked alongside him towards the altar, feeling awkward.

"Can I help you with those?" she asked, pointing to the collection of books under his arm. They had become unruly and were threatening to fall out of his arms in at least three directions.

"Oh, no thank you. I'm used to this," Gregory replied, straightening the pile in his arms. "You know," Gregory observed, "Truth be told, I never thought to see this many people in a church without a ceremony going on either. We have a very active congregation here." He smiled proudly at the thought and then added, "Julie is a big reason why."

Kate looked at the stained glass windows as they walked. There were various religious stories depicted in each window. Some Kate knew, like the birth of Christ and the arrival of the wise men. Others,

Kate had no clue what they depicted nor their significance. "Julie has always been very religious. I never really could understand her," Kate admitted.

"So, what brings you to us today then?" Gregory queried.

That was the question Kate was struggling to answer. Why was she here? Kate put her head down and stared at the floor, looking for her answer. When it wouldn't come she fidgeted with her hands a bit and then finally said, "I guess I want to understand."

Gregory smiled softly at her and asked, "How would you like to begin?"

~

Kate and Gregory walked together in the park. Kate felt uncomfortable. This wasn't at all what she had expected. Gregory had suggested the walk in the park and Kate agreed because she didn't really know what else to say. Gregory had remained quiet, waiting for her to explain her visit. That silence was getting on Kate's nerves and she had a sneaky suspicion that Gregory knew that.

"I have no idea what I am supposed to do. Should I tell you all the curses I've said or something?" Kate ejaculated, unable to stand the silence any longer.

Gregory laughed and replied, "It's a start. How about we talk? Just talk."

Kate settled down. She felt more relaxed now. With a renewed sense of ease, Kate said, "Okay. That sounds good. What should we talk about?"

Gregory looked down at the grass and suddenly seemed deep in thought. When he spoke again there was an unmistakable sadness to his voice. "Why don't we talk about your relationship with Julie?" Gregory said. "She's very important to you, isn't she?"

Kate smiled shyly. Gregory looked to the sky as if he was avoiding tears. "This is just between us, right?" Kate asked.

"Uh-huh. Just the three of us," Gregory said, pointing to the heavens. Kate smiled as she watched some children playing with a Frisbee in the park.

An Absence of Faith

Kate began, "Julie is so strong and sure of herself. I've respected her for that for as long as I can remember. I've spent my whole life asking questions that she just seems to know the answers to."

The Frisbee landed at their feet and Kate picked it up. She tossed it back and waved to the kids. "I guess I envy her. She lives her life joyfully. She never doubts her faith. I don't even know if I have any faith at all to doubt." They continued to stroll and Kate continued to talk. "I love her. I wish I could be like her. I wish my life could be full of joy and free of all the trouble I seem to attract."

Gregory stopped Kate and placed his hands on her shoulders. With a great deal of seriousness Gregory said, "Kate, the presence of trouble in one's life does not mean the absence of God. The two CAN coexist." Gregory breathed deeply, trying to settle himself. "Believe me, Kate. I understand sibling rivalry. My brother has spent most of his life trying to show me that he's smarter than I am. That he knows more than I do."

Kate couldn't meet his gaze and dropped her head. She had never considered that she was simply jealous of Julie.

"Have you ever thought that Julie might face a great deal of problems in her life?" Gregory asked. "It is her faith that brings her joy. It is her faith which makes her life seem so untroubled." Gregory shook his head and added, "Maybe the trouble you feel in life is not the absence of God, but rather an absence of faith?" ·

Kate pondered that for a long moment. She had been wrong about Julie. Worse, she had wronged her. Kate always saw Julie's life with rose-colored glasses. Gregory had helped her to see the reality of it. Julie didn't live the perfect life; she just focused on the better parts of it. Where Kate had seen all that God did not do, Julie had seen all that He did do. Julie chose to see the good, despite the bad, where Kate couldn't overlook it. Maybe, Julie saw it and just chose to focus on the better things life had to offer, Kate thought. She smiled and said, "Thank you, Father. I needed to see things in a new perspective. You've been a great help to me."

The two walked again, and silence dominated once more. This time, however, it was Gregory who broke it. "You know where to find me any time you need to talk," he offered. Kate smiled at the kindness of the offer.

She coyly asked, "So what are you doing for the next hour or so?"

Gregory burst out in laughter. "Forward as always, Kate. No one may doubt you on that. How about we walk back to the church together?" Gregory offered his arm to her.

Kate slipped hers through and they walked together. "I'd like that. I'd like that very much."

The two ambled along the city street with the church never more than a short distance from them. They spent the better part of an hour discussing Julie, Anna, and Donald. They talked about church and about baseball. They talked about her father and about Mike. A great deal of time was spent sorting out her feelings for him. Though the topics were varied, Kate felt as if a weight had been lifted from her. As they approached the church, Gregory said to Kate, "It has been a pleasure, Ms. Manning. We must do this again some time."

Kate gratefully acknowledged him, "I owe you one, Father."

Kate walked Gregory up the stairs to the church. Several people were seated on the stairs reading or relaxing. Gregory stressed to Kate, "Remember, Kate, that you are always welcome here." The two hugged and said goodbye. Gregory walked to the church door while Kate watched him go.

Kate took a deep breath and started down the stairs. A thick, muscular man sat in the corner with a newspaper obscuring his face from view. He folded the paper and tucked it under his arm. Kate now saw he had a small wrapped gift box that sat on the far side of him. He rose and pulled his jet black suit down, straightening it. Then, he called out to her, "I sincerely hope my brother has helped to cleanse your soul."

Kate stared uncomfortably at this man who had chosen to be so forward with her. He was broad shouldered, powerful and well dressed. It was the eyes that helped put it together for Kate though. He had said, "brother" not father. Father Gregory shared the same steely blue-gray eyes as the man in front of her.

She quickly replied to the stranger, "Father Gregory has been very helpful." She smiled and bade him good day. With that, Kate walked away under the watchful gaze of the man she herself was hunting.

Chapter 24

"It is not in the stars to hold our destiny but in ourselves."

William Shakespeare

Kate stared into the bathroom mirror with her towel wrapped around her. She didn't particularly care for the reflection. Brown hair and brown eyes, skin that wasn't exactly perfect and bone structure that was perfectly average, stared back at her. "Nothing spectacular," she said aloud to herself as she pushed her cheeks up and down and wondered what she would look like if she could change every little thing she disliked about herself.

"Kate," Julie's voice penetrated the bathroom door, "Come on, Girl! We have work to do!"

Kate had called in reinforcements for tonight. She called her sister and mumbled some unintelligible stuff about Mike and a date, and suddenly, Julie was knocking on her apartment door with a suitcase full of clothes, makeup and hair care products.

Kate opened the door and gave Julie a look of misery.

"This is impossible," Kate said sullenly.

Julie held up two dresses, both purple. Kate had loved the color purple since she was a little girl and Julie knew it was her color of choice. One dress was a strapless with two silver sparkly bands that accentuated the waistline and then allowed the dress to flow outward at the knees. It was pretty, but the other took her breath away.

"Where did you get this?" Kate gushed as she took the dress from her sister.

"I bought it for you," Julie said, beaming with excitement.

Kate couldn't believe it. "But?" Kate muttered, wondering how and when she could have done it.

"I bought it for your birthday. I figured you might need it early, so, happy birthday!"

Kate hugged her sister tightly.

Julie relished the affection from her normally reserved sister. She also knew they were on a clock. "We don't have time for this right now. You can admit I'm the better sister later. Right now, let's focus on you!"

Kate ran into the bedroom and came back in a few seconds.

"What do you have planned for this evening?" Julie asked giving her the stink eye while looking at her sister's underwear.

"Is it too slutty?" Kate asked in a panic.

"No, it's perfect . . . ly slutty," Julie joked. "Come on, hair and makeup time."

~

Mike tugged at the wads of toilet paper stuck to his face. He had cut himself at least four times while shaving. "Who knew it was so difficult to get the perfect shave?" he thought. He had been Q-tipping an ear, shaving and trying to brush his teeth all at once. It had required a third hand and far more coordination than Mike apparently had. Only one of the small wounds on his chin was still bleeding, but he had run out of time to deal with it. He would have to treat it on the move. Mike dressed in slacks and a blue checked, collared shirt his mother had given him. She had said it made him look respectable. He doubted that.

"Don't be nervous," his mom had told him.

"I'm not nervous, Mom," Mike lied.

"Michael, you love this woman and she loves you. The two of you just can't get out of your own way."

She was always a smart lady.

"Be yourself. Be the man she is already in love with and you'll do just fine. Oh, and wear that shirt I bought you."

He was wearing the shirt. He hoped the rest of the night went that easily.

~

Jasmine wasn't the type to accept a date with someone she had just met. So, she wasn't really sure why she had taken one with a man who was an absolute stranger to her. She had said yes before she could stop herself and now she was regretting that.

She was curling her hair with a hot iron and chastising herself through the mirror. "In the future, think before you speak," she told herself. She had told her friend that she was going to cancel, but she talked her out of it. "Go," she had said, "Have fun. Be wild for once." Jasmine didn't feel wild, she felt nauseous. "Ugh, I swear I could puke out my insides right now," she said to herself as she finished her makeup.

~

Victor observed the gashes on his neck were healing nicely and probably wouldn't scar. He had been thoroughly cleaning and caring for the wounds since he had received them. He put some ointment on them again, but didn't feel the need to bandage them at this point. He dabbed shaving cream on his face and used the brush to spread it around. He glided the straight razor over his face and then ran his fingers over his cheeks to check his work. Once he was satisfied, he wiped his face clean and finished getting ready to meet Jasmine. He had met this one in the grocery store. To Victor, the beginning mattered little. It was the end that he was focused on.

~

Kate slipped on a pair of high heels while Julie fidgeted with one of the pins in her hair.

"Stay still!" she yelled.

"I'm gonna be late," Kate returned.

"Then, you can make an entrance. Okay. You are good," Julie said finishing.

Kate stood up and nearly fell over. High heels were a rare occasion for her. "Well?" she asked.

Julie smiled at the vision her sister had become. Then, just as suddenly, Julie dashed off into the bathroom. When she returned, she had a pair of long, sparkling diamond earrings. Julie put them on Kate and gently kissed her cheek.

"If I cry, I'm going to smack you," Kate said, choking back tears. The earrings were her mother's. Kate hugged her sister.

"Go! You're going to be late," Julie sniffled and sent her big sister out the door.

~

"Where are my keys?" Mike yelled as panic was setting in. He had searched the bedroom, the kitchen, and the living room. They were not in the couch, on the counter, or under the bed. Spanky used his considerable size and slobbery nose to nudge Mike from behind. Mike brushed him off, but the dog wasn't having it. "We just came back from a walk! Go lay down," Mike chastised him.

"Oh!" Mike ran to the front door and looked at the small table near it. He fumbled around through the junk mail and the leash he had tossed there. "Bingo!" he exclaimed and stuffed his keys in his pocket. He rubbed the dog's head and headed out. "Don't wait up for me!"

~

"Be a good girl, Patches," Jasmine gave the tabby cat a scratch under the chin as she left. She had decided she would try to make the best of this. Maybe the guy wasn't the pompous ass she had remembered him being. "Why would you say yes?" she asked herself again as she recalled Victor's arrogant air as he asked her out. He wasn't her type and she knew it.

Jasmine headed to the restaurant where they were to meet. More than once she thought about turning around but didn't. She wore slacks and a conservative blouse with a pair of flats. The outfit said, "I'm not interested." She just hoped the guy would listen.

"Hi. We have a reservation. It will be under Sloan," Jasmine told the hostess.

"Is your whole party here?" she asked indifferently.

Jasmine shook her head no and was politely told to wait. She headed to the bar to stiffen her resolve with a drink. "You could still leave," she reminded herself.

~

Before Victor left for his date, he liked to lay out the items he would need upon his return. He laid out a box and top on the table along with scissors and tape. He went to the closet and selected a bright metallic green and purple wrapping paper. Then, he chose a lighter green for the ribbon. He laid them on the table with the small box. Satisfied that all things were in order, he headed out to meet Jasmine at the restaurant. She had chosen a quaint Italian place just at the border's edge of Brooklyn and Queens.

~

Kate arrived at Paulie's Restaurant with three minutes to spare. The place was expensive for her tastes but it was nice too. No paper napkins or plastic covered table clothes here. It was elegant and gave diners the feel that they were eating on a city street in Italy. Not gaudy, just classy, Kate felt. Classy wasn't exactly how her night had gone thus far though. She had been harassed the entire way to the restaurant. She had even stopped to curse out the fourth guy who had made some of the more inappropriate cat calls towards her. She wasn't used to that kind of attention. The first guy surprised her, the second one flattered her, the third pissed her off and the fourth got a badge in his face and a stern talking to.

She stood in the small foyer of the restaurant and looked around to see if Mike had arrived. She thought about texting him, but didn't want to seem over eager. She lingered a few moments, looking at the door each time it opened and then decided to see if Mike had already been seated.

The hostess greeted her warmly and asked if she had a reservation.

"Yes. It would be under Cooper. He's meeting me here," Kate thought how desperate that all sounded. "No, I'm not getting stood up. That can't happen to me," Kate figured the hostess was thinking exactly that. She smiled apologetically at Kate, "He hasn't arrived yet." Kate heard the condescending tone and thought about schooling the woman, but decided against it.

"Thank you," Kate replied, not meaning it.

She sat on a tall barstool next to a pretty young woman.

"Hi. Waiting for your date, too?" she asked.

Kate shook her head in the affirmative. "He'll be here in a few minutes," Kate swore, but there was a part of her that was starting to get nervous about that.

"I'm Jasmine," she said, putting out her hand to shake.

"Kate. Is he late, too?" Kate asked, hoping that she had met a kindred spirit.

"No. I'm early. I'm always early. The curse of good parenting, I guess," Jasmine joked.

"I'm always early myself," Kate said and the two talked away the minutes waiting for the men in their lives to arrive.

~

Mike was late. He stood in front of a small flower stand and pondered what to do. He mumbled to himself as he picked up one premade bouquet and then put it down. "Do I buy her flowers? Will she get mad and say I'm pushing her too hard? What if I don't buy her flowers and she's expecting me to? Why the hell does this have to be so complicated?"

"All women love flowers," the old vendor said, responding to Mike's indecisive behavior.

"If I get her a dozen roses it might scare her or make her think I'm desperate for something more. If I get her one rose, she'll think I'm cheap," Mike said, unintentionally ignoring the man.

The old man started to pick red roses from a wooden bucket and gather them in a bunch. "I don't know of a single woman who does not want a man to bring her roses," he said as he stuffed baby's breath into the bouquet.

"How much for a dozen?" Mike asked, still feeling torn.

"Forty" the man replied as he wrapped the bundle up.

"Robbery is a crime you know," Mike said and handed the man the money.

~

Victor arrived at the flower stand a few moments later. "Good evening," he said to the old vendor. The man smiled and offered his assistance, but Victor politely refused. Victor was very particular about his selection. He hand selected a single rose after rejecting the first six he looked at. "There is beauty in death," Victor thought, smiling to himself.

~

Mike raced in to the restaurant a few minutes late. He entered the foyer of the restaurant and looked around for Kate. His eyes passed over her twice before he realized it was her. She was seated next to another young woman and the two chatted amicably.

"Oh, wow," he said, smiling at her and walking towards her like a moth to the flame. He inadvertently bumped into another patron and apologized to them without ever taking his eyes off of Kate.

Kate blushed and smiled bashfully in return. She rose to greet him.

Mike took her hand in his and looked at her. Kate's hair looked amazing. She had a tight braid that ran down the side of her head that ended in soft, flowing curls that rested gently on her shoulder. She wore glittering earrings and a necklace that had a simple glittering bead that brought just the right kind of attention to her cleavage. She was stunningly beautiful in the dress. Thin purple straps that led down to a shimmering hourglass shaped silk with soft white muslin edges, bordered with sparkling stones. The dress hugged her hips and flowed loosely down to her knees. The combination of high heels, curls and an incredible dress had left Mike speechless.

"Hi," Kate said trying to break the awkwardly long silence.

"Hi," Mike responded, still holding her hand.

"You look nice," Kate said, not knowing what else to say.

"You like nice," Mike echoed.

Kate snickered at the parroting he was doing.

That seemed to break him from the trance. Mike handed her the flowers like he was transferring a newborn baby to her. "These are for you," he said, feeling embarrassed now at the gesture.

"They're beautiful. Thank you," Kate said. Nobody had ever bought her flowers before. She didn't date much. The guys she had dated never did this. She loved it, but didn't know exactly how to handle it. "I don't know if I even own a vase," she thought, feeling panic rising inside her.

"Aaawww," Jasmine interjected. "You two make such a cute couple."

Mike's eyes went wide. "Thanks, but . . . uh," he stammered, but Kate interrupted him.

"Thank you. It was nice meeting you, Jasmine," Kate waved at her and smiled warmly.

Mike felt like he was sweating profusely. "Should we get a table?" he asked.

Kate nodded and looked down at their intertwined hands.

~

Kate sat at the table and leaned close towards Mike. They held hands across the table, their arms interwoven between glasses of wine. The two whispered and laughed together. It was odd. They were on a first date but already knew each other intimately. Their friendship was strong and it made tonight feel all the more warm.

Kate watched as the hostess seated Jasmine. Her date had arrived, apparently a few moments after Mike and had brought her a single rose. Mike followed Kate's eyes and saw what she was looking at.

"So, are you having a nice time?" Mike asked even though they had been there for all of five minutes.

Kate ignored Jasmine's single rose man and focused on her own date. "I am, thank you," she said and meant every word of it. For Kate, it had not been five minutes, rather five hours in Heaven.

"You look beautiful," Mike said, his voice suggesting that it was impossible for him to deny.

That's what this night was for them; a night of truth and honesty. They couldn't pretend it wasn't a date. They couldn't pretend they didn't have feelings for one another. Tonight, the curtains were open and there was no hiding.

They lingered over every morsel of food, nursed their glasses of wine and made every second count. Kate saw Jasmine from the corner of her eye and knew that the woman was bored. "Should I go rescue her? Pretend I ran in to get her?" Kate asked Mike. "Maybe, I can fake an emergency or something," she suggested.

Mike shook his head. "No. No can do. I promise you, everyone in this place knows you are here."

It took Kate a second to register the compliment before she blushed. Jasmine looked as miserable as Kate was happy. "Poor girl. We've all had those dates," Kate lamented.

"All mine have been perfect so far," Mike said.

Kate understood the suggestion and called him out on it. "Come on, this is your first date?"

Mike nodded. "I never dated in high school. Then, I went into the Corps, then college at night while I worked at the lumber yard during the day, then, the academy. Then, I met you."

Kate felt her stomach nearly burst. He just said he didn't date other woman because of her. "That's the type of thing that could go to a girl's head, you know," Kate suggested, considering they had known each other for five years.

"It should," Mike replied confidently, not bothering to hide from it.

The evening rolled on and they shared old stories and new ones. Mike told Kate a new story about a family vacation they had gone on. "So, my brother and I are carrying my mom down Mount Washington in the pitch black and all my father could do was scream like a three year-old girl. Every time he heard a sound he would squeal, 'Bear' at the top of his lungs!" Kate had met his parents a few times and the story was one she intended on using in the future when she saw them again.

The night was getting late and they were running out of excuses to stay. The idea of a movie had long since been jettisoned as they sat and talked for hours. It was time to go. Kate reached across the table and touched his hand. "Would you excuse me for a minute?"

Mike leaned back in his chair and watched Kate as she walked towards the restroom. It was an inspiring sight. He put his arms up over his head, clasping his hands behind, and allowed his eyes to drift south from Kate's head all the way down to her bottom. He smiled widely as he took her in and dreamed about taking her to bed.

"You did it, Cooper," he said to himself. "You finally got her to notice how incredibly spectacular you are." He considered his amazing feat for a moment and thought, "I should write a book, *How to Get Great Girls to Notice You in Five Years or Less.*"

~

Victor excused himself. He walked away from the table feeling more than a little confused. The woman didn't fawn over him. She didn't flirt with him. Jasmine could barely even bother to hold a conversation with him. Victor didn't understand. No woman he had ever encountered had ever behaved quite like this one. He had invested several hours into this one and was feeling frustrated. She was talented at hiding who she was, but that only made him more determined to expose her.

He stormed towards the bathroom and bumped into a woman in a purple and white dress. She was done up, her hair and makeup clearly well-planned. She was a whore, no doubt. "This one, I understand," Victor thought as he pushed past her. "Excuse me," she said snottily, but Victor ignored her. He was busy trying to sort out what was happening with Jasmine.

~

Jasmine slumped in her chair feeling more than a little despondent. "Way to go, kid," she thought, "I think you've managed to attract every emotionally distant man in the tri-state area." The thought frustrated her and she wasn't one to focus on the negative for long. "At least this one was easy on the eyes."

~

Kate looked at herself in the ladies room mirror. She tucked a few stray hairs back into her braid and tried to tighten it. She huffed audibly and rested her hands on the sink counter. "You cannot do this," she said, speaking to her reflection, trying to convince herself. "Things are going to get really complicated really fast if you do this," she reminded herself as if any of that mattered anymore. "So, you are going to walk out there, say goodnight and thank him for a nice time. That's it!" Kate lied to herself. "Do you understand me?" she chided, pointing her finger at her reflection.

"Honey, things are always complicated," an attractive middle-aged African American woman said to Kate as she exited the stall behind her. "That's what love is all about."

Kate smiled at her and the two walked out together. The woman joined her husband, a matched set of boy/girl children and two grandparents. They walked out together and Kate couldn't help but look on feeling just a bit jealous of the life the woman had. She swore to herself that she wouldn't mess this up.

~

Victor checked his reflection in the mirror of the men's room. He leaned into it as if to whisper something to himself. He was frustrated and the anger was beginning to show on his face. "She is a master of her craft," he had decided, "deliberately coy, trying to tempt me into knowing more." He washed his hands and rubbed the warm water over his face. "This one is steady, determined. In every way she works to deceive me and misguide me." Victor smashed his fists down on the counter in frustration. "She wants me to chase her. I will. This one will suffer a great deal."

~

They had taken a cab back to Mike's apartment. They rode in silence. Mike had not let go of her hand, just like the evening they came back from the fair. He had caressed it, moving his thumb gently over the lines on her palm. Kate hadn't taken her eyes off of him the entire drive. She watched his hand in hers, his eyes as they looked at her. She drank him in like a woman who had just finished a marathon, parched and needy.

When they arrived, they walked upstairs together, still holding hands. With each step they climbed, anticipation rose within them. Kate understood how different this time was. They couldn't blow this off as a drunken night of fun. Tonight didn't come from frustration or need or impaired judgment. No, tonight was purposeful. They both wanted, longed, for this.

They entered the apartment and Mike shut the door snugly behind them. Kate leaned against the door and stared at him. She could hear Spanky snoring in the background and it made her smile. This was becoming a part of her. It felt like a child's favorite blanket.

"Kate, I . . ." Mike tried to speak although he didn't know what to say. Were there words in the English language that could describe this moment, Kate wondered. Were there words in any language that could describe how happy she was in this moment? She feared it was only going to be a moment. It would fade and the real world would come stomping all over her happiness. Just not right now. Kate was living in, and for, this moment.

"Sssshhh," Kate whispered, putting her finger to his mouth. He kissed it instinctively. Mike watched as the strap of her dress fell from her shoulder. He put his hands on her hips and pulled her close. Kate could feel his excitement, his desperate need for her.

"Can I . . ." he started to ask. Kate kissed him fervently in answer to his question. She felt his hesitation, his uncertainty and it made her want him all the more. Kate broke away from him and turned her back. She reached behind her and started to unzip her dress. Then, she stepped towards him and let him finish the rest.

Mike gently unzipped her and held the dress by the sides as it slipped from her body. Kate stepped out of it and stood before him. He treated the garment reverently, as if it were his ticket into Nirvana. He walked away from her and went to the hall closet. Taking a hanger from within, he delicately hung the dress for her, zipping it back up to make sure it didn't fall.

Kate moved towards him, an inexorable need to be close to him. She took his hands and passionately slammed them onto her hips. Mike looked at her with ardent desire in his eyes and Kate, knee bent, began to tap her toes on the floor. Mike lifted her swiftly into his arms and carried her into the bedroom. Sex wasn't in their near future. For the first time, they would make love. A purposeful, meaningful expression of all they meant to one another.

~

Mike watched as Kate got out of bed. He was hoping tonight would be different; that she would stay. She had never stayed before. She looked back at him and smiled coyly. He didn't pretend that he wasn't looking at her. He stared with unabashed abandon at her naked body and there was a part of him that thought Kate liked that.

Kate picked up a piece of clothing and Mike felt crushed. She then held it high, letting his shirt hang from one finger. "I didn't bring pajamas," Kate said. Mike felt a rush of relief wash over him and beamed at her as she slid her arms into his shirt, fastening only the lowest buttons. She climbed back into bed and nuzzled into his arms. Mike held her tightly as he waited for her to fall asleep. Finally, he had what he had really wanted all along. They were no longer lovers, they were in love.

He listened to every breath as he waited for Kate to slowly drift off to sleep. Mike gently guided her tousled hair behind her ear and leaned in. Carefully trying not to wake her, he pressed his lips to her, barely touching her cheek as he kissed her softly. "I love you, always and forever, Kate," he whispered, seemingly into the warm night air. He rolled over on his side and pulled her into his warmth.

On the other side of the bed, Kate held tight to her share of the blanket and smiled so wide she feared her cheeks would crack.

~

Jasmine had tried hard to be nice about cutting the date short. "I had a very nice time. I need to wake up early for work tomorrow though," she said, trying to excuse herself. "I'll take you home," Victor said, not taking no for an answer.

Now that they had arrived, Jasmine tried again to end the night gracefully. She put out her hand to shake his and Victor looked quizzically at it. After a moment, he shook her hand and said good night. She watched as he began to walk away before she took out her keys. Jasmine opened her apartment door and then turned to look at the stairs.

"Oh!" she exclaimed, startled to see that Victor stood less than an arm's length from her. She had never heard or felt him approach.

"I'm sorry for startling you," he said. "May I just use your bathroom?"

Chapter 25

"There is no surprise more magical than the surprise of being loved. It is God's finger on man's shoulder."

Charles Morgan

Victor placed the plastic bag on the counter of his vast kitchen. He went into the bathroom and turned the shower on. Removing his clothes, he packed them into a white kitchen garbage bag with a red tie strip that had been waiting for him on the sink counter. A change of clothes was there, as well. Victor liked to arrange as much as possible in advance.

He showered, carefully cleaning each part of his body. He toweled off and checked himself in the mirror. Victor looked at the scratches that were on his neck. They were barely visible now, merely light pink scuffs that needed no care.

Returning to the kitchen, Victor took up the plastic bag, held it over the sink and unceremoniously dumped the contents into the basin. He turned the water on warm and began to rinse Jasmine's heart free of congealed blood. Using the sprayer, he forced water through the valves and coagulated blood sputtered from the organ and began to clog the sink. Victor took gobs of it and broke it up with his fingers, allowing the water to flow freely again. Once he was satisfied, he towel dried the heart and placed it on the counter to air dry further.

Victor sat on his favorite antique upholstered chair feeling proud of his achievements and flicked on the TV. He had a few hours to kill before he could go visit Gregory and he was too amped up to sleep. He considered reading, but his eyes were tired. He wanted something mindless. He channel surfed for a while until he found an *I Love Lucy* marathon. Settling in, he lost himself in the ridiculousness of the show. "This is who society laughed at?" he wondered. A woman who constantly lied, concealed, and deceived her husband and friends.

Maybe, mankind did understand somewhere deep in their brains that Lucy really did represent women. Deception, manipulation, they were the keys to her success.

Victor watched until the sun began to creep into the apartment from under the thick window shades. He left the TV on as background noise and headed back into the kitchen. He took the heart and shook out some stubborn water that had hidden in the recesses of a valve. He towel dried it again and then, headed into the dining room.

A large dark stained oak table was covered with neatly stacked trimmings for wrapping a present. Victor placed the heart in a box that had already had decorative tissue paper placed within it. He packed additional paper into the box, neatly filling the empty spaces and then covered it. He considered the options he had laid out in gift wrapping and chose a metallic green and purple paper. It shimmered in the glow of the early morning sunlight as Victor measured out the appropriate size and cut it to fit. He sealed each edge with a small piece of clear tape and then selected a white strip of satin ribbon to tie around the box. Victor made a neat bow and adjusted its size a few times before he was satisfied with the work.

Victor had a very specific routine before he visited Gregory. He liked to make things beautiful before he presented them to his brother. Gregory had always said that God was responsible for all the beauty in the world. Victor knew that wasn't the case. That was one of many things Victor intended on teaching his older brother.

~

Spanky wasn't used to this. His routine was decidedly off. He sat at the edge of the bed, his chin resting softly on the mattress and his jowls splaying out to the sides. His nighttime walk had not happened. He couldn't sleep in his spot last night and now his breakfast was delayed. He whined and whimpered, but no signs of life came from the bed. If an image of depression could be captured, this was it.

Finally, he had enough. Spanky slapped a paw up on the bed and it landed on Mike's chest. As the dog brought his paw back to the floor it scratched across his chest and Mike woke with a startling pain.

"Owww! What the Hell, Spankster?" Mike said slowly bringing the volume of his voice down, trying not to wake Kate. He glanced at the alarm clock and realized he had been a neglectful owner. He threw on a pair of pants and a t-shirt and grabbed Spanky's leash. The dog leapt like a gazelle and happily followed him out of the bedroom practically knocking him over in his urgency and excitement.

After a nice walk around the block and a lengthy stream of urine, Spanky was ready for breakfast. "You aren't the only one, Pal," Mike said as he pushed the hungry dog away from his bowl in order to fill it. Spanky ate with a voracious speed, consuming a healthy-sized portion in twenty seconds. He spent the next two minutes licking the rim, bottom, and periphery of the bowl in the off chance that he missed a morsel.

Meanwhile, Mike had started to take out eggs, bacon and cheese from the fridge. He filled the teapot and began frantically looking for honey for several long moments until he found it buried behind some spices. He threw on the apron his mother had given him when he first moved in and got cracking. Soon, the smell of bacon and eggs wafted through the apartment. As always, Mike and Spanky split the first piece of crispy bacon. Spanky grabbed the flying piece of meat from midair and swallowed it whole. He gave Mike a sideways glance with puppy dog eyes, but Mike shuffled him away. "Go away, Big Guy. No more," Mike scratched his head and side as he said it.

Kate woke to the muffled sounds of Mike's voice in the kitchen. She lay in bed and listened, trying to make out what he was saying or doing but couldn't. It sounded like the TV was on, too. She rolled around in the bed, wrapped herself in a cocoon of blankets and smelled the sheets. Kate loved the warmth and aroma of the place. She could feel him everywhere here.

She could also smell the aroma of breakfast beginning to seep into the room. Kate felt the cool breeze generated from the air conditioning and resisted getting out of bed. Mike's shirt was comfortable and smelled like him, but it didn't keep her as warm as he would. Finally, she decided to wrap herself in a single sheet as if it were a Roman toga. She had seen it done in the movies; but, the practical application of it was a bit more difficult than she had imagined it would be. She wound up needing to tuck a few parts around her and then holding the rest like a bridal train. She slithered quietly into the bathroom and rummaged for toothpaste and anything that resembled a brush. He had the dental necessities; but, there was nothing to help with her hair. Her braid had long since come undone and it added to the tangled mess she faced. She tried to mat it down, running her fingers through it in a last ditch attempt to make it presentable, but her head was too far gone.

A lumbering knock at the door told her she was out of time. When Kate opened it she nearly jumped out of her skin. Two big black eyes stared at her with a long tongue hanging limply to the side. "Good morning, Spanky," she whispered as the dog barreled forward and nudged his head between her legs, presenting his back-end for scratching. Kate leaned down to give the dog some love and her makeshift toga fell apart. She scrambled to reassemble it and then walked into the kitchen with Spanky prancing next to her.

She heard a thick Hispanic accent on the TV, "Lucy! You've got a lotta splainin to do." Boy, did she ever. Lucy's voice responded, "But Rickie . . ." and the theme song to *I Love Lucy* came on and the show cut to commercial.

Mike stood at the counter in the kitchen making breakfast. He was whisking eggs in a glass bowl and Kate stopped to admire him. Spanky's paws tapped on the floor and Mike looked over to see what he was up to.

"Oh," he said surprised to see her, "I was going to bring you breakfast."

Kate could tell he was a little disappointed that she had ruined the opportunity. She, of course, made it even worse. Kate burst out into laughter as Mike turned towards her revealing the *Kiss the Cook* apron. It was the uncontrollable kind of laughter, like when you were a kid and someone knew just where to tickle you. The toga started to peel apart and Mike's face drooped as he missed out on seeing her naked. As a small consolation, it was his shirt she was wearing. Kate pulled herself together, realizing she had pretty much ruined the moment.

She pointed at the apron and held her laugh in with the other hand. Mike looked down at the apron and shrugged.

"Gift from my mom," he said, "sort of like a horrible Christmas sweater."

Kate laughed again and tightened her hand over her mouth.

"It's not that funny," Mike said defensively.

"Can we start over?" Kate asked apologetically.

Mike took a deep breath and said, "Good morning. How do you like your eggs?" It was a question to which he already knew the answer, but Kate appreciated him hitting the reset button.

Kate replied with a smile, "Scrambled. Thanks."

She sat at the small table and struggled to control her sheet. She saw Mike grin as she pulled up the front. He brought over the tea and filled a mug for her. "There's honey," he said. He was the most considerate man she had ever met. When they first became partners, she noticed that he listened. He paid attention to the little things that she liked and always made sure that he had them around.

Spanky made his way over to Kate and rested his head on her lap. He was a champion beggar, made so by Mike's utter lack of discipline or doggy parenting. "No, silly, you cannot have my tea," Kate said as she gave him a kiss on the bridge of his nose.

Mike placed some eggs on Kate's plate and put a plate of bacon on the table in the center. He filled his plate with a heaping pile and then put the frying pan back on the stovetop. Kate glanced at the table, noticing the salt and pepper shakers but no other condiments. She picked up her fork to eat, but Mike stopped her. "Hey, I know you," he reassured her, "Don't worry, I know you need ketchup. You can kill everything with plenty of ketchup." Mike handed her the ketchup bottle as if he was a waiter getting her approval on a fancy bottle of wine.

"Thank you," Kate said as she took the bottle from him and slathered ketchup all over her eggs. Mike watched her as she ate. Kate could feel his gaze and she felt suddenly awkward. They ate in relative silence, both trying to find the right words and failing to do so.

Kate cleared the dishes from the table when they were done. She went to the sink and started to wash them but Mike came behind her and stopped her. His strong arms wrapped around her and she could feel him press against her from behind. "I'll do these," he said as he rested his chin on her shoulder. Her arms took his and her head pushed against his. Kate instinctively squeezed him with every part of her body. It was the type of hug that made the world disappear for just a second or two.

Mike kissed her shoulder. He kissed her neck and then turned her around to face him. She was pressed against the sink, her makeshift toga unravelling around her. She kissed him hard and then stopped suddenly.

Kate looked down and examined her bare feet. She loved him. There was no doubt on that. Now, since last night, she knew he felt the same. If life worked like the movies, this would be the euphoric climax where everything that kept them apart would melt away in some sort of comical Dues ex Machina event. But it wasn't. Life was complicated and it never allowed Kate any simple solutions.

Her mind raced. They couldn't be partners anymore. Lovers, but not partners. She also worried incessantly about how that would all work out. Her history didn't give any relationship much of a chance. The Vegas odds-makers would find the line on their love story laughable. Kate didn't want to hurt him, but she wanted him so badly she was willing to risk all the pain and sorrow that might just be inevitable for him and for her.

She lifted her head and caught him smiling at her. It was a goofy one, full of the "*I'm going to Disneyworld*" sort of exuberance that little kids get when they can't hold in their excitement.

"God," he said and hesitated before he finished, "you are so beautiful."

Kate felt her face flush. She couldn't help but smile. The unabashed compliment wasn't one she was used to or to which she knew how to respond. She also understood that it had risen from him out of a need to verbalize it. He couldn't keep those things inside anymore. They were welling up from the depths of his soul, impossible to pack down. It was a rumbling she knew well.

Nervously, Kate said, "We have to talk."

Mike's cell phone vibrated on the counter. He snatched it off the counter as it danced away from him and looked at it. Three missed calls. He flicked his thumb across the phone and said, "What's up?" A few seconds later he was writing down an address and Kate knew that her movie moment wasn't to be. There would be no romantic comedy ending for her. "Thanks a lot, God," she thought sarcastically.

Mike looked at her and he saw the sadness creep into her face. He walked towards her and gently put his hand behind her neck. He nudged her forward and kissed her forehead. "We'll talk. I promise," he said, "but we have to go to work first."

Chapter 26

"If there are no miracles then we need to find another word for the existence of life – the existence of you and me – on earth. Call it a gift from spirit (God or god in whatever form works for you), serendipity, happenstance or plain good fortune. I invite you to look at your life as if it were a miracle. To treat your life in any other way seems to me to be a terrible waste of your unique presence on this planet."

Robert White

"Your refusal to speak to me is not unexpected," Victor informed his brother.

Gregory seethed on the other side of the confessional wall.

"However, you must know that it will not deter me from my work," Victor continued, immune to his elder brother's new tactic.

He fingered the neatly tied bow on the box that rested on his lap.

"Brother, this is all I can offer you," Victor said, his voice betraying a hint of disappointment.

Gregory was confused, but remained resolute in his determination not to feed his brother's ego.

"These gifts I give you. You do not appreciate them. Yet, I give you the greatest of gifts; the gift of knowledge."

Gregory balked at that. He went to counter but caught himself. "Don't participate," he chided himself.

"Here, in this box, I give you the very truth of existence."

His brother bit his lip and remained silent, wanting to respond, but refusing to do so. Gregory thought, "No. It is a young woman's heart. You killed her. That is the only truth I see in it."

"You may try to deny it," Victor said, almost as if he could read his brother's thoughts. "Ignore it as you will. Ignore me as you will. Your God will not intervene on your behalf."

Victor waited for his brother's strength to fail. He waited to hear him lash out and defend the indefensible.

"I wonder, what do you do with the gifts I bring you?" Victor mused, ratcheting up the one-way conversation. Victor had already surmised the answer long ago. "I would imagine they make wonderful fertilizer for your rose garden." Victor added a sharp prick of a thorn, "Mother would be proud."

Gregory's fingers curled into fists. He wanted to smash the walls. He wanted to bash his brother's skull in. "Don't give him what he wants! Don't give in to him!" Gregory screamed in his mind. He felt claustrophobic, trapped within the walls of the Confessional, unable to escape the trap his brother had set for him. He stayed silent, simmering with frustration.

"As you will. I will visit again soon," Victor promised. "Don't forget to gather up your present."

~

They had started early in the morning, arriving at a few minutes after seven. Those few minutes set Mrs. Kraus off into a considerable mood.

"When you are late, you are telling people that their time doesn't matter," she wagged her finger and corrected them like a terrifying Sunday school teacher.

Paul, the artist they brought with them, wasn't the type of person to take a dressing down without answering back. "Look, haven't you ever been stuck in traffic?" He spat back sarcastically before Mike could stop him. That first impression set the tone for a very long morning.

Paul was young, prideful, and impatient. Mrs. Kraus was old, prideful, and impatient. The two mixed like oil and water. He tried to use the iPad that had the latest computer software to make a digital image of the suspect but Mrs. Kraus would have none of it. "No," she would repeat over and over again as he asked her qualifying questions regarding features or dared to show her what he felt was a finished product.

Mrs. Kraus made a comment under her breath that no one heard and then stormed off into the kitchen.

"Can I help you with something?" Kate asked as she followed her into the kitchen and tried to take a page from Mike's "sweet talk the witness book."

"Could you grab me that bowl, Dear?" Mrs. Kraus asked amiably. She seemed to reserve all of her venom for Paul.

Kate offered her the bowl. Mrs. Kraus instead handed Kate two eggs. Kate nearly dropped them and fumbled like an amateur juggler as she managed to get the bowl to the counter before the two eggs could jump from her hand.

"You're a natural at this," Mike joked as he leaned on the counter.

Kate playfully stuck her tongue out at him and tried to crack the egg the way she had seen it done a thousand times on TV and in Julie's kitchen.

Mike laughed as Kate gently tapped it on the edge of the bowl. He took it from her and gave it a solid rap and then split it, letting the yolk drop into the bowl. Then, he laid the second egg at the edge of her fingers and held her hand over the bowl.

Kate let him guide her arm back and then forward as the egg cracked against the bowl. She could feel his comfort with this, his confidence. She looked back at him and smiled brightly at her success.

"I see the two of you have finally decided to give it a go," Mrs. Kraus said without turning to look at them.

That separated the short cooking lesson and sent them scurrying away from each other. Mike went back out to talk Paul off the ledge, and Kate remained to offer what help she could in the kitchen.

The breakfast that the two ladies presented was a bountiful home cooked meal reminiscent of the best Southern homes.

Paul dug in too quickly and Mrs. Kraus rapped his knuckles with a wooden serving spoon.

"Boy! Do you have any manners?" she said chastising him.

He looked as if he were going to take the old lady over his knee and spank her, but he didn't respond.

"Would you say grace, Dear?" she asked Mike, as if the angry outburst was a distant memory.

Mike bowed his head and said grace. Kate awkwardly followed suit but Paul refused to participate.

They ate and chatted about Mrs. Kraus's deceased husband, a Navy man. She forgave Mike for being a Marine and said her husband always liked to beat them up. Kate was beginning to adore the old lady. She was tough, spunky, and sweet all rolled into one.

Mike cleared the dishes and Kate decided to do the washing. Mike took the opportunity to speak to Paul about his approach.

The two men couldn't be more different. Paul was slight and baby-faced while Mike was broad and square jawed. Where Mike had a sort of been there done that, what's the rush approach to life, Paul never seemed to be in the moment. Rather, he was always worried about where he was going next.

"Let's go a different route, okay?" Mike said to Paul more as an order than a request.

Paul took the pencil and pad from Mike and started to draw out the features Mrs. Kraus has shared. He complained about the antiquated methods but begrudgingly did as he was instructed.

"Well?" Paul asked, turning the fifth drawing so Mrs. Kraus could condemn it again.

"No, no, Dear Boy. That's not it at all. The eyes are all wrong," Mrs. Kraus protested.

Paul balled the sheet up and tossed it to the side. It tumbled and stopped when it hit the small pile of failed attempts growing behind him.

"I quit. That's all. I just quit!" he exclaimed.

Mrs. Kraus barked at him, "I don't know how else to explain it to you. You, young people, don't listen these days. Always in a rush to get somewhere other than where you are."

Kate couldn't help but snicker from the kitchen as Mrs. Kraus pinned the kid's description perfectly.

"THAT'S IT! I have taken quite enough from you, Old Lady!" Paul fired back from his seat in the living room.

"You disrespectful, untalented hack!" she retorted and aggressively stepped towards him.

"Hey! Hey, you two. Go to neutral corners!" Kate said as she entered and tossed a dish towel at Paul.

She took a position between the two combatants and held up her hands in a stopping motion.

"Manning, this lady is a psycho!" Paul yelled. "I've been working on this for two days! Not two hours! Two friggin' days and she's still not satisfied."

Paul did have a point. He had worked intermittently on it for two days, hence the personal visit to the apartment. Kate could understand a level of frustration, but she started to wonder if he had grandparents. He showed no patience and even less respect for the elderly lady.

"It would have gone much faster if YOU HAD ANY TALENT!" Mrs. Kraus overemphasized the last few words, letting her anger flow freely.

Kate soothed them, "Okay, Okay. Let's take a look at what you've got so far, officer," Kate tried to soothe them both, but also subtly reminded Paul of his rank.

Kate knelt down and picked up the most recent sheet of crumbled paper. She felt her stomach twinge a bit as she bent over. It was the third time this morning she felt sick to her stomach. Mike walked to her and looked over her shoulder.

Kate whispered, "The two of them need a time out."

She unfolded the piece of paper and looked at it. Mike watched as her face went white.

"Kate?" he said, growing concerned.

She pushed him out of the way and sprinted to the bathroom. The apartment erupted with the sounds of her retching over the toilet, a heavy breakfast pouring out of her at high speed.

Mike walked into the bathroom and took her hair in his hands. He bunched it behind her head and rubbed her back.

"No," Kate said drained. "Not here."

Mike understood her meaning. The last thing they needed was the cocky young ass getting wind of their budding relationship.

"Wow, Manning, that's some pile you got going there," Mike said in an exaggerated tone, trying to cover his concern for her.

By the time Kate had emptied her stomach and returned to the living room Paul felt he had something.

"Please, let this one be it," he pleaded.

Mike looked at Kate and furrowed his brow. It was his way of asking if she was okay. Kate waved her hand in front of her, low so nobody else could see. She mouthed silently, "I'm fine. It's nothing." But, Mike's brow only went deeper; he knew her well enough to read the lie.

Mrs. Kraus gave Paul a hard slap across his back as if he had just scored the winning run. "That's it, Dearie! You finally listened!"

Paul gave her a snide look, but refrained from comment this time.

"Get that out to everyone, suspect in multiple homicides, include the descriptors on file. Got it?" Kate said still looking green.

She glanced at the rendering and for a second felt she had seen that face before. Then, her stomach spasmed and she ran back to the bathroom for salvation.

~

Victor walked crisply up the stone steps towards the large wooden doors of his brother's church. In his hand he carried another offering, a small box wrapped with a bow, as always. Victor was happy to be here. It had been only three days since he last visited. That conversation, if it could be called one, left Victor unsatisfied. His brother was not seeing the light and Victor was determined to push him to the truth.

The sun burst into the church as Victor entered. Each ray of sunlight seemed to choose a different color of the spectrum to highlight.

The glittery bow that wrapped around the present shimmered in the light and Victor had the sense that today, Gregory might finally see things his way.

Victor stood in the doorway of the church, a dark shadow amidst pure light, with a small smirk on his face.

Gregory sat near the altar reading a passage from the Bible, too deep in the church for the light to reach him. He scribbled in a notebook that sat at his side. Working on his next sermon, Gregory was oblivious to Victor's entrance.

"I have come to offer more proof brother," Victor's voice boomed and echoed in the empty church.

Gregory stood to face his younger brother. The Bible in his hand hung limply, ready to drop at the slightest agitation.

Victor stretched his hands out, presenting the box to his brother, offering for him to come take it, to accept it.

Gregory shook his head defiantly. "Get out! You offer no proof!"

Victor's hopes were dashed. He brought the box down to his side and walked it towards his brother and the altar. The two men stared at each other, but said nothing. Victor gently rested the box in the center of the offering table, as if it were to be divided and offered up as a sacrament.

"I do this for your sake, Gregory," Victor whispered as he adjusted the position of the box, ensuring the placement was perfect.

"No," Gregory said through gritted teeth.

Victor knelt, and prayed to the box and its contents, mocking the traditions of the church. "Sooner or later you must accept the truth."

"Stop it!" Gregory said as firmly as his racing heart could muster. Victor ignored him.

"Laura will be next," Victor threatened. "Will your God save her?" he asked as he raised both of his arms to the crucified image of Christ. "Is she somehow more special to Him than any of these others? They are meaningless, Gregory!" Victor grasped the chalice from the offering table. "Empty vessels," he said as he tossed it down the aisle.

As the golden cup crashed to the floor, the sacramental bread used in the Eucharist tumbled onto the red carpet as well, each one marked with the cross. A single piece rolled and crashed into Gregory's shoe. He stepped back instinctively from it, as if it burned him. "Empty," Victor said more quietly this time. "Why will you not see this?"

Recovering himself, Gregory dropped the Bible from his hand and went to gather the Host from the floor. "Get out," he hissed.

Victor walked from the altar and stood next to his brother. Gregory, on his knees before the altar and the image of Christ, picking up communion chips, seemed a sad sight to Victor. He put his hand on his brother's shoulder and looked up at the box on the offering table.

"The longer you deny it, the harder I will work to prove it to you."

Gregory remained motionless, kneeling on the floor as his brother's footsteps echoed out of the church. He held several pieces of the Host in his hands, staring down at them. As the anger and frustration consumed him, Gregory's hands squeezed tightly, crushing the sacramental bread. "I can't. I can't keep this promise," he whispered through gritted teeth. "God, why do you challenge me so? How can I be faithful?" With his question left unanswered, Gregory sobbed and let the shattered Host fall to the floor.

~

"I'd like to go back to the restaurant," Kate whispered as she held tight to the toilet bowl.

"You can think about food right now?" Mike asked, stunned. The smell of Kate's vomit eliminating any appetite he might have had so early in the morning.

Kate rose and rinsed her mouth, feeling as pale as she looked. She brushed past Mike and looked for Paul, but he had already left. "Damn," Kate said quietly, wanting another look at the sketch if she was going to play her hunch. She pulled out her phone and called Paul. He picked up on the third ring and didn't even say hello.

"I'm not coming back there," he said, half-serious.

"Kate ignored him and got straight down to business, "I need you to take a picture of the sketch and send it to my phone."

"Okay. I'll do it as soon as I get back to the precinct," Paul replied.

"No. Do it right now," Kate ordered, then added, "Please."

"Alright. Will do," Paul obliged.

Less than a minute later, Kate had the image on her phone. They made their apologies to Mrs. Kraus and headed back to Paulie's Restaurant.

~

Mike and Kate had to knock to get into the restaurant. They flashed their badges and a waiter who was filling salt shakers decided to let them in. They explained themselves to the waiter who quickly handed them off to the owner. Luckily for them, he wasn't the type to stonewall the police.

"I'll get the credit card receipts for you and I'll help you look through them," Paulie offered. "I'm afraid the security footage you asked for will be a bit more difficult."

Kate and Mike stared at the aging man, who had given up trying to comb over his hair and had accepted his fate, waiting for an explanation.

"I don't know how to work it," he admitted. "I'm not very good with technology. I'll call my son and he can help us," Paulie offered.

"Would you mind if I look at it?" Kate asked, offering her services.

"If you can figure it out, by all means," Paulie agreed.

I took more than an hour to sort through the receipts. Mike was happy to do it in order to avoid the lengthy process of court orders and a battle with the credit card companies. The effort was fruitless, but at least it hadn't taken weeks and mountains of paperwork.

Kate's day had been decidedly more productive. She had found the images of Jasmine. Her date had been stunningly careful about keeping his head down when he entered or exited the restaurant. Thankfully for them, Paulie's had a problem with a waiter several years back who was skimming money from a register and had installed a camera inside, near the waiter station, which just so happened to catch passing images of people who were coming back from the men's room.

There was no way Kate could print what she needed so she took snaps of the images with her phone.

"Is that our guy?" Mike asked as he put his hand on her shoulder.

Kate leaned her cheek onto his hand and took a deep breath, "Part of me hopes so, part of me hopes not." Kate suspected that her friendly conversation with Jasmine bore a terrifying finality to it. Kate couldn't bear to think it, but she knew in her heart that Jasmine's date had ended very differently than her own.

Then it hit her. "Are these the bar receipts?" Kate barked at Paulie.

"No. Do you want those?"

"Yes!" Kate said excitedly, "Look for a first name of Jasmine."

Within minutes, they had what they needed. Kate held the thin paper in her hand.

"I'd say that's probable cause to get an address and search her apartment, don't you?" Mike suggested.

"Let's call for a court order. When we get this guy, I don't want anything the D.A. will balk at," Kate said.

Mike shrugged his shoulders and took out his phone. He would go through the motions to satisfy her, but he didn't think the order would matter. Secretly, he knew that this guy would never see a courtroom. He would make sure of that.

~

They knocked on Jasmine's door several times. After pounding on the door for nearly a minute, they had decided to breach it. Mike moved back to throw his shoulder into it. Instead, Kate just wiggled the doorknob to discover the door was unlocked. That wasn't a good sign.

There on the couch, Jasmine rested one final time. She was positioned as all the others had been. Kate fought back tears as Mike called it in. They had a face now. They were close, but it didn't matter. Jasmine was dead.

Chapter 27

*"I do not feel obliged to believe that the same God who has
endowed us with sense, reason, and intellect has intended us to forgo
their use."*

Galileo Galilei

G regory stood upon the altar in his church, alone with his thoughts. At least, he thought he was alone. Seated in a pew near the back of the church was a visitor who had come to discuss something very important with him. That visitor had gone unnoticed by Father Gregory.

"Days such as these make us all feel powerless," Gregory said, speaking to an imaginary crowd of parishioners. "We feel weak in the face of threats and danger. Yet, it is not true," he shook his finger to emphasize the point. "We all have power over one another. Each of us has the ability, the strength to make changes not only in our lives, but in the lives of others." Gregory paused for breath and then continued, his voice lowering an octave, though growing louder. "Many of us choose to believe that we have no power. Others wish only to use their power for selfish goals. Yet, God has given us this power for a higher purpose. He wishes us to use our power." He shook his head as he said it. "Yes, to help ourselves, but also to help others. It is in how we wield our power that we will be defined. It is upon the use or non-use of this gift that we will ultimately be judged. When you stand before God and He asks what you have done with this gift He has granted, say to Him but one thing; Let the work I have done speak for me." Gregory ended, poking himself in the chest.

Gregory stepped down off the altar as the visitor rose and approached him.

"Father," Kate said trying to gain his attention.

"Oh!" Gregory jumped, grabbing his chest and taking hold of the cloth of his t-shirt. He was clearly stunned that there was someone so close to him of whom he was unaware.

"I'm sorry," Kate demurred. "I was trying to stay quiet while you rehearsed. I didn't mean to startle you."

Gregory smiled at Kate and waved his hand to suggest the shock was nothing to be concerned about. "Well, Kate, what did you think of this Sunday's sermon?"

"It was excellent," Kate said with forced enthusiasm.

Gregory grinned and didn't call her out on the lie. "I don't normally give sneak previews you know. I always feel better going in with a bit of practice though."

"I'm sorry to have just dropped in on you like this," Kate said, her eyes darting around the church and avoiding his. "I just needed someone to talk to."

Gregory could see she was a woman in crisis. Her face was tired, tense. He put his arm around Kate and walked with her towards the front of the church.

"You know what, Kate? I have some time right now. How about we go get ourselves a hot dog or two and talk things over?" Gregory asked, genuinely happy to see her. After all, the only other visitor he had of late was his brother.

"My treat this time," Kate said as her way of thanking him.

Kate and Gregory stepped out into the warm sun and walked down the steps.

"So, what has you coming to church on a Wednesday afternoon?" Gregory asked. He watched as Kate dropped her head and grew concerned that he might have shut her down before she even started to talk. "Not that I'm complaining mind you," he added quickly in apology.

Kate couldn't bring herself to speak. She tried. Her mouth opened but no words came out. Her eyes spoke everything Gregory needed to hear.

"That bad, huh?" he asked and held out his arms to her so that she could come in for a hug. She hesitated and then dropped into his arms. Gregory could feel her quiver as she lost control and began to cry. He held her until she loosened her hold on him. When they made eye contact again her tears were gone, but her face was puffy and red.

They walked in silence to the hot dog vendor on the corner. They placed their order and the man chatted idly with Gregory. The two must have known each other well as they cracked various jokes both obvious and inside.

Gregory applied the same methods on Kate this time as he had previously. He walked with her and stayed quiet, waiting for her to begin. This time, he had to wait quite a bit longer. He had finished his hot dog long before she uttered a word.

"I can't seem to get anything right in my life," Kate finally blurted out.

Gregory remained silent.

"Everything feels as if it's just out of reach. Then, when I do reach for it, I feel so guilty for trying."

Gregory let out a muffled, "Uh-huh."

They walked together a while and Kate didn't elaborate on her guilt at all. She just seemed to sulk. Gregory tried to console her a bit with idle chatter. When it had failed, Gregory tried to get her to open up.

"Kate, what is it that makes you feel so guilty? What do you think you have done that is so horribly wrong?"

Kate sat on a faded green bench and put her head into her hands. Gregory stood next to her and placed his hand on her shoulder.

"I slept with someone," Kate said, not taking her hands from her face. "That's not really true. I've been sleeping with someone," she corrected.

"That's not exactly uncommon these days, Kate," Gregory said, trying to alleviate the guilt that was tormenting her.

Kate ignored him. "He's very special to me and I was always afraid that if our relationship went this far it would be doomed. I feel like I just got what I've always wanted and now I know in my heart it's going to be taken away."

She started to cry again. Gregory knelt in front of her. He put his hand on her leg and tried to comfort her.

"Kate, I don't think . . ."

"I just want to be happy," Kate cut him off. "I want a family and a husband. I want what Julie has. Why does it have to be so hard?"

Gregory smiled at her as he wiped away a tear from her face. "Heaven knows how to properly price its goods. Things as wonderful as love and children should never come easy. If it comes easy, it is often times taken for granted."

Kate smiled at Gregory and let out a half laugh, half cough.

"Thanks," she sniffled. "I'd pay anything for this one to work out." She shook her head and added, "To not screw it up."

"Does he know that?" Gregory asked.

"I was going to tell him, but we've been trying to solve these murder cases and, well, work got in the way," Kate made excuses for herself.

Gregory shuttered at the thought of Kate being on the trail of Victor. Julie had said enough to clue him in that Kate was one of the detectives responsible for the case. He didn't fear for his brother. He feared for her.

"Tell him," Gregory urged, not looking at her.

Kate shook her head in agreement but said, "I don't know how."

Gregory offered her his hand and helped her from the bench.

"You just tell the truth. Nothing more or less. Don't be afraid of it. Once you let it out, you'll feel free," Gregory suggested.

Kate got the sense that he understood what it was like to keep a secret. Hell, he probably kept half the borough of Queens's dirty little secrets, Kate thought. They walked with one another awhile before Kate began again.

"Father, I have to ask you this," Kate said firmly. "How can God allow these innocent girls to be murdered?"

Gregory looked as if someone had run past and punched him in the gut. Kate immediately felt as if she had insulted him and tried to apologize.

"I'm sorry Father, I didn't mean . . ."

"It's all right," Gregory stammered through the lie. His face was white and the corners of his head were starting to sweat. "I sometimes have a hard time with that one as well. I think we're here and there's a plan for us," he offered in explanation.

Kate had heard it all before. This was the stock response she had gotten time and again. She expected better of the man she had grown to like and to trust.

"What would light be without dark? How would we know good, if evil did not exist?" Gregory proffered. "Evil is a product of free will, not God. Sometimes, I think that evil exists, so that we may know the gift of goodness."

They had returned to the church stairs; but, Kate wasn't satisfied with his answers.

"So, in the face of this ultimate evil we are supposed to better understand what good is?" Kate asked with obvious disdain refusing to accept his interpretation of the events. "How is that possible?"

Gregory desperately wanted to avoid this conversation. He responded with a hint of anger in his voice, trying to assuage her concerns, "As this man tears out the hearts of his victims we see the heart in so many of us. Families coming together, citizens working together, cops working overtime to protect us." He gave a slight nod of his head as if to say, "See, I told you so."

Kate had suddenly stopped on the stairs and Gregory had continued on. He stood three steps above her and looked down at her in confusion.

"So, why do you think he takes the hearts of his victims?" Kate remembered her sister, Julie, asking.

Kate had thought about that question before. As a trophy, she considered. The heart was the vessel of love. Maybe, he was the jilted lover of his victims. Yet, they had found no connection between the women. Why the cross then if he was angry at being rejected by them? Kate had gone over it and over it. Nothing made sense. "I don't know. I just don't know," Kate murmured.

"Excuse me?" Gregory said, not understanding why she was mumbling

"I don't know," Kate seemed to chant. Then, she seemed to come out of the trance. "Excuse me?" Kate repeated him. "What did you say about the hearts?"

"I was just saying that this killer who is removing the hearts of his victims is helping all of us to see how much we care about each other, our lives, and maybe, even God." Gregory replied full of false confidence. Maybe if he said it aloud, he would start to believe it himself.

"No one knows. Not even the press." That's what Kate had told Julie. She told her not to speak to anyone about it. Kate stood frozen and Gregory came down the stairs to see if she is all right.

"Kate? Kate, are you okay?" Gregory asked.

Kate remembered Julie walking across the kitchen, dropping a stack of pancakes onto her plate.

"Does the press know about the . . .?" Julie asked but Kate had cut her off.

"Maybe she told him," Kate considered, her mind racing.

She thought about the last time she was on these steps. The man who spoke to her. There was a small wrapped box sitting next to him. The words came spinning back to her. "I sincerely hope that my brother has helped to cleanse your soul." He said brother. Not Father, brother. Kate remembered the dinner at Julie's. She remembered Father Gregory's words. "The body is simply a vessel for the soul that resides within us all. Its loss is sad to those left behind; but, it does not mean that the spirit dies with it." Kate recalled the disastrous meeting with Mike in the bar. "I know. I know what he's looking for!" she had said. Visions of the victim's heads flooded her. The blood stained cross on their forehead. Kate could feel her stomach go queasy as the memories crashed into her brain. Gregory and Kate had walked in the park together. What was it he said? She tried to remember it. "Believe me, Kate. I understand sibling rivalry. My brother has spent most of his life trying to show me that he's smarter than I am. That he knows more than I do." The reservation at Paulie's; It was under the name Sloan. Kate could barely breath as the epiphany crashed over her.

Gregory stood in front of Kate on the church steps. He held her by the shoulders. Kate felt as if she were just waking from a dream. She was pale and her knees were shaking.

"Kate? Kate, do you need an ambulance? Are you all right?" Gregory asked.

"Uh-huh. I'm okay," she muttered breathlessly and pulled away from him.

Gregory let go of her shoulders begrudgingly.

"Are you sure you're okay? You looked pretty woozy there for a minute," Gregory showed genuine concern for Kate.

"Father Sloan, what did you say your brother's name was again?"

Gregory quickly replied without thinking, without registering that Kate had used his last name. "Victor. . . . Why?" As soon as he asked, the realization crashed down on him. She had put it together. What had he said that had given it away? How had he broken his promise? "No! No!" Gregory had thought, his mind scrambling for what he could say or do.

Kate watched as the terror cut across his face. Kate screamed at him. A guttural, violent scream that shocked bystanders and froze their steps.

"You knew. All this time, you knew," she spat.

"No, I . . . no," Gregory stuttered desperately.

"You could have stopped him," Kate said, reeling from the shock. Tears started in her eyes. "All those girls, dead."

Kate shook with rage and fury. "You bastard! How does it feel? Tell me! I want to know what it feels like to be such a hypocrite. You preach about power, and yet, you do nothing. Why? Why would you protect him?" She couldn't fathom it. It didn't make sense. How could she have been so wrong about him?

Gregory tried to explain, "Confession is one of the most sacred rites in the Church," he began, desperate for absolution. "The Sacrament is based on the belief that the seal of the Confessional is absolute, inviolable." He looked at her pleadingly. "I am not permitted to disclose the contents of any Confession, or even allowed to disclose that an individual did seek the Sacrament." The Confessional seal could only be broken at the cost of excommunication and Gregory was not one to break a promise, especially to God. He chose to cover Victor's crimes with that seal. He needed time to convert him; to convince his brother of the error of his ways. Gregory looked at Kate and held his hands out in front of him in supplication. "A priest who violates that seal suffers automatic excommunication from the Church."

Kate boiled over with indignation at the excuses. He protected his position in the church. He protected his brother. The one thing he didn't protect was innocent women!

Gregory collapsed onto the hot stone stairs. His pulse resonated in his ears like a tribal dance. There was no escape. It could no longer be hidden. He should have felt relief, but it was fear and confusion that reigned in him.

"I promised. I made a promise," he cried.

Kate took several steps away from him, leaving him there on the stairs with his head in his hands. Several people, parishioners maybe, stared at them as they fought. Kate thought about the betrayal that she had suffered. Gregory was a hypocrite. Kate felt her heart pounding in her chest, like one of those aliens in the movies. She thought about arresting him but didn't know if she could. Confused and devastated, Kate let out a guttural moan that echoed off the façade of the church and returned louder than she thought possible. As she began to run away from him, Kate's scream sliced through the air, "I hope you burn in Hell!"

Chapter 28

"Pray as if everything depended upon God and work as if everything depended upon man."

Francis Cardinal Spellman (1889-1967)

"Please God, let him be home," Kate prayed. She had already tried his cell phone three times with no answer. There was no answer at home either. Kate left the same message at his apartment that she did on his cell. She had also texted it to him. "Mike, it's me. Meet me at the station. I know who the killer is."

Her hands shook. She felt woozy and light-headed. She shivered even though it was warm. Kate felt like she was going into shock. She stopped and looked over her shoulder. She had only made it two blocks from the church. She could see the church through a haze. It was like she was looking at it through a pair of cheap binoculars. Black circles seemed to frame the church and pull in on it, making it smaller and smaller. Then, everything went black and her knees buckled. Kate collapsed on the sidewalk and fell, unconscious.

~

Victor sat quietly in his apartment sipping on a glass of ice water. He was bored and more than a little frustrated. So, when the phone rang, he was happy to hear it. It could be only one of three things; Laura, who he did not expect to call, telemarketing, or his brother. He looked at the caller ID and smiled.

"Hello Gregory," Victor said evenly.

"They know," Gregory blurted.

Victor could hear him on the verge of hyperventilating. "Good," he thought.

"Do you hear me? They know! The cops, Victor! They know who you are," Gregory yelled, the urgency in his voice growing with every word.

"Ever the loyal brother, eh Gregory?" Victor whispered coolly into the phone, in stark contrast to his brother's terror.

"The cops, they know," Gregory repeated. "You have to stop. You have to get away and stop all of this, please," he implored, seemingly frantic to save his younger brother.

Yet, Victor remained tranquil. "You were always so weak," he observed. "Everyone always thought you were strong, but I have always known the truth."

Victor could hear his brother's footsteps stamp through the phone as he paced back and forth.

"This isn't about me, Victor, it's about you!" his brother yelled. "Run and hide. But for God's sake, stop this madness!"

Victor grinned widely, satisfied now. "You really are an idiot aren't you?" he asked sarcastically. Victor waited as his brother tried to sort out his meaning in silence. Then, calmly, he began to explain, "This has everything to do with you. After all that I have shown you; do you still believe in the salvation of God?"

Victor waited for a response that would not, could not come.

"What must I do?" Victor asked. "What must I do to show you how foolish it is to believe? How do I prove it to you, Gregory?"

"I do! I believe! Stop this!" Gregory was incensed. "You are insane! I believe in God and you do not. Let it be. Please, Victor, just let it be."

Victor was slow to respond, always careful with his words. "I cannot. I believe in you. You are my brother. You must see the truth."

"I will not forsake Him," Gregory promised.

"Careful," Victor suggested, shifting his weight on his favorite chair. Finally, it felt less like a chair and more like a throne. Victor sensed that his victory was near. Gregory must see the truth now. Deliberately, Victor said, "Promises are what got you into this mess in the first place."

"Damn you, Victor!" Gregory railed.

Victor interjected before Gregory could curse him further. "You leave me no choice. Laura Moles must die."

The name hit Gregory hard. Gregory felt as if he were placed on a medieval rack, being pulled in different directions. His muscles ached as he felt his body and soul rending from the torture. He began to plead, "Victor please, don't do this! She is an innocent child."

Gregory waited but instead, Victor let silence speak for him.

"She has nothing to do with our quarrel. None of these women did. You hate mother. I understand. But, I could not, cannot hate her. Why must it always be your way?" A lifetime of resentment was contained in a single statement. It had always been about Victor. Gregory's life was defined by his brother's needs, his mother's, God's, never his own.

"Mother deserved . . ." Victor had begun, but caught himself. His voice was angry now, though still controlled. "Again Gregory, you behave like you do not understand the rules of our struggle. You know what you must do to save her and I know that it will not work."

"What must I do to convince you?" Gregory begged.

"Make Him stop me," Victor hissed. "That is the only way you will prove that I am wrong and you are right."

A loud thud echoed through the phone.

"Victor, I am on my knees. I am begging you to spare her life."

Victor walked to the window of his apartment and opened the shades. It was late afternoon now and the sun was beginning to fall below the tallest buildings on the horizon. Victor understood that this may well be his last opportunity.

"Why do you continue to waste your time with me?" Victor asked. "I won't listen to your groveling. Pray to your God and you will find He is more like me than you. He will not listen! That is because He does not exist. You have only to admit that to stop all of this, but you cannot. You made a promise, didn't you? After all, my brother never breaks a promise. Isn't that why you called to warn me?"

Gregory began to sob. "Yes," he cried. "I swore to mother and to God I would protect you and I have. Couldn't you please spare her?" he pleaded.

"Yes," Victor stated with a chilling carelessness, "but I will not. Only you or your God can do that."

Victor waited for his brother to forsake his vows. He waited for his brother to swear that God wasn't real or that he would leave the church. All he heard were sobs.

"Then, Laura is already dead," he said and dropped the phone to the floor.

"Victor! Victor! VICTOR!" Gregory's screams could be heard reverberating through the receiver, echoing through a cold apartment where no one and nothing cared to hear them.

~

Kate awoke in the hospital to the smell of iodine and plastic. A heavy set nurse in blue with thick dreadlocks was lingering over a plastic tray set on her bed.

"What happened?" Kate asked, getting right to the point. She tugged at the IV stuck in her arm and decided against yanking it out.

The nurse smiled at her and started to take her vitals. "You collapsed on the street. They brought you in and we've just been keeping you under observation."

Kate was confused. "Why would I have collapsed?" she wondered. The nurse seemed to read her mind.

"Have you been feeling sick lately? Tired?" the nurse asked, staring at Kate as if she had discerned a secret she had been hiding. Somewhere in the recesses of her mind, the word secret made her shudder, but Kate was still cloudy as to why.

Now that she mentioned it, Kate had been feeling exhausted and she had thrown up more in the last month than she had in the last ten years.

"I guess," Kate replied.

The nurse leaned in and glanced back as if to ensure no one would overhear her in an empty room. She smelled like she had recently eaten a brownie. Quietly, she said, "Just between us girls, congratulations!" She winked suggestively. As she started to walk out of the room she turned and formally told Kate, "You'll have to wait for the doctor to come in to discuss your results."

Kate was utterly dumbstruck.

"Oh, by the way, I think the daddy is waiting to see you," The nurse added in a false whisper, "I'll send him in."

"Don't tell him," Kate said quickly before the nurse could let the heavy door close behind her. She poked her head back in and gave Kate a thumbs up, then disappeared on her rounds. Kate's heart went leaping from her chest. She grasped her bosom and tried to quell the pounding of her heart. Then, slowly, she reached down to her belly and caressed it lovingly. The first pangs of excitement washed over her. She was going to have a baby. Mike's baby!

Then reality came crashing down on her. They weren't married. Hell, they weren't even a couple. He loved her. She was certain of that now. She loved him. The thought of that made her smile again. Would it be enough, Kate wondered.

Mike burst into the room, concern hanging all over his face. He carried a pink stuffed bear and a gold foil get well balloon trailed behind him, all obviously bought at a gift shop within the hospital.

"These are for you," he said, jutting his hands out and offering the bear and balloon to her.

"Thank you," Kate smiled and accepted the gifts. She hugged the bear tightly and then shifted it to the side as if she were holding a newborn baby.

"So what happened? Any guesses yet?" Mike asked worriedly.

"I'm pregnant," was what Kate thought. She couldn't bear to tell him. She was terrified of complicating things further than they already were. Avoidance would only get her so far, she knew, though it would get her through today at least. She would keep the secret for now. There it was again, the word secret.

"Oh my God!" Kate blurted.

Mike lurched forward and his eyes searched for a problem. "What? What's wrong?" he queried.

"Gregory. That's what happened," Kate realized suddenly, remembering everything now. "I was talking to Father Gregory."

"Your sister's priest friend?" Mike asked, confused.

Kate nodded and then blushed, realizing what she had gone to talk to the priest about.

Mike stared at her, waiting for her to elaborate. It wasn't exactly like Kate to visit a priest. Mike was no less confused when Kate spoke again.

"I solved the case," Kate said.

Chapter 29

"Say nothing of my religion. It is known to God and to myself alone. Its evidence before the world is to be sought in my life: if it has been honest and dutiful to society the religion which has regulated it cannot be a bad one."

Thomas Jefferson (1743-1826)

Victor cut into the muscle with precision. The knife was sharp, making quick work of the flesh. He diced it into a small, neat section and held it up to his face, examining it. The chef had done an exquisite job with the filet. It was a beautifully marbled piece of meat that Victor savored as he ate.

"Is everything to your liking, sir?" a waitress asked. She was a blonde with a terribly trendy, partial-dye job that had streaks of pink and purple throughout her hair. She was in her mid-twenties, probably just out of college but unable to find a job in her field. Maybe, she was a struggling actress. A half dozen clichés ran through Victor's mind before he nodded and smiled.

"Excellent. May I have another glass of wine, please?" Victor said. As the waitress walked away, Victor watched her carefully. If his brother had not exposed him, Victor was certain that this woman would be his next target. But, he had other plans now. The timetable had changed.

Victor swirled the red wine that remained in his glass, watching it flow. It was a 2007 Les Lezardes Syrah and Victor had been pleasantly surprised by it. The wine had a sort of black pepper hint with smooth tannins that paired perfectly with his filet. It was inexpensive, as was the entire restaurant he now ate in, but of stunning taste and quality. He had always preferred the more elite eateries within the city. Now, he was finding that great food could be found in unlikely places. He would never have imagined such a place could exist.

The waitress returned with a second glass. She smiled and told Victor to yell if he needed anything. Clearly, the service at Pattie's was as classy as the décor, he observed. The place was a dark old watering hole with oak stained furniture and matching paneling that had chipped with years of use and neglect. It reminded Victor more of an old Irish Pub than a fine restaurant. He didn't have time to make reservations at his normal establishments. Moreover, he didn't want to waste time traveling to them. Victor needed a quick meal so that he could go to Laura's apartment.

After Gregory had called him, Victor had called Laura on the prepaid cell. He had arranged an impromptu date for this evening.

"I'm so excited," she beamed over the phone. "I've never been to the ballet before. I used to do it as a kid, but . . ." she trailed off not wanting to seem like she was about to tell her life story.

"I'll pick you up around seven, if that is all right with you?" Victor asked as if he was imposing on her.

"That would be wonderful," Laura dismissed his bashful concerns.

"Perfect. Could you tell me your address, please so that I can inform the driver?"

He could hear the gasp in her voice. The excitement of a world of money and opulence made the woman giddy. She quickly informed him of her address and then added a question, "Victor, what should I wear?"

"Anything you wish, for it will not matter," Victor responded suggestively.

"Very sweet, but you are no help!" she chided. "I'm going to buy a dress."

Victor ended the conversation, "I look forward to this evening."

~

Father Gregory did not know how long he had remained motionless on his knees. His legs ached. Pins and needles shot through his feet where the weight of his body rested on his heels. He still held the cell phone he had used to call his brother limply in his hand. He didn't want to put it down. If he did, he was admitting that he could do nothing more to stop him; to save Laura from Victor.

When he finally did move, his body screamed out in pain. "Good," he thought, "No one deserves it more." He wanted to punish himself further but seemed to lack the courage to do so. Gregory limped out of the back of the church and towards the rectory. He paused and reflected on the rose garden of which he had been so proud. Victor had tainted it. His brother had poisoned so many things in his life. Gregory could not see life in the garden any longer, only death and decay. He swore he must be wrong for his nose felt the smell of rotting hearts overpowering the scent of roses.

When Gregory had entered the seminary, Victor had sworn to prove him wrong. "Your faith in God is misplaced, Gregory," Victor had said with cold ferocity. "How can a benevolent God have put us under the care of such a woman?" Victor had said the word woman as if it were something that cut his tongue. That happy day was ruined by his brother's bitterness.

Victor would, over the next two or three years, pop in from time to time while Gregory studied. He would challenge him; probe the limits of his understanding. Gregory had welcomed the conversations. He felt it was good practice for speaking to non-believers. Somewhere inside of him, Gregory believed that he could help Victor to see. If he could convert his brother, Gregory could change the world. One of the many things he had failed at in life, Gregory concluded.

"Promise me, Gregory," his mother had begged, "Promise me, you will always protect him?" She was dying in a hospital bed, a lifetime of abuse and neglect had finally caught up to her. She was frail, barely more than skin and bones. Her eyes sunk in and her cheeks had collapsed, making deep inroads into her face. "I don't want to die," she cried. Gregory remembered the fear in her eyes, the longing for someone or something to help her. At the time, he was confident that God would accept her, take her into his loving arms and allow her soul to rest in a better place.

An Absence of Faith

"He's a special boy," she had said, coughing harshly as her lungs gave out. "You know he will need you to help him," his mother had explained. "Help him to understand." Those were her last words to him, before he left her to be buried in an unmarked grave; before he abandoned her to protect his reputation. "Help him to understand."

Victor had always been smart. Smarter than Gregory. He was also angry. Gregory had always thought his mother had tasked him with a mission. That it was his task to save Victor, to help him see God; to see good in the world. Gregory believed he was God's hands and feet on earth. Through him, God would save Victor's troubled soul. Saving him would have been the greatest test of Gregory's life as a servant of God. Gregory could not save him. Now, he could only hate him.

He found himself standing in the center of the garden. He had tried so hard to make it beautiful. Gregory had tried, but his brother refused to see his efforts as anything but foolhardy. Gregory had protected him, tried to guide him, but it had all been for nothing. Bitterness washed over him. Suddenly, Gregory stomped on one of the rose bushes. His foot crashed down and branches splintered. He stomped again, and again and again. He kicked and thrashed with pent up rage at Victor, at their mother, at himself, and at God. The thorns grabbed at him, catching his legs, tying him to them.

He slipped and fell amidst the broken branches and torn up bushes. The thorns dug into him and soil stained his clothes. Petals of red, mashed and mutilated, surrounded him, but he could not escape. Gregory cried. He cried the tears of a man who had no reason to hide his anguish. Heavy sobs from a heavy heart.

He picked up a single rose, one that had survived his thunderous assault. It was beautifully formed. The deep crimson petals were velvety and thick. They folded over at the top, without a hint of the scars that most wear as proof of their survival. This single rose had lived without pain, without sorrow or betrayal. It was pure and perfect. Gregory thought of his mother. How she would have appreciated such a flawless rose. He took hold of it and broke the stem about six inches below the flower.

He took the rose with him to the rectory and laid it on his pillow. There, he stripped off his dirty clothes and left them in a pile on the floor. He took out his collar and formal robes from his closet and laid them on his bed, careful not to crush the rose. He went into the bathroom and cleaned himself up before dressing. He lifted the rose reverently and carried it with him as he left. Gregory returned to the church, taking the longer route so as to avoid seeing the destroyed garden. The church was quiet, empty.

Gregory climbed the two flights of red upholstered stairs up to the balcony. He remembered the first time he had climbed these stairs. He had looked down upon the church with such hope, such promise. But it was promises that had undone him. Promises he had made and could not keep. Promises God had made and did not keep.

Gregory looked towards the altar. The large statue of Christ, crucified, dominated his view. He had died for our sins, Gregory thought. Christ had died so that we could be reborn. Gregory lamented the thought of it. He should have chosen that path long ago. Victor would not have needed to prove him wrong if he was not alive to be wrong. Oh, how promises had destroyed him. "Promise me," Gregory could still hear his mother's weak words ebb from her lips.

Gregory knelt and then began to pray aloud.

"I beg of You to spare her," he began. "I know that You won't. I have asked You before, and each time, You have not answered."

His hands clasped in front of him and he shook them high above his head, in protest.

"My prayers fall upon deaf ears. All my service has meant nothing. You do not listen. You do not care," his voice had risen to a howling fury, hopelessness and disappointment infecting his every word.

"You have tortured me. Twisted my promises. Made me into a thing of evil," he grieved bitterly. "I no longer wish to serve You."

Gregory rose from his knees and climbed up onto the ledge. He steadied himself and then stood, straightening his body, expanding the distance between his eyes and the floor two stories below him. Gregory closed his eyes and allowed his body to wobble and then fall. There was a brief moment, a tiny instant, where Gregory felt as if he were being lifted up. Then, gravity took hold and pulled him to the ground. Seconds later, he crashed into the pews, where his parishioners had listened to him extoll the virtues of faith. Something he no longer had.

The impact had shattered him. That his body was broken, Gregory had no doubt. He could taste blood in his mouth. Every synapse fired with heightened emergency signals, overloading his conscious mind. He yearned for a release from the pain, but it did not come. Gregory tried to move; to drag himself on the floor, but his legs would not obey. "Was this what death felt like?" he wondered.

He saw a Bible that had been jettisoned from the pew he had crashed into. He reached his arm forward and searing pain shot into his shoulder. His eyes darkened, as if a tunnel was collapsing in on him but Gregory strained for the light, pushing through it. He sought salvation. He sought hope and a release from all the pain. He shuddered in agony. Gregory could feel his breath shorten. As each breath became shallower, his fear deepened. Judgment was upon him.

With his last breaths, Gregory reached one final time. His forefinger lightly gripped the book, dragging it closer to him. Gently, he rested the rose on the top and prayed that God would forgive him, for he could not forgive himself.

~

Kate stood back from the door, her gun drawn, praying that God was with her. Gauze was still strapped to her arm with a thick piece of medical tape where she had taken out the IV. She felt bad about yelling at the nurses and not waiting to be discharged through appropriate channels, but time wasn't something she had to give.

A loud crack signaled that Mike had kicked the side of the door a second time and the framing started to give way. "He won't be here. Gregory would have warned him," she thought. Kate knew she should have taken him into custody. She panicked and it might cost a woman her life tonight. Another quick front kick busted the frame completely and the door swung wide.

"He was right under our noses the whole time," Kate thought as she cleared the entryway. Mike moved in behind her and in a matter of seconds they had cleared the entire apartment. The space was large but sparse. Kate would have called it almost Spartan were it not for its obvious elegance. The place felt temporary, like he had just gotten it, so he could keep an eye on his brother. Kate's heart sunk with the thought that the killer might have two addresses.

"He'll leave us breadcrumbs for sure," Kate whispered to Mike as if the walls had ears. "He wants to show everyone his power," she thought, keeping that idea to herself. Kate was trying to get into his head.

They started to look around, careful not to touch anything unless they thought it could lead them straight to him.

"Think like him, Manning," Kate told herself. "He wants to convince us that he is right. He wants to show us that God will not intervene." Everything had become so clear to her once she linked Gregory and the murderer together.

Kate looked around the bedroom. A single dresser, large closet and bed with nightstand. Nothing that told a story. Nothing that gave them a clue as to who this man, Victor Sloan, was or where he might be. "A singularity of purpose. You are very focused Victor. Not much time for anything else," Kate whispered into the air. "I'm afraid. What if he's right?" Kate pondered internally.

Kate watched as Mike moved through the bathroom. He glanced at her and shook his head.

"I used to think I didn't believe in God," Kate considered. "This guy wants to prove it. He wants to eliminate any mystery."

Mike passed by Kate as they worked in different directions and their free hands almost brushed together. She felt an energy between them; a connection that was very real to her. Kate had sort of reached for him and she wondered if he did the same. They gave each other quick, nervous smiles and continued on in the direction they were headed.

"First pass is clear," Mike reported, clearly disappointed. "Let's take a closer look."

"I'm scared of being that alone. I want to believe." Kate thought. She didn't quite know how to do that though.

Kate walked out of the bedroom. She stopped at the doorway and tried to imagine Victor here. What would he do here? She imagined the organs he took. He didn't seem the type to store them or display them. Where then? Why? Kate looked at the art on the walls. She recognized Eve in the Garden of Eden, but not the other woman in the opposite painting.

"Hey Mike, do you know who that is?" Kate queried.

Mike stopped and looked back at the wall. He nodded.

"Pandora. You know, Pandora's box and all the trouble you ladies cause," he blurted sarcastically as his eyes continued to scan the apartment.

Kate waved her hand at him telling him to shut up.

"Yeah, yeah, I know the . . . Holy crap!" Kate exclaimed remembering Gregory's heroin addict comment at dinner.

"What?" Mike turned and took three steps towards her, the concern in his face obvious.

"He blames women. He hates his mother and he blames women. He's killing them to send a message that they are the cause of all the world's troubles! Hah! Got you, you bastard!" Kate shook a clenched fist in celebration towards the paintings on the wall.

"It would be nice if that led us to his location, you know," Mike castigated her for the early celebration.

They continued their search. Mike started to go through the drawers of the end tables in the living room. Kate attacked the closets in the entryway. The second one she opened revealed a stack of wrapping materials and more than forty flattened gift boxes. In any other place, the scene would have been perceived as generous or somewhat normal for a storage area. Here, the enormous pile had rather grim undertones. "He must be giving the hearts as gifts to his brother," Kate considered. It was obvious that Victor planned to continue his spree a long time.

"Jesus!" Kate exclaimed. "Hey Mike, come take a look at this."

Mike walked over and examined the find. Again, it did little to give them a location, but it did serve to further motivate them.

"We gotta stop this guy," he said flatly.

"That's a fact," Kate replied.

Mike returned to sorting through the papers he had removed from the end table. Kate walked into the living room and stood, gazing at the walls.

"So, where are my breadcrumbs, Victor?" she asked aloud.

Kate scanned the room. She imagined Victor walking in. Where would he put his keys? Where would he go first, to unwind or escape?

"I know you want me to find you. It's a test. You think you'll win."

There was an ornately covered chair in the corner of the room. A small oak table stood next to it. To Kate, it looked like an antique that came from the Cloisters. The whole affair seemed decorative. But somehow, it didn't fit in the room. It matched the elegance, but not the Spartan philosophy. It was as if they meant something to him.

"Over here? Did you keep track of the ones you wanted? The ones that offended you the most?" Kate narrated aloud as she moved closer to it. She sat on the chair and looked down at the table. "You had to be able to contact them. Track them somehow." There was a small drawer in the table, but it faced the back of the chair. She would never have noticed unless she had sat. Kate pulled it open and found a sheet of paper. "Jackpot!" she exclaimed quietly.

Mike continued looking through the drawers, feeling around the tops and bottoms for hidden papers. Kate unfolded the single sheet of paper she had withdrawn from the drawer.

"MIKE!" Kate called out urgently.

Mike came barreling towards her and she immediately regretted the emergency tone she had used.

"Sorry," she said, shrugging her shoulders and handing him the list she had found. She admittedly was shaken by what she had seen on the list.

"I think we've got our breadcrumb," she offered.

Mike looked at the list and concluded exactly what Kate had.

"That's a list of victims and they are in order," he saw.

"Uh-huh," Kate agreed. "Look who's next," Kate said.

"Laura Moles," Mike read. "We have to find her."

"Mike," Kate said shaking, "I know her. She's sweet." Kate watched as the list shook in her hand. She tried to steady herself but could not. "She's a member of Gregory's congregation. I volunteered with her. Made burgers and stuff," Kate could feel the tears welling in her eyes.

"We'll find her first," Mike reassured her.

He wasn't one to make empty promises, but Kate felt the bottom drop out of her stomach. She was terrified. She remembered Mike's oath to Mr. Curtin and shivered at what might come.

"Do you know where she lives?" Mike asked.

Kate shook her head and then said, "No. But Julie does," and was already on her cell phone making the call.

"Hey, I need an address on Laura Moles right now. It's urgent," Kate said, her voice quivering as she tried to make Julie hurry while not putting her in a panic. Julie came back on the line and read the address to her. "What's happening, Kate?" she pleaded but Kate had already started to hang up. She jotted down the address on a small sheet of paper picked off of the desk and handed it to Mike who was already dialing the precinct.

Mike called the whole thing in with military efficiency. "Okay, got it. Send anybody and everybody you got in the area. We'll need an ambulance too. We are only fifteen minutes away and heading there now."

Kate followed him out the door and prayed they were close enough to save Laura.

Chapter 30

"We fear the thing we want the most."

Robert Anthony

They left the siren off, but the lights pulsed in time as they raced to save Laura. Kate drove, winding her way through cars that seemed to stand still. Mike stared straight ahead and barked orders into the radio. He repeated everything and ended with, "Two plain clothes detectives will be on scene." Kate listened intently, making sure he didn't forget anything.

Two blocks from the apartment, Mike drew his weapon. Kate saw it out of the corner of her eye and asked, "By the book, right?" One block from the apartment. Mike flicked the safety off but ignored Kate. She repeated her question, "By the book, right?" He didn't look at her.

"Yeah, by the book, right," Mike said flatly unlocking the door by hand.

As Kate brought the car to a halt Mike leapt from it and was running up the stairs to the apartment before Kate could fully stop the car.

Kate yelled after him, "Mike! Mike! Wait!" but it was already too late. He was inside the building before Kate was out of the car. "Stupid! Stupid! Stupid!" She could see the edges of his sneakers as they bounded up the stairs. She could hear his thunderous steps above her and she tried desperately to catch up. Suddenly, the thuds stopped and she heard Mike's voice ring out.

"Police! Open the door!" Then, Kate heard a powerful smash and the shattering of wood. Mike had kicked the door in.

"Why did we separate?" she wondered as she bounded up the stairs, pulling herself along the railing. Kate begged in her mind, "Please be careful, Mike. Wait for me. Please wait." But, she knew he would not. She was so close now. Twelve more stairs maybe. "Just a few more seconds. Wait for me," Kate pled silently with him, hoping he could hear her thoughts. "Someday, you are going to get yourself killed," she chastised. Kate remembered saying it to him once before. His response then, was classic Mike. "Greater love hath no man than this, that a man lay down his life for his friends," he had said pensively. His father had given it to him on a pendant when he joined the Marines. Mike buried it with a friend. Kate never asked why. Someday, she hoped to understand.

She threw herself against the side of the door and took a quick glance in. Moving with all the speed she could, Kate began to clear rooms. "Clear! Where are you, Mike? Clear! Talk to me, Mike. Clear! You are scaring me!" Then, Kate saw his sneakers jutting out into the hallway. Mike was down. Kate leaned on the far wall and aimed into the door. She wanted to look down at Mike, but knew even a glance could be fatal for both of them.

Laura, dressed in a beautiful yellow and white gown, was on her knees in front of Victor. Tears streamed down her face and she was half undressed, but otherwise unharmed. Victor smugly stared at Kate, pulling Laura up to shield himself. He held the knife tightly to her throat. "Drop the knife," Kate demanded from ten feet away. Victor did not move. He did not respond at all. He simply stared with a smug smile and waited for Kate. She knew at that moment that at least one of them was not leaving this room alive.

"Drop the knife dammit!" Kate screamed feeling like she was running out of time.

"Drop the gun," Victor ordered coolly as he tightened the blade against Laura's throat. She screamed out in pain as the blade cut her. Laura winced in pain, Victor stated, "I will not ask again."

His voice was emotionless. Kate had seen first-hand what he had done to his victims and she had little doubt that he would cut Laura's throat if she failed to drop her weapon. She considered firing, but felt that would guarantee Laura's death as Victor fell. She couldn't risk the shot.

Kate knelt down and put her gun on the floor. She raised her hands, showing herself as no threat. "Think, Kate! Think!" Victor, satisfied, eased the knife off of Laura's throat. A trickle of blood flowed down to her collar bone and Laura shook with fear. Kate glanced at Mike and saw blood flowing from his mid-section. He was face down and Kate couldn't see how bad the wound was beyond the growing pool of red ebbing out from under him.

"Hold on, Mike," she whispered as she nudged her gun towards his hand, hoping he was still conscious; still alive.

Victor began, "I see that confessing your sins to my brother served no purpose."

That sealed it. Kate knew she had met him. Now, she knew that Victor had recognized her, as well. Kate wondered if that was why Laura had become a target. Was he following her? Is that why she had met Jasmine? Her mind raced trying to see a pattern where none may exist. Maybe he was just guessing? Kate wasn't willing to risk anything. She thought quickly of Julie and promised herself that Victor would not walk out of here alive, no matter the cost.

Kate wiped a tear from her face and asked, "Did Gregory tip you off?"

Victor nodded his head, "He promised to protect me; and so, he has. I promised to disprove his religion; and so, I shall."

Kate saw Mike shift his weight on the floor and thought she just needed to buy time. She let the tears flow giving Victor exactly what he wanted. She could hear Mike trying to whisper something to her, but couldn't make it out.

"Why?" Kate asked, trying to get Victor to talk. She needed to buy time and figured his ego was her best weapon.

He obliged eagerly, "Because there is no God. Gregory would not believe this; so, I needed to prove the fact to him." Victor removed the knife from Laura's throat and waved it around as if everything in sight was proof of his opinion. "He still has not learned," Victor spat angrily.

A blend of anger and fear swirled like a vortex within Kate. She tightened her fists and screamed at Victor, "You murder innocent people to prove your brother wrong! How can you do this?"

Victor stood triumphantly tall, pushing out his chest. "If God exists how can he allow me to do the things I do?" Victor asked. "Everyone needs to see the truth. There is no soul, no Heaven or Hell. No God. There is only us."

Kate wanted to lunge at him. "Get your head together, girl," she thought. Kate calmed down from her rage, but her eyes were still full of tears. Kate decided to poke the proverbial bear and see if she could get him to attack her and throw Laura to the side. "Your mom was a heroin addict, probably a prostitute. That doesn't mean every pretty girl has to die because your childhood sucked."

Victor pointed the knife at Kate in anger. "My mother was a lie," he screamed. "You are all liars! Whores! I will prove it to you!" Victor took the knife and pointed it towards the floor. "Kneel," he demanded. Kate's plan had not worked at all. Victor was angry and utterly unwilling to surrender his victim.

Kate dropped to her knees. She glanced quickly at Mike, but saw no movement. A wave of terror came over her. She didn't want to live through this without him.

Out of a desperate fear, Kate quietly said, "Killing me won't prove anything."

Victor smiled and brought the knife close to Laura's throat again. "I'm not going to kill you," he said. "I want you to pray for her life." Victor's face was stone cold. "A little test to see if your God will answer."

Kate was on her knees. She bent her head low like she was a child at bedtime. She could see no way out of this. The darkness was unescapable.

An enraged Victor screamed at Kate, "I WANT TO HEAR YOU PRAY! PRAY FOR THE WHORE'S LIFE!" Kate shook feverishly. She had thought of church when she was a child. All of her unanswered prayers flooded her mind. She had thought of Gregory and how he had said that her problem wasn't the absence of God, but the absence of faith. Kate had faith in Mike. She trusted him in ways she had never trusted another person in her whole life. She wanted him to survive this. She wanted to survive it with him. Kate couldn't help but mourn all the time she had lost being afraid, stubborn, and stupid.

Kate began to stutter, "God . . . God please . . ." and in moments she found herself praying earnestly and loudly, "God, I am begging you to please spare this girl's life. I know I haven't been very faithful . . . I know I've given up hope in you but please . . ."

A terrifying shriek broke her train of thought.

Kate looked up to find Victor slowly digging the knife into Laura's throat. Kate screamed, all of her frustration with God, her fear into one long lament, "NO!" Kate pleaded, "Please, God, save her! Don't let him kill her! PLEASE!"

Then, the deafening report of gunfire split through the apartment. Victor's face turned first to shock, then to a sort of blank nothingness. He dropped to his knees and then crumpled into an awkward mass on the floor. Kate could see a large exit wound in his back where the bullet had torn through his chest. She looked to see from where the shot had been fired. Mike still held the gun a few inches off the floor, holding his wrist, steadying his firing hand with the other. He fired again and Kate quivered at the unexpected shock of the sound. The crumpled mess that had been Victor shifted slightly as the second bullet tore through his head. Mike, drained of all energy, dropped the gun and seemed to surrender to his fate.

Kate slid across the floor and reached Mike in a fraction of a second. She dug her hands into the tear in his shirt and ripped. Blood poured from the wound in his side. Frantically, she wiped trying to ascertain both the length and the depth of the cut.

"Tis but a scratch," Mike choked out, quoting the Monty Python Boys. Kate wasn't in the mood for jokes.

"Keep pressure on it. I'll be right back," Kate ordered.

Kate took his hand and forced it onto the gash. Mike let out an agonizing groan that confirmed Kate's worst fears. He was hurt badly.

Kate ran into the bathroom looking for towels and any first aid she could find. She heard Mike cough behind her and the sound sent shivers down her spine. She tore through closets and drawers.

"Laura! Bandages! Do you have any bandages?" Kate screamed; but, Laura did not answer. She could not answer. Kate knew her friend was bleeding badly from the wound in her neck and going into shock. Kate grabbed a few towels and started to take off her belt as she ran back down the hallway to where Mike was bleeding out. Kate knew that Laura could wait, despite the fact that she didn't think so herself.

She wrapped two towels over the wound and tried to secure her belt around them. It was too small to fit him. She should have known that! Instead, she ran to Laura and wrapped her neck securely. She was unconscious, but breathing. The wound in her neck was deep, but it had not cut her artery.

Kate returned to Mike. He was pale and losing a great deal of blood. She held pressure on the towels as they turned a dark crimson and looked frantically around the room for something she could use. Nothing. The frustration welled up in her. She wanted to scream.

"Kate," Mike said in a whisper. "She okay?" he asked.

Kate nodded, "She'll be okay, thanks to you."

Mike forced a smile, "I promised I'd kill the bastard," he said and then tried to hide a wince of pain. "I keep my promises," Mike said solemnly and closed his eyes.

"Hold on," Kate begged, tears thudding from her eyes like rain in winter. Mike's eyes began to roll and flutter. "Please Mike, hold on. Stay awake. Help is coming. Can't you hear the sirens?" She could feel panic setting in. There was nothing more she could do. "Dammit, Mike, open your eyes!" She screamed and then started to sob. "Please, Mike! Please!" she yelled. "I should have been faster! Please forgive me. I should have been faster." Then she collapsed on top of him and wrapped her arms around him, "Please stay with me. You promised to love me forever. Please, Mike, I love you."

Epilogue

"Impossible is just a big word thrown around by small men who find it easier to live in the world they've been given than to explore the power they have to change it. Impossible is not a fact. It's an opinion. Impossible is not a declaration. It's a dare. Impossible is potential. Impossible is temporary. Impossible is nothing."

Muhammad Ali

She prays every day now. If someone had told Kate Manning that prayer would be part of her everyday routine, she would have laughed in their face. Kate never considered how much she had to lose. Back then, Kate's life was dominated by routine, skepticism, sarcasm, and futility. "Kate," her father would say, "the world is full of bad people and decent folks are just trying to get by without getting taken." For Kate, seeing the world in any other way would have been impossible; a miracle even. Kate was starting to believe in miracles.

Donald and Julie, dressed in requisite black, stood waiting at the front door of her apartment. Kate took a last look at herself in the hallway mirror before grabbing her purse and keys. Her eyes were weary with anguish. She pushed on the puffy bulges below her eyes and realized no makeup was going to hide them. The three of them walked silently out the door and down to the car. Donald opened the rear door for them and ushered the ladies in. They smiled and gave thanks with a nod. He would drive them, sit with them, hold them, so that they could say their goodbyes to an important man.

The ride was silent. None of them wanted to talk about what had happened. How their lives had been invaded by this great evil and irreparably changed by it. Kate stared out the window allowing the morning sunshine to wash over her, dreaming of the path not taken. She thought about a dozen different moments. How could they have gone differently? What would have happened if? In her mind, she played out those scenarios as Donald drove them to the funeral.

The church was packed solid; standing room only. The air was Hellish, humid, and rank with the odors of people wearing too many layers of clothes for the temperature. Kate and Julie sat several rows from the back, seats given to them by a young man and his father. The ladies protested, though the father had insisted, arguing that youth have to be taught manners and respect. Kate wasn't a feminist exactly, but she wasn't traditional by any means. She didn't like it, nevertheless, she took the seat, worried she might collapse if she stood in the hot church. While they waited for the service to begin, Donald stood and quietly talked up the coming football season with the two gentlemen. Kate smiled at the thought of something she remembered Mike would say. "It's always football season." That was his philosophy. Kate grasped her hands together, the whites of her knuckles peeking through her rough skin. She prayed. For what must be the hundredth time in the last three days, Kate failed to hold her emotions in. Her nose stuffed up, her eyes filled with tears and her shoulders shuddered. Kate cried. Julie wrapped her in her arms and Kate tucked her head into her shoulder. The two girls wept with one another; a loud, wailing song of unimaginable grief and pain.

The priest had begun the ceremony and Kate had tried to pull herself together. A lifetime of tamped down emotion had sprung up within her. Buried no longer, it had taken on a life of its own that Kate could not control or even begin to understand. Julie sniffled and whispered commands to Kate, so that she knew what to do and when to do it. Kneel, stand, sit. It was like Christian calisthenics. Kate knew that it was only a matter of time now. She took Julie's hand and held it tightly. Julie squeezed back, silently communicating the dread they felt. "And now, a reading from Julie McMahon," The priest said stoically.

Julie rose slowly, still holding Kate's hand as if she would bring her to the podium with her. Their fingers slipped away from one another but their eyes remained mirrors of each other's for the long walk to the altar.

"A reading from the Book of Wisdom."

Julie's voice cracked and Kate began to leave her seat; ready to run to her. She resisted the urge and quickly sat back down. Kate couldn't protect her from this and she hated that. The reading would be the same one Julie read at their father's funeral. The memory of his loss undulated through them today. Kate and Julie didn't discuss it; but, both were overcome with waves of grief followed by bouts of exhaustion and a void that rivaled the largest black holes in the universe.

Julie took a deep breath and began,

"But the souls of the righteous are in the hand of God,

and no torment will ever touch them.

In the eyes of the foolish they seemed to have died,

and their departure was thought to be a disaster,

and their going from us to be their destruction;

but they are at peace."

Kate's eyes welled up again. She choked the tears back. Julie remained strong. Kate was proud of her and that feeling only added to an already overburdened emotional torrent crashing down on her.

"For though in the sight of others they were punished,

their hope is full of immortality.

Having been disciplined a little, they will receive great good,

because God tested them and found them worthy of Himself;

like gold in the furnace He tried them,

and like a sacrificial burnt-offering He accepted them.

In the time of their visitation they will shine forth,

and will run like sparks through the stubble.

They will govern nations and rule over peoples,

and the Lord will reign over them forever.

Those who trust in Him will understand truth,

and the faithful will abide with Him in love,

because grace and mercy are upon His holy ones,

and He watches over his elect."

Julie walked from the podium quickly, as if her strength had seen its final moments and lingering one moment more would break her completely. Kate hugged her upon her return and they sat holding hands until the end of the service.

Burial occurred in the small cemetery on the side of the church. Ancient tombs, long since erased by time and neglect punctuated the manicured grass. These tombs had no flowers adorning them. They were forgotten by all but a dark skinned Hispanic man who tended to them with the same level of care as he would his own garden. That same man lingered near a tree in the corner of the cemetery now. He rested his hand on the bark, the hint of a shovel peeking out from behind his hiding spot.

Six men carried the simple wooden coffin to the hole that had been dug. A metal frame was set up above it and they rested the box on it. Several people tossed roses, none of which came to rest above the coffin. Each flower floated through the air, briefly kissed the edge of the coffin, then, slipped into the six foot pit disappearing forever.

Solemnly, the priest began to speak. Several people began to cry, knowing that the ceremony was concluding as if somehow the finality of the event assured the reality of it. "In sure and certain hope of the resurrection to eternal life through our Lord Jesus Christ, we commend to Almighty God our brother Gregory; and we commit his body to the ground; earth to earth; ashes to ashes, dust to dust. The Lord bless him and keep him, the Lord make his face to shine upon him and be gracious unto him and give him peace. Amen."

Julie found comfort in Donald's broad chest. Kate stood alone, staring at the coffin. The church had said he had fallen to his death. An accident. Kate doubted it. She would keep her secret though. Kate approached the coffin and laid a flower gently in the center. She kneeled on the plastic grass mat that surrounded the hole in the ground.

"Be at peace, Father," Kate whispered. She silently prayed to God that He would be more understanding than she had been.

Four bagpipers marched forward with exaggerated steps. Dark blue and green kilts, big black hats and ornate bagpipes made each man look nearly identical. One began to play Amazing Grace while the others waited. Soon, one at a time, the pipers joined in the haunting lament. As the fourth and final piper began, the first executed a crisp about face and began walking away from the grave. He continued to play as the coffin began to lower into the earth. Each piper in turn followed suit. The song lingered in the air, fading away as the men walked off into the distance. By the time the attendee's looked back to the coffin it had descended into its final resting place and the funeral was over.

Kate knew this day focused on loss. The death of Father Gregory, his suicide, bothered her. Conflicted was about the only way to describe how she felt. He was a man who she had seen as doing so much good; yet had hidden so much evil. Over the last few days, Kate had hated him, pitied him, resented him and loved him. But, Kate had discovered something about herself as well, in these last few days. As much as today was dominated by death, Kate could not take her mind from something even more profound. She brought her hand to her tummy and gently rubbed it, looking around to ensure that no one was watching. Kate smiled at the thought of the little miracle of life growing inside her. She silently thanked God and started to cry. They were tears of joy. Kate couldn't wait to go to the hospital and visit Mike. She hadn't decided how she was going to tell him; but, she knew in her heart that happiness wasn't impossible for her anymore.

The next novel by David W. Gordon

The Count of Mount Collier High

Also by David W. Gordon

The Outhouse

Book Club Questions:

1. Did *An Absence of Faith* entertain you as a reader? Why or why not?

2. Which character did you most closely identify with? Why?

3. Do you think Kate and Victor have anything in common? How has each of their journeys been similar yet profoundly different?

4. What did you think of Gregory's choices? What might you have done differently?

5. Are we, like the characters in the novel, the sum of our experiences or our choices?

6. Do you feel the novel's theme was universal? Why or why not?

7. Has there ever been a moment in your life when you had an absence of faith? How did you resolve it?

8. Did the novel end the way you expected it to? If it had ended differently, would you have been more or less satisfied?

9. What do you think the future holds for the characters?

10. Would you recommend *An Absence of Faith* to other readers?

The following pages contain some of the artwork produced when *An Absence of Faith* was going to be a graphic novel. I included it here with the permission of the artist, Sten Miller, so that readers could have a glimpse of what might have been.

Since a novel differs greatly from that of a visual medium, some story elements that were in the graphic novel did not make it into the book. Conversely, some of the elements from the graphic medium were altered because the novel allowed more freedom and space to develop characters.

Enjoy!

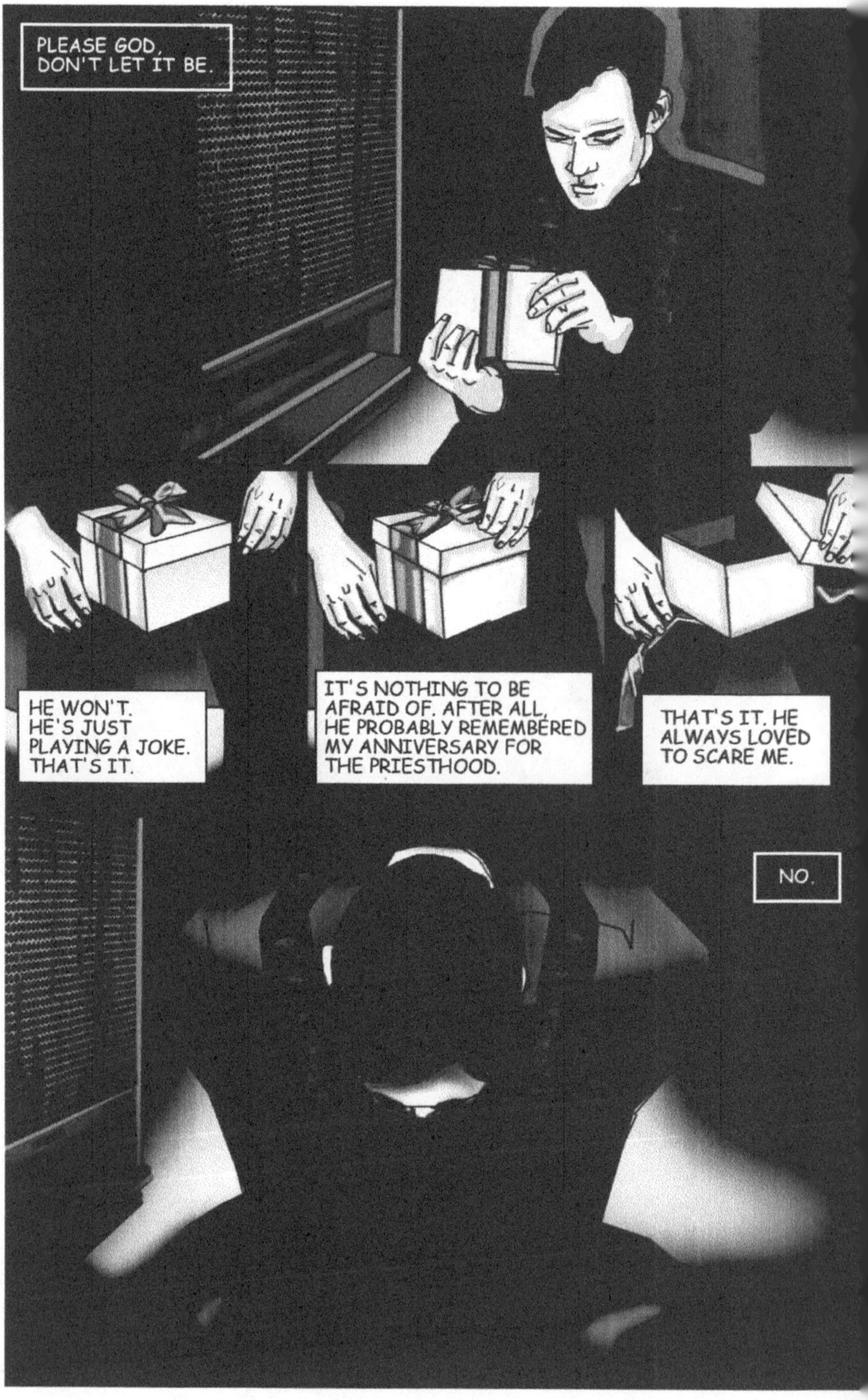
PLEASE GOD, DON'T LET IT BE.
HE WON'T. HE'S JUST PLAYING A JOKE. THAT'S IT.
IT'S NOTHING TO BE AFRAID OF. AFTER ALL, HE PROBABLY REMEMBERED MY ANNIVERSARY FOR THE PRIESTHOOD.
THAT'S IT. HE ALWAYS LOVED TO SCARE ME.
NO.

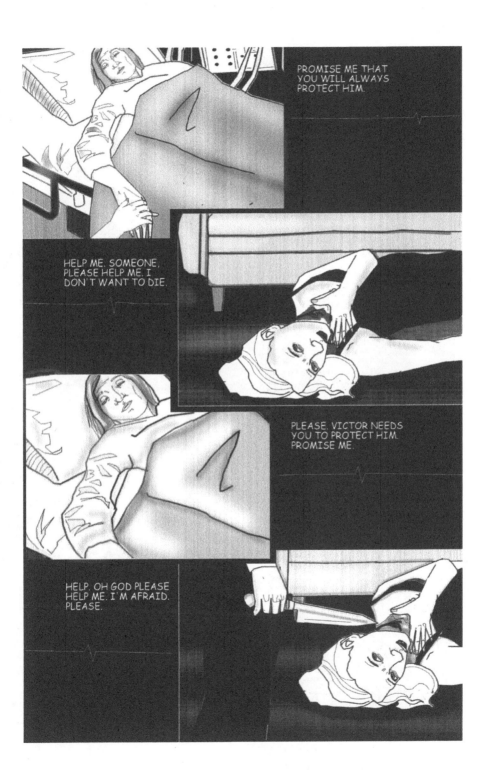

SWEAR TO ME GREGORY. SWEAR THAT YOU WILL PROTECT HIM.

HAIL MARY FULL OF GRACE ... PLEASE DON'T!

YOU MUST SWEAR TO PROTECT YOUR BROTHER

THIS ISN'T HAPPENING ... I WANT TO GO HOME. OH GOD, PLEASE...

I FIALED YOU BOTH. FORGIVE ME.

GOD? WHERE ARE YOU? PLEASE DON'T LEAVE ME HERE.

I SWEAR I'LL PROTECT HIM.

I FORGIVE YOU.

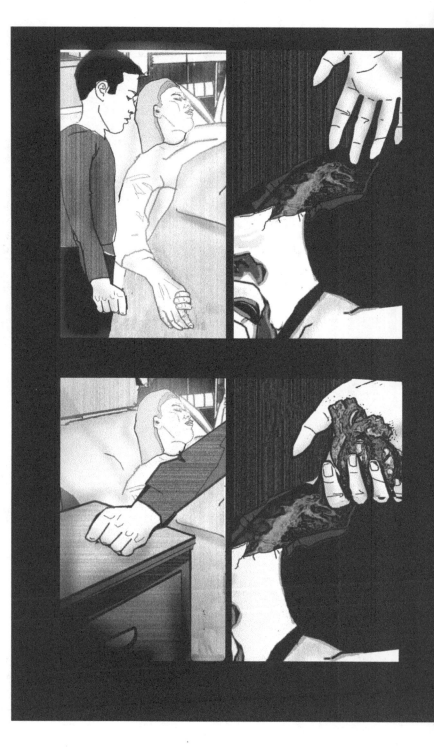